DON'T MISS THE OTHER BOOKS IN THE
WINTERHOUSE SERIES

Edgar Award Finalist • Agatha Award Finalist • Indie Next List Pick

"Guterson provides readers a treat:
mean caregivers à la the Dursleys; a vast,
luxurious hotel where oddities abound;
a new word-puzzle-loving friend; a
shrouded history for Winterhouse;
and sinister circumstances . . .
Clever and captivating."
—*Kirkus Reviews* on *Winterhouse*

"Filled with puzzles and magic,
Guterson's debut keeps suspense high."
—*Publishers Weekly* on *Winterhouse*

"A charming, atmospheric mystery . . .
for fans of Kate Milford's *Greenglass
House* and Trenton Lee Stewart's
The Mysterious Benedict Society."
—*School Library Journal* on *Winterhouse*

"An engaging blend of sleuthing, puzzle-solving, and magic."
—*Kirkus Reviews* on *The Secrets of Winterhouse*

"Guterson's rich mystery and lively characters . . .
will keep readers turning the page to solve the puzzles
within and leave them eagerly anticipating the next
book in this intriguing and magical series."
—*Booklist* on *The Secrets of Winterhouse*

THE WINTERHOUSE MYSTERIES

BEN GUTERSON

With illustrations by **CHLOE BRISTOL**

Christy Ottaviano Books

Henry Holt and Company
NEW YORK

Henry Holt and Company, *Publishers since 1866*
Henry Holt® is a registered trademark of Macmillan Publishing Group, LLC
120 Broadway, New York, NY 10271
mackids.com

Library of Congress Control Number: 2019941051
ISBN 978-1-250-12392-3

Our books may be purchased in bulk for promotional, educational, or business use.
Please contact your local bookseller or the Macmillan Corporate and
Premium Sales Department at (800) 221-7945 ext. 5442 or by email at
MacmillanSpecialMarkets@macmillan.com.

First edition, 2020

Printed in the United States of America by LSC Communications,
Harrisonburg, Virginia

1 3 5 7 9 10 8 6 4 2

For Jan, John, Dave, and Mary

"Bruno Gesten's earliest novel, *The Flinders Deception*, mentions a character's fabricated quotations from imagined books, an endeavor both futile and splendid."

—From *Marbella Everlasting* by Pierre Menard

PART ONE

THE PERIL A STORM BRINGS

CHAPTER 1

AN UNSETTLING DISCOVERY NEAR THE EAST RANGE

On a frozen Saturday in mid-March, Elizabeth Somers was skiing alone when she noticed a crimson cloth tied to an alder branch on the trail ahead. She'd been about to return to Winterhouse, not only because Norbridge, her grandfather, had asked her to be gone no longer than two hours, but because the afternoon sky was darkening with clouds and she hadn't yet even touched her weekend homework. Now, however, as she eased into a slowing glide on her cross-country skis, her attention was caught. A red kerchief—the only burst of color in the otherwise vast whiteness through which the trail wound—was fixed to the limb of a tree.

Elizabeth came to a stop and examined the cloth, which

was frayed and appeared to have been on the branch for some time. She tugged at it with her gloved hand; the knot was strong. Her breath came in puffy clouds, and the sweat on her brow chilled as she considered that she'd never before come quite this far on the trail when she'd gone out skiing. She turned to look at the snow-covered valley in which she'd paused. There were no houses in sight, only stands of wintry fir and alder and, far to the east, high mountains beneath a graying sky. All was silent.

Who would have tied this out here in the middle of nowhere? Elizabeth thought.

She glanced around once more, and then she studied the ground before her. In the powdery snow was a set of

footprints leading away from the tree and toward a slight, snow-covered incline beyond the iced curve of a creek about a hundred yards to the north.

The feeling came over Elizabeth, her by-now-familiar intuition—a sinking in her stomach and a buzz in her head—that there was something more to her surroundings than met the eye: a surprise awaiting discovery, an incident set to unfold, maybe even a person nearby.

"Hello?" she called, looking toward the low hill. "Anyone out here?"

No answer came; the wind sighed through the heights of the trees for a moment before the silence returned.

"I will not be afraid," Elizabeth whispered to herself.

She tugged her cap over her ears as she looked up and down the trail once more, and then she loosened the bindings from her skis, steadied herself on her boots, and began walking, following the faint tracks as they led forward.

Just past the frozen creek, the footprints continued up an enormous rim of earth covered by snow and as high as the surrounding alders. Elizabeth climbed a few feet more and then came to a stop along the perimeter of an immense and treeless circle—wide enough that if the ice-skating rink at Winterhouse were multiplied ten times, it would still fit inside comfortably. Snow-clad boulders covered the entire expanse. She was staring at what amounted to a plain about as large as a good-sized pond and dotted with enormous rocks, the whole thing set within a bordering berm atop which she now stood.

What is this place? Elizabeth thought.

The footprints led down to a little clearing amidst the boulders, and Elizabeth followed them. When she reached the bottom, she noticed a listing metal post, and atop it, a battered beige sign barely recognizable as something man-made against the snowy rocks. Elizabeth rubbed her glasses to clear them of snow, and she peered at the sign. In orange letters so faded they were difficult to read was the following:

DANGER! THE RIPPLINGTON MINING COMPANY DECLARES THIS MINE, THE SILVER CORRIDOR, DEFUNCT! IT HAS BEEN SEALED AND IS NO LONGER ACCESSIBLE! FOR THE PROTECTION OF ONE AND ALL, WE HAVE FILLED THE ENTRANCE, BUT WE CAN ACCEPT NO LIABILITY FOR INDIVIDUALS WHO MIGHT PROCEED PAST THIS POINT! TURN AROUND! IT IS NOT SAFE TO CONTINUE!

Elizabeth felt a flutter in her chest. She knew that the Ripplington Silver Corridor's hundreds of passageways—abandoned well over a century before—sprawled in all directions beneath the ground from this spot and created a maze of tunnels under Winterhouse itself. It had been in one of these passageways, nearly three months before, that Elizabeth had overcome Gracella Winters, Norbridge's sister and the sorceress who'd attempted to gain power over her; she also knew that, although Gracella had been defeated, her body still lay deep within a dark corridor underground. By some evil magic, her physical form had become not only stone-solid but immovable, and Norbridge—as a precaution—had entombed her where she lay and sealed the doors in Winterhouse that gave access to the passageways. The only other possible way in or out, Elizabeth realized, would be the opening above which she stood, though it was blocked by tons of rock. With a shudder, she read the battered Ripplington sign once more.

Elizabeth was about to reverse her steps when she thought she felt the slightest rumbling beneath her. It was something like the sensation of distant thunder, and one part of her wasn't certain she'd really felt anything. She stood and waited to see if the rumbling would come again, but all remained silent and still.

The wind blew, and as Elizabeth began to turn away, the faintest tint of crimson seemed to shimmer upon the snow at the center of the plain of boulders. She shook her head quickly and put a hand on her jacket above where her silver-and-indigo pendant—with the word "Faith" on it—lay.

"I will not be afraid," she said.

Once more, the wind blew, harder this time. Elizabeth looked again at the sign before her. A breeze pressed down and across the wide bowl of the sealed mine, and Elizabeth turned and scrabbled up the slope to the top of the rim. When she glanced back one last time at the treeless plain, it appeared the center of it gleamed with a dull reddish light. But this seemed so improbable, and her fear at that point was so close to bringing her to panic, she focused only on making certain she didn't stumble in the snow as she raced back to her skis. When she reached them, she felt the ground rumble slightly again. She grew still and listened. The sky was darkening even more.

Thunder, she thought as she latched her boots onto her skis, though she wondered how she had missed the flash of lightning. *That must be thunder.*

The red kerchief fluttered before her on the tree as the wind kicked up once more. Elizabeth snatched at the cloth, snapping the thin alder branch as she did so, and then she balled up the kerchief and flung it into a pile of snow. She hopped onto the trail, began pushing as fast as she was able, and raced away, back toward Winterhouse, all the while fighting off a thought that kept forcing itself on her: *What if Gracella isn't dead and gone after all?*

The ground rumbled once again.

CHAPTER 2

A NOTEWORTHY RUMBLING

The foremost thought Elizabeth had as she moved farther away from the mine and the red kerchief was that she needed to tell Norbridge what she'd found. She was scared—both by what she'd seen and how it had made her feel. She'd been living at Winterhouse since the Christmas holiday, with pleasant days at a new school, evenings to read and drink hot chocolate and visit, hours alone in the hotel's massive library, and weekends outside to ski or skate or simply walk beside frozen Lake Luna—and yet she remained intrigued by something alluring that Gracella represented but that she couldn't define. This thought was unsettling.

She was reflecting on all of this when, after fifteen

minutes of hard skiing and with the snowfall increasing, *the feeling* came over her again and she stopped. There was a fork in the trail, and although she knew which way returned to Winterhouse, she had the certainty that someone was approaching on the trail with which she'd just converged. She'd traveled it a few times herself, so she knew that if she veered onto it, it would take her south to Havenworth—where her school was—five miles distant. She listened, waiting to see if anyone appeared, and then, from around the bend no more than one hundred yards away, someone in a silver jacket and red hat skied into view, gliding quickly along the trail in her direction.

"Elizabeth," the skier called out, at the very moment she recognized him. "Hello!"

"Hyrum!" she answered, and all the fright and anxiousness of the previous half hour blinked out. For here was teacher-in-training Hyrum Crowley, whom Elizabeth had known at Havenworth Academy for ten weeks now since they'd both started at the school. Although he only taught English on Tuesdays and Thursdays (he was, after all, just learning how to be a teacher), he seemed to Elizabeth well on his way to being an outstanding instructor. That he was twenty-one years old, attended prestigious Bruma University thirty miles away, wore his black hair trimly styled, and seemed to have read almost as many books as Elizabeth had (including one of her recent favorites, *The Secret of Nightingale Wood*) only bolstered her assessment. He was nice, too—just old enough to be an adult, but not so old that he'd lost all touch with what it meant to be younger, even twelve and three-quarters, as Elizabeth was.

"Wow," Hyrum called as he drew near, "I guess all the cool people are out skiing today."

Elizabeth laughed. "Are you coming from town?" she said as Hyrum stopped before her. He was breathing heavily, the snow falling thickly now and the wind continuing to press. Elizabeth had run into him on the cross-country trails outside of Winterhouse at least a half dozen times and knew how much he loved to ski.

"I am," he said, his eyes bright. "And very nice to see you out here." He glanced at the trail behind her. "You just coming in?" And as she nodded but before she could speak, he said, "I bet you're racing back to finish up Mr. Karminsky's bio assignment before Monday."

Elizabeth laughed again. "I'll get it done." She pressed at her glasses with a glove.

"I'm heading to Winterhouse to meet the headmaster," Hyrum said. Elizabeth recalled Norbridge mentioning that Professor Egil P. Fowles, the headmaster at Havenworth Academy, would be joining them for dinner. Mr. Fowles, who was a kindly if very proper man who seemed to order his day by frequent examinations of his watch, was another reason Elizabeth loved her new school. Unlike the school she'd attended in Drere, the small town where she'd lived with her aunt Purdy and uncle Burlap from age four through the Christmas just past, the teachers and staff at Havenworth Academy seemed to genuinely love not only the subjects they taught, but the students themselves. And to this, Elizabeth attributed the guiding influence of Egil P. Fowles.

"Are you going to have dinner with us, too?" Elizabeth said, barely concealing her hope that he would say he was.

"One thing I've learned during my time here," Hyrum said with mock solemnity, "is that if Mr. Norbridge Falls invites you to a meal at Winterhouse, you don't say no." He glanced at the sky. "But why don't we talk while we ski? I don't think the sun's coming out anytime soon."

Over the next half hour, as the tracks along the trail became obscured by a layer of fresh snow and as the sky grew darker, Elizabeth realized how glad she was to have run into Hyrum. He skied beside her as they discussed Havenworth Academy, Winterhouse, the well-maintained ski trails, and a topic that was a favorite for both of them: books. The one thing she decided she wouldn't bring up was what she'd seen before they'd met—the strange, abandoned mine and the red kerchief on the tree. As she thought back, a shudder ran through her, and she felt frightened to think of that still and lonely place inside the bowl of the old mine.

"So, have you read anything else by my grandfather lately?" Hyrum said after Elizabeth mentioned some of the books she'd finished over the past couple of weeks.

One of the many interesting things about Hyrum Crowley was that his grandfather Damien Crowley had not only lived near Winterhouse years before but had also been a writer of spooky and macabre mystery novels that

Elizabeth loved. She hadn't yet read all his books—by her understanding, he had written ninety-nine in total—but she hoped to do so one day.

"I just finished *Every Rainbow Has a Black Lining*," Elizabeth said as Winterhouse, gleaming gold and with its silver "W" banners flapping atop the roof all around, came into view far off through the thick snow.

"I love that one," Hyrum said. "When the leprechaun turns out to be a vampire? Wow. I don't know how my grandfather came up with that stuff."

"I want to read *Darkness at the End of the Tunnel* next."

"Good luck falling asleep if you do."

"I think my favorite so far is *Colin Dredmare's Chamber of Despair*," Elizabeth said.

"Maximum creepy factor in that one," Hyrum said. "My favorite is *Malcolm Ghastford and the Mystery of the Expanding Dungeon*."

Something that had remained in Elizabeth's mind for over a year was a strange discovery she'd made in Gracella's old room at Winterhouse on the one occasion she had sneaked inside. The room—which was strictly off-limits—had turned out to be very ordinary and, aside from a few pieces of furniture, empty. But in a drawer of the room's only bureau, she had discovered a Damien Crowley book entitled *The Secret Instruction of Anna Lux*, which she'd glanced at quickly and then left in place, never mentioning it to anyone. Elizabeth had occasionally been tempted to enter Gracella's room to look at the book again, especially because even Leona Springer, Winterhouse's elderly librarian and Elizabeth's good friend, had been unable to locate an edition of it anywhere, even through her many librarian friends. But Elizabeth knew she shouldn't return to Gracella's room—curiosity about it had overwhelmed her once, and she'd never confessed to Norbridge what she'd done—and so she told herself she wouldn't try again.

Elizabeth was considering asking Hyrum about the Anna Lux book. But before she could, and as they left the final stand of trees and entered the broad expanse before Winterhouse, he said, "You know, Professor Fowles mentioned you might be running Winterhouse someday, seeing as you're next in line in the Falls family. Is that true?"

The question startled Elizabeth—not because she hadn't heard it before but because she hadn't yet figured out how she felt about it. She loved Winterhouse with all her heart and believed she was the luckiest person in the world to now live there, but the thought of carrying on after Norbridge, of being responsible for the hotel and everyone in it—that was too much for her to contemplate. She was twelve years old, and it was enough to pitch in at the Winterhouse library a few days a week and finish her homework on time.

"I don't know," Elizabeth said. "I guess . . ." She felt the way she often did back in Drere when her aunt Purdy would interrogate her about a sock that had gone missing or something else she, Elizabeth, had nothing to do with: Hyrum's question left her anxious and uncertain. The sound of their swishing skis seemed louder suddenly, as she considered what to say next.

"Almost there!" Hyrum said, and Elizabeth was glad he'd filled the awkward silence. They were, indeed, drawing near to the enormous hotel; through the swirling snow, Elizabeth saw, in the covered roundabout before the lobby, a car parked and people disembarking.

"Aren't those the puzzle guys?" Hyrum said, looking ahead.

Sure enough, Elizabeth saw Mr. Wellington and Mr. Rajput, the two gentlemen who'd been working on a thirty-five-thousand-piece puzzle in the lobby of Winterhouse on and off for nearly two years, assisting their wives out of the car as they all moved to enter the hotel. She was about to call out a greeting to them, but the distance was still too great and the snow was a distraction.

"I didn't think they were coming till next week," Elizabeth said.

Hyrum gave a flick of his head toward the hotel. "Let's go say hi."

Elizabeth pushed forward on her skis. As the distance to Winterhouse diminished, she found herself wondering why the arrival of Mr. Wellington and Mr. Rajput felt so odd to her. An image of the crimson-tinted snow at the mine flitted through her mind. But then she and Hyrum reached the roundabout of the grand hotel, and she dismissed all troubling thoughts.

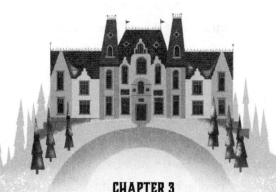

CHAPTER 3

A PUZZLE RESUMES—BUT A BLEAK PROSPECT FOLLOWS

The lobby of the Winterhouse Hotel was so elegant and so massive, Elizabeth never failed to be awestruck by it, even after all the times she'd been there. The chandeliers, the polished wood of the paneling, the plush carpet with its diamond patterns, the paintings and elk heads on the walls, the gentle string-quartet music lilting from the speakers, and the aroma of firewood mixing with the sugary-sweet smell of Winterhouse's world-famous confection known as Flurschen—all of it enchanted Elizabeth anew on each occasion.

"This place is the best," Hyrum said, shaking the dampness from his now-cap-free head as he and Elizabeth, having left their skis beside the front doors, stepped into the lobby. He was gazing at the high ceiling and smiling. "You're so lucky to live here."

Elizabeth was about to agree when Sampson, a bell-hop only a bit older than Hyrum, called out to her. "The world-famous alpine skier Elizabeth Somers returns!" he said from behind his clerk's stand, displaying his buck-teeth with a wide grin.

"Hello, Sampson," Elizabeth said. Since she had known him, Sampson had proved to be not only one of the best but also the friendliest bellhop at Winterhouse.

"And hello, Mr. Hyrum Crowley," Sampson said. "Great to see you. And glad you both made it in before the storm really started dumping."

"Hi, Sampson," Hyrum said, jabbing a thumb above his shoulder to point behind himself. "It's getting pretty snowy out there. Has Mr. Fowles arrived?"

Sampson peered through the glass of the lobby doors. "Any time now, we expect."

"It's getting a lot colder out, too," Elizabeth said, though her gaze drifted to the far corner of the lobby where, on a long table, lay the enormous puzzle to which tall and bald Mr. Wellington and short and round Mr. Rajput had devoted scores of hours over the past many months. The two men and their wives generally stayed at Winter-house for two weeks at a time, at least three or four times a year, and the men spent most of their hours working to fit in pieces. They'd last been for Christmas, when they'd made great progress on their puzzle—which featured a beautiful picture of a temple in the Himalayas where

Winterhouse's founder, Nestor Falls, had once lived—and were increasingly eager to complete it. Elizabeth assisted them whenever she could, both because she loved puzzles and because she'd turned out to be an uncanny discoverer of pieces. The two men were ever glad to have her help.

To Elizabeth's surprise, the men stood beside the table now (their wives nowhere to be seen) and were examining the massive sprawl of pieces before them as though they'd been at work for hours, although Elizabeth and Hyrum had entered Winterhouse only a few minutes after them. It struck her as peculiar that Mr. Wellington and Mr. Rajput would resume their work immediately without even visiting their rooms first.

"I didn't know they were coming today," Elizabeth said to Sampson, pointing to the puzzle table.

He leaned in close. "Surprised us, too," he said in a low voice. "Mr. Wellington was super excited to be here. He kept asking Mr. Rajput to hurry up so that they could get started on the puzzle, and then they headed right for the table like they couldn't wait."

Hyrum turned to Elizabeth and gave her a *that seems strange* look. But then he shrugged and tipped his head toward the two men to invite Elizabeth to follow. "Let's say hi, huh?"

They strolled over to the puzzle table, but Mr. Wellington and Mr. Rajput seemed not to notice anyone approaching; they remained fixated on studying the pieces lying before them.

"Hello, Mr. Wellington," Elizabeth said. "Hello, Mr. Rajput."

The two men flicked up their heads and turned to Elizabeth. They looked not only startled but slightly uncomprehending, the way a person appears when you meet him in an unaccustomed place and he knows he's seen you before but can't recall just how he knows you.

After a moment of this, Mr. Wellington's typical, friendly expression arranged itself on his face. "Ah, yes!" he said with exuberance. "Dear Elizabeth! How good to see you." He came to her and took her hand in his, and then he looked to Hyrum. "And the young schoolteacher, as well. Wonderful to see you again, sir." He turned to Mr. Rajput, who was reluctantly shuffling forward. "Mr. Rajput, no dawdling, sir. Come here and greet our friends."

The shorter man ambled to them, his expression fixed in its typically cheerless cast, as though he'd just gone through an indescribable disappointment and needed everyone to realize it; he held out his hand to Elizabeth. "We remain, as always, pleased to find our prodigy joining us," he said. His heavy-lidded eyes moved to Hyrum. "Although I'm guessing you're engaged already in an afternoon of young person's enjoyments and will find yourself unable to remain here with us as we resume our laborious—very laborious—trudge toward completing—"

"Mr. Rajput!" Mr. Wellington said, interrupting him and gesturing toward Hyrum by way of directing Mr. Rajput to shake his hand. "Enough of your grumbling." He smiled at Elizabeth. "We are overjoyed to be here, and we are so very thrilled to resume our efforts."

"I can see," Elizabeth said, glancing at the puzzle. It was, she guessed, one or two visits away from completion. Although she enjoyed working on it when the two men were guests at the hotel, she avoided advancing it by even a single piece in their absence out of respect for the fact that the puzzle was their project. There was even a sign left on the table while the men were away—*Mr. Rajput and Mr. Wellington, the two gentlemen who have been toiling away on this puzzle for months now, are absent from Winterhouse at this time. Please do not disturb the puzzle in any way. We thank you. Mr. R and Mr. W*—and which seemed to keep all potential contributors to the effort at bay. As bizarre as it was to Elizabeth, not a single guest ever seemed moved to violate the request on the small sign; she'd seen plenty of people admiring the puzzle, but she'd never seen anyone attempt to fit in a piece on their own.

"Well, you two sure got right down to business, didn't you?" Hyrum said.

Mr. Wellington, beaming, turned to look at Mr. Rajput. "We're determined to finish this puzzle by Easter," Mr. Wellington said. "We originally arranged our arrival for next Wednesday, but then, in consultation, Mr. Rajput and I decided to adjust the time frame in order to accelerate the schedule." He leaned forward and said, in a chipper and confidential tone, "If we can begin each day before breakfast and continue into the late hours of evening,

I'm confident we can finish within the next two weeks! There's no time to waste, yes, Mr. Rajput?"

Mr. Rajput shrugged wearily and moved back to the puzzle. "I'm not the one who's frittering away my time in conversation," he said somberly.

Elizabeth, who'd been staring at the puzzle herself and thinking—not for the first time—how odd it was that this huge box and the thousands of wooden pieces even existed, felt something familiar stir inside her.

"Hey!" she said brightly, pointing to a piece beside Mr. Rajput's hand. "I think I see where that one goes."

Mr. Wellington looked to Hyrum and beamed like a man who'd just found a twenty-dollar bill on the carpet. "She is remarkable, she is," he said. "We all know what's coming now."

"I must give the young lady her due," Mr. Rajput added. "She puzzles with remarkable aptitude."

The piece Elizabeth had spied was pure blue, a part of the thousands of pieces that made up the sky in the picture, but some telling angle of its shape or how it lay on the table caused something like *the feeling* to arise in her, and she plucked it up, moved to a cluster of pieces near the upper rim of the picture, and snapped it in snugly.

"Right there!" she said triumphantly. She had no idea how she was able to do this; she only knew she often had the sensation, while working with the two men, of grasping instinctively that a certain piece was destined to fit in a definite spot. This time, however, with the eyes of the three others on her, she recognized there was an unaccustomed degree of satisfaction in having found a piece that fit, something a notch more pleasing than she could recall feeling before.

"Whoa!" Hyrum said. "Talk about skill!"

"It's a gift," Mr. Wellington said. "She has a gift."

"And she has an appointment with Mr. Falls in one hour," someone said.

Elizabeth turned to see Jackson—Winterhouse's head bellhop and Norbridge's right-hand man—looking as smart and dapper as ever in his red bellhop's outfit, his pillbox hat, and the brass of his buttons and nameplate polished to a bright shine. Jackson was the most experienced and competent worker at the hotel, and he had Norbridge's—and Elizabeth's—complete trust.

"Hi, Jackson," she said as Hyrum greeted him, too, and the two men at the table moved to shake his hand.

"You have arrived, Mr. Wellington," Jackson said properly. "And Mr. Rajput." He glanced about. "Your wives are with you, too?"

Mr. Wellington pointed toward the stairs. "They've made their way to our rooms."

Jackson paused, smiling graciously. "We are overjoyed to have you as our guests once more." He turned to Hyrum. "And you too, young sir. Very glad to see you. Your headmaster, Mr. Fowles, will be arriving shortly. We have baked trout and roasted yams for dinner and then a violin concert by Miss Sunny Chen, who will be playing the Vinteuil Sonata in Grace Hall at eight o'clock. I am confident you will enjoy it." He nodded to Elizabeth. "And as Miss Somers knows, tomorrow afternoon we will be showing *The Floating City of Isfaheen* in our theater, followed by an evening lecture on the art of voice throwing by the renowned ventriloquist Mr. Isaac Igbinedion. You won't want to miss any of it."

"It's always so great to be here, Jackson," Hyrum said. He pointed to the corridor. "But you know, if you don't mind, everyone, I'd like to head to the library for a few. There's a couple of books I need for class next week."

"Of course," Jackson said. "Dinner at six thirty."

Hyrum gave a salute and a smile to the others and aimed for the hallway. "See you then."

An awkward silence fell over Elizabeth and the three men as they watched Hyrum depart. Elizabeth had the distinct feeling Mr. Wellington and Mr. Rajput wanted nothing more than to resume working on their puzzle.

Jackson cleared his throat. "Gentlemen," he said soothingly, "given that you've already discovered one piece— with help from Miss Somers, I believe—perhaps you will want to join your wives and rest before dinner. The puzzle will be waiting whenever you return."

Mr. Rajput shrugged at Mr. Wellington. "Perhaps we ought to take the gentleman's recommendation. It's clear that because our young helper is unable to remain, our prospects for success this gray afternoon are most likely slim. We are both out of practice." He rubbed his forehead. "And I am fatigued."

Mr. Wellington darted his eyes furtively across the

pieces on the table, stroked his chin, and then smiled at Jackson. He took a deep breath.

"You're very right, Jackson," he said. "I suppose a brief intermission won't do any harm. To our rooms we go!" He waved Mr. Rajput forward, and the two men strode toward the elevator doors. "As we prepare to enjoy yet another stay at the Winterhouse Hotel." He pushed the button for the elevator and turned to Jackson and Elizabeth. "Until this evening."

Mr. Rajput waved listlessly as the door slid open. "We shall see you at dinner, assuming nothing happens to us between now and then."

"Sir!" Mr. Wellington said as he and the other man stepped into the elevator. "Of course we'll see them. And then we'll get right back to our work on—"

The door closed. Elizabeth stared at it as though the two men might change their minds and return. She looked to Jackson, who was staring at the door himself.

"They sure seemed eager to work on their puzzle," she said.

"Travel can be disorienting for some people," Jackson said with an arch of his eyebrows.

He glanced around the lobby; if this had been a Saturday afternoon three months earlier, during the giddy slide into Christmas, there would have been so many people scurrying in all directions—staff preparing for the big feasts and concerts, guests heading out to skate or coming in to drink hot chocolate in Winter Hall—the place might have seemed as bustling as a train station at rush hour. Now, however, a dark day in mid-March, with Easter still two weeks away, Winterhouse was about as empty as it ever got, with fewer than half the rooms filled and relatively placid evenings of movies or quiet concerts. Elizabeth loved Christmas season at Winterhouse, but she realized she loved these calmer weeks just as much now that she lived at the hotel.

"You said Norbridge wanted to see me?"

"In the observatory at four o'clock."

The observatory was on the thirteenth floor—the topmost floor—and it was there that Norbridge kept a powerful telescope in a glassed-in overlook so that it was possible to view the world all around Winterhouse during the day, or the stars and planets at night. He also had an office in the room, where he conducted the most important business of the hotel.

"I believe," Jackson said, "he wants to discuss something about Elana."

Elizabeth felt a shudder go through her. *Elana.* It had been on New Year's Eve in the gloomy passageway under Winterhouse, that an awful tragedy had befallen Elana Vesper—or, rather, Elana Powter, as Elizabeth now knew her. Elana, who was the same age as Elizabeth, had been enlisted by her unpleasant parents in a plot to bring Gracella back to her full, evil strength. Gracella had been defeated when Elizabeth chose—decisively—to retain her own powers for good and not share them with Gracella. But in the battle in the twisting mine beneath Winterhouse, and in a final desperate measure, Gracella had magically drawn years out of Elana's body in a futile effort to preserve herself, leaving Elana as feeble and withered as a woman of ninety. It was a shocking and frightening fate, all the more so because it became clear in the aftermath that Elana had been an innocent pawn of her wicked family. In fact, after the terror of New Year's Eve passed, Elana's parents and brother disappeared, leaving her alone.

Elizabeth felt sick about the entire thing and believed Elana was suffering far more than she deserved for the slight contributions she'd made to her parents' schemes. If there was something that could be done to assist her, Elizabeth wanted to figure out what it might be—and she knew Norbridge felt exactly the same way. For now, Elana remained in a room on the fourth floor in a state of sadness and confusion so severe, it was difficult to know if she fully understood where she was or what had happened to her. At times, Elizabeth wondered if Elana's mind had become permanently clouded; perhaps, sadly, there was no hope for her.

"Did something happen to her?" Elizabeth said.

"I believe she wants to talk to you and Norbridge," Jackson said. "From what I understand, she seems to be doing better. Let's hope she's turned a corner."

This news was startling to Elizabeth—and very welcome. "That's great to hear." She glanced at the clock by the clerk's stand. "I'll be sure to meet Norbridge at four."

"Absolutely," Jackson said. He nodded, turned toward the desk where Sampson was examining some papers, and began walking to him. "Do not slump, sir," he called. "Bad for the back, bad for the spine. Upright! Upright!"

Elizabeth was about to head for the stairs when she examined the puzzle once again and realized she felt inexplicably drawn to continue fitting pieces, if she could. She looked at the letters—in a language unknown to her—above the temple doors in the picture. Mr. Wellington had once told her they stood for the word "Faith," and Elizabeth found this comforting whenever she reflected on it. With a finger, she touched the word, drew a line across it as if smoothing a fold in a piece of paper, and put the finger to her sweater, just above the pendant on which was written the very same word in English.

A chill ran through her, something like *the feeling* but oddly cold and sharp. Before she considered what she was doing, she picked up a single piece of the puzzle—a nondescript cutout of pure blue—and examined it. She peered over her shoulder to see if Jackson or Sampson or anyone else was watching, and when she was certain no one was, she tucked the piece into her pocket, took a deep breath, and then strode toward the staircase and out of the lobby.

She'd stolen one of the thirty-five thousand pieces of Mr. Wellington and Mr. Rajput's puzzle.

CHAPTER 4

AN ENIGMA ILLUMINATED

Elizabeth's room on the third floor, number 301, was as bright and cheerful as her bedroom in her aunt and uncle's shabby home in Drere had been gloomy and dull. If you've ever imagined living in a hotel room, where everything is well arranged and fresh, but then you also have all your own belongings in it—your books on a huge oak shelf, your clothes inside a cherrywood bureau, your posters (huskies leading a sled, young Arthur removing Excalibur from the stone, the cover of *The Thief Lord*, the platypus from the third Cattle Battle movie *The Return of the Heifers*) on the wall, and strings of trinkets and small flags and glittering lights strung across the ceiling—then you'll have something of the idea of what it was like in

Elizabeth's room. She loved it. And at times she could hardly believe it was all her own.

What she loved most was sitting on her sofa, turning on the Tiffany-shaded lamp beside it, and reading for hours. If the window curtains were open to reveal a snowy sky and Lake Luna and the mountains beyond, all the better, though a dark night with a half-moon was just as good. A close second to relaxing on the sofa and reading was sitting at the small desk beside her bed and working through school assignments or drawing pictures or adding to one of the lists she kept in her journal ("Reasons Why Havenworth Academy Is Better Than Drere Middle School," "Best Lectures at Winterhouse This Year," "Songs I Want to Play on the Guitar When I Learn to Play the Guitar," and "Tattoos I Would Never Get, Even Though I'll Probably Never Get a Tattoo Anyway" were recent additions). She found it straightforward and easy to focus at her desk—and infinitely less distracting than attempting to complete a math assignment in her room in Drere, where the blare of her aunt's television shows (*Car Crash Chaos* and *Let's All Laugh at Other People* were huge favorites) or her uncle's elaborate complaints about his job often broke her attention. Living in Room 301 at the Winterhouse Hotel was a dream come true.

On this afternoon, however, as she locked her door and changed out of her ski clothes, her mind was occupied with several things that hadn't been there three hours before: the creepy sights at the mine, the odd behavior of the men at the puzzle table, the possibilities for Elana's condition, and—most immediately now—her own reasons for removing a puzzle piece from the lobby. She took the small wooden shape from her pocket, set it on her desk, and examined it: blue, with the curving lines and precise arcs of any other puzzle piece she'd seen. Completely ordinary. What hadn't been ordinary, she thought, was how difficult it had been to depart the lobby with it—Elizabeth attributed this to a strong pang of guilt she felt, though she'd also had a peculiar feeling of *resistance*, as though some slight tug was drawing her back to the table.

I'll put it back soon, she thought, ignoring the question of what, exactly, had moved her to take the piece. She dropped it into the top drawer of her desk, took a quick shower, and sat down to begin one of her favorite things on Saturday afternoons: logging on to the new laptop Norbridge had bought for her (and that she allowed herself to use for no more than half an hour a day, three days a week) and enjoying the emails that her best friend, Freddy Knox, sent.

Elizabeth loved working in the library with Leona—something she did at least three afternoons a week and usually once on the weekend; she liked leading an hour-long demonstration of the camera obscura up on the thirteenth floor for any interested guests on Saturday mornings, something she'd promised to do after Freddy had restored the device weeks before. She also found she loved attending Havenworth Academy and had even made friends with a few of the kids there. But what she looked forward to at least as much as any of these things was hearing once a week from Freddy, with whom she'd shared adventures the two previous Christmases and who would be visiting with his parents for Easter and was due to arrive in five days.

Freddy was a year older than Elizabeth. His incredibly wealthy parents, though, were so much more interested in the things they bought and the places they traveled to, Freddy himself had become an afterthought to them: For four years in a row, during the one time of year when most families would make an effort to spend time together, they'd left him alone at Winterhouse. Which was fine with Freddy—he had come to love the hotel as much as Elizabeth did. One of the main things Elizabeth liked about Freddy was that, although he was rich and could have been a very stuck-up person, he was actually nice and intelligent without a trace of arrogance. He was an ace inventor, too, having fixed the camera obscura and created the Walnut WonderLog—a log made from compressed walnut shells—the year before. Elizabeth found she and Freddy were so much alike in so many ways—primarily in the natural curiosity they both had and their love of anything related to anagrams and codes and puzzles and all sorts of wordplay—they had become good friends even though they had only spent two Christmas holidays together.

As she started up her laptop, she looked to the uncovered window. In the glow of the lamplights outside the hotel, snow was falling through the afternoon twilight like a torrent of spray on an arctic coast. The flakes were everywhere, driving thick and fierce through the darkening sky. Wind pressed against the windowpane, and Elizabeth pulled her sweater around her and turned to her computer to read Freddy's email:

Set Ginger, Hazel Bite! *Er, I mean:* Greetings, Elizabeth *(just in case you couldn't figure out the anagram)!! I hope your week was better than mine. I broke my glasses on Monday. On Tuesday, my dad was supposed to take me to the hockey game, but then he said he couldn't go, so he had me go with our chauffeur instead. It was fun, actually. Jacques is a really nice guy, and we ate a lot of popcorn and I had three ice-cream sandwiches (but the Albatrosses lost in a shoot-out, which was not good). Anyway, then on Wednesday I came down with a cold. At least yesterday we got our third-quarter grades, and I have all A's. Some things never change. Just kidding! (Well, not really kidding about that part. How are you doing at school, by the way?)*

How is everything at Winterhouse? How is the camera obscura? Have you read six thousand of the books in the library by now or only five thousand? Is Norbridge doing well? And Leona? And everyone else? I'm still kind of jealous that you get to live there, but I'm happy for you, too. Maybe you can ask Norbridge to let me move in. Hint, hint! Do it! Yes! You should! (Please?!)

Okay, I've been continuing the research on my end, and I have some updates for you. Prepare to be amazed. Because: FRED> FEED> FEND> FIND> FINE> WINE> WISE. See what I mean? Anyway, I keep studying that genealogy website I told you about, sojustwhereyoufrom.com, to figure out all the connections between the people who were helping Gracella. Here's what you and I already know: Riley Granger (or, as I think of him, "The Guy Who Created All the Bizarre and Mysterious Things at Winterhouse a Long Time Ago, Mainly to Drive Us Crazy") was the father of Ruthanne Sweth Granger, who married Monroe Hiems, and their son was Marcus Hiems (which is why he knew about The Book), and he ended up marrying Gracella's daughter, Selena Winters. Also, Riley's cousin, Jenora Sweth, married a guy named Peter Powter, and his son is Ernest Powter, who is the father of Rodney and Elana. The Powters are related to Selena, and so that's how all of them knew so much about Winterhouse. But here's the new thing I just found out! Peter Powter had a sister named Patricia, and she was the one whose name you found in the old guest book! You know, the lady who came to Winterhouse with Riley Granger when he was an old man. Spooky. And interesting!

One other thing I found out. I kept doing research on the Dredforth Method without any luck. But a *couple of days ago I landed on this website called the Crimson Scarab. I don't know who put it together, but it's all about magical stuff. Anyway, I'll paste in the important part here for you to read:*

> *The Scottish charlatan and evildoer Aleister Winters often alleged that he and his circle of followers had discovered the secrets of preserving everlasting life through a ritual he named the Dredforth Method. Winters believed that souls could separate themselves from human bodies and await reunification if conditions were optimal. However, Winters claimed, if the physical body had perished, the "disconnected soul" would need to undergo the aforementioned ceremony on the eve of the third full moon after physical death, or else it, too, would be lost forever. In a peculiar addendum to Winters's career, the writer Damien Crowley, who fell under Winters's sway in the 1950s, was said to have revealed the secret of the Dredforth Method in a work of fiction that remained unpublished. Most scholars find the entire story of Winters and Crowley to be without merit.*

Bizarre, huh? Basically, Gracella's husband came up with this magical ceremony that you and I have been trying to learn more about, and then Damien

Crowley wrote about it in a book! We'll definitely need to talk about this when I see you.

Okay, I better get going. Oh, and be sure to save some Flurschen for me. I hope my parents don't change their mind again, last minute, like they did at Christmas. But even if they do, I'll make sure they send me!

See you!

Freddy

P.S. Seriously, I hope Elana is doing better. Let me know.

Elizabeth felt more than slightly stunned by what Freddy had shared. She'd first come across the words "Dredforth Method" in a letter she'd discovered in Selena Hiems's hotel room two Christmases before—signed, simply, "D." And although she was unfamiliar with the method referred to, it was clear it was some magical way of separating a person's spirit and body in order to preserve both, albeit in a weakened and suspended state. Despite some research she'd done in the library, Elizabeth had been unable to learn anything more about the Dredforth Method.

Elizabeth stood and went to the window. The snow seemed to be falling even harder. She pulled the curtain closed and returned to her laptop to do a search for details about the recent lunar cycles. A table of dates appeared on the screen before her, and as she made sense of it, an awful thought resolved in her mind: *The third full moon after Gracella's death will be in two weeks—the night before Easter.*

She wanted to type out a quick note to Freddy—about what he'd found, about what she'd seen at the mine, about how glad she would be when he arrived—but she didn't want to be late. Her interest in learning what had developed with Elana was keen, and she absolutely had to tell Norbridge about the red tint she thought she'd seen in the snow at the abandoned mine.

The Dredforth Method, too, she thought. *I'll tell Norbridge what Freddy discovered.*

She shut down her computer, rose from her seat, and headed for the thirteenth floor.

CHAPTER 5

A MAGNIFICENT ENSEMBLE OF TILES

Elizabeth knocked on the door of the office observatory, and when she heard a hearty "please enter!" from inside, she slipped into the room. It was small and almost without furnishings, though the brass telescope within its glass-enclosed balcony was impressive. Norbridge had shown Elizabeth everything from Saturn's rings to distant Mount Arbaza through the scope; the most tantalizing thing he'd shown her was the statue of Winifred, Elizabeth's mother, set on a pedestal far across Lake Luna. The trail to that side of the lake wasn't clear enough yet to make a trip there, but Elizabeth hoped that day would arrive soon. She'd been waiting for it eagerly.

"Elizabeth, my dear!" Norbridge said, emerging from

the door at the end of a short hallway just off the living room. He was dressed in his customary wool blazer and white shirt, along with a black bow tie and sturdy boots; his pure white mustache and beard were as trim as ever, and his ruddy face—eyes glinting lightheartedly, as though he was always ready to say something to make you smile— was as cheerful as Elizabeth had come to expect on almost all occasions. He spread his arms in greeting. "You have arrived."

Elizabeth smiled. "Jackson said you wanted to see me."

"I do." With an upward tickle of one finger and a quick pivot to show her his back, he said, "Please, in here. I wanted to share a few things with you."

Norbridge's office—carpeted with a silver-and-black Navajo rug, lit softly by two lamps, and filled with cabinets and bookshelves and a cluttered desk—looked out at the black sky through a floor-to-ceiling window. The most remarkable thing about the room, however, was the shiny murals made of blue and white tiles. They showed scenes from Winterhouse's past—illustrious feats of mountaineering and cross-country skiing and snowshoeing by members of the Falls family, along with incidents such as the time the renowned balloonist Hector Velasquez landed beside Lake Luna at the end of his remarkable "A Continent Conquered by Dirigible" tour, or the evening the famous fado singer Helena Ferreira recorded her melancholy, chart-topping live album *I Long for the Powdered Sugar of My Youth* in Grace Hall before a packed house of fans snacking on Flurschen. Dozens of scenes adorned the walls in ornate blue upon creamy white. Elizabeth thought they were the most beautiful things in the entire hotel. There was even a mural of her mother when she'd been a girl. "The Youngest Person to Make an Ascent of Mount Arbaza—The Intrepid and Fearless Winifred Falls, Eleven Years Old," read the caption beneath a picture that showed Winnie in a thick parka standing atop a snowy peak. Elizabeth felt transported—proud and resolute and, most of all, sad at having lost her mother eight years before—every time she looked at that picture.

Beyond the beauty of the room, though, lay a deeper significance: When Norbridge had first taken Elizabeth here a few months before, he'd explained she was only the fifth person ever to enter, after Norbridge's grandfather Nestor, Nestor's son Nathaniel, Norbridge himself, and Winnie. The first three were the men who'd run Winterhouse over its 120 years of existence, next was the daughter who'd been destined to oversee the hotel before her disappearance and untimely death, and finally came Elizabeth herself. She recalled Hyrum's question from an hour or so before, about her carrying on after Norbridge someday.

Norbridge gestured toward the sofa, inviting Elizabeth to sit; he lowered himself into his enormous oak chair and studied her for a moment before saying, "How was the skiing today?"

"Something strange happened," she said, and then recounted the events from the moment she'd seen the red kerchief on the tree. Norbridge listened attentively, nodding here and there and asking for small clarifications along the way. When Elizabeth mentioned she'd run into Hyrum, Norbridge stared at the carpet and stroked his beard.

"Well, all this concerns me," he said, looking up. "That mine's been sealed since 1887, and there's no way inside from that end. . . ." He allowed his sentence to die and looked to the enormous window as he stroked his beard again. "You say that strange feeling came over you? And there was a crimson cast to the snow? Shaking of the ground?"

"That's right," Elizabeth said. She knew her news was worrisome, and she'd been wanting to share it all with Norbridge; now, seeing him this agitated, she felt even more alarmed herself. Another part of her, though, was heartened to see him taking her seriously. There had been times when she'd been frustrated because Norbridge hadn't given her concerns their due. That he was genuinely unnerved now and didn't seem to have an ounce of doubt about her take on things gratified Elizabeth.

"What if Gracella is trying to come back?" Elizabeth said. She thought of the red kerchief once more and how it had been left so deliberately. "And what if someone is trying to help her?"

Norbridge hesitated. "But then the question becomes: who?"

This was what Elizabeth had been thinking herself, almost from the moment she'd raced away from the sealed mine. The likely culprits were few. Gracella's daughter,

Selena, had perished in the underground passageway at the same time Gracella had drained years of life from Elana, and Elana's parents and brother had fled on New Year's Eve. Norbridge had put out feelers to locate them, but nothing had turned up other than a vague report from a hotel owner friend of his in Malta that a family meeting the Powters' description had been seen at a resort near Venice named the Malstella Villa. Beyond Elana's family, Elizabeth couldn't imagine who might want to assist Gracella.

"I can't think of anyone," she said, "but Freddy did some research on the Dredforth Method that you should know about." She shared the details from the Crimson Scarab, as Norbridge leaned closer throughout, his interest deepening.

"Perhaps you can help me look at that internet web spot later," he said. "Is that the right way to say it? Internet web spot?"

Elizabeth smiled. "You can just say website."

Norbridge said nothing in return. Instead, he pointed to his eyes with two splayed fingers as if to say, *Let's both keep a close watch on things.*

"On a different note," he said, "I want to share some news with you. You know I remain deeply troubled by Elana's condition and have been trying to determine what we can do to help her. Ideally, we'd make her twelve years old again, but that's not as easy as it sounds."

Elizabeth squinted at him. "That actually doesn't sound easy at all."

"Exactly," Norbridge said. "Which makes this whole thing a difficult nut to crack. We seem to be up a creek without a paddle and may be likened to the snowball that finds itself amidst the fires of—" He abruptly waved his hands before himself and sighed, dismissing the little expressions he favored and that Elizabeth always found so amusing. "I'm at a loss over it. However, short of reversing the aging process, I've been wanting to find a way to ease Elana's sadness and see if we can't help her become more alert. And I'm happy to report this seems to be occurring naturally." Norbridge leaned forward in his chair and fixed Elizabeth with a somber gaze. "I spoke with her this morning for one hour, and she is—finally—a bit like her old self again after all these weeks. She's very sad, of course, but she's communicating at last."

"That's great news!" Elizabeth said, even as she wondered if there might be a downside to Elana's improved awareness: Perhaps she would understand even more certainly that her situation was most likely hopeless. "I just wish there was something I could do for her."

"Well, I think there is. In fact, she wants to talk to you. After dinner tonight, I'd like us both to head to her room for a little get-together. If nothing else, you can help cheer her up."

Elizabeth wasn't sure this was such a good idea. She'd been inside Elana's room already on several occasions, but only to look at her as she slept and—as frequently as she could—to offer a prayer or two or three for some sort of recovery and comfort.

"You're sure we should?" Elizabeth said.

Norbridge held up a hand. "I'm sure. But I want to tell you something first. She knows a great deal about matters of interest to you and me. Her parents talked a lot, and she listened well. It turns out Gracella absolutely was behind the death of your parents." He lowered his eyes, and his voice became quiet. "I'm sorry to share the details with you. I know how painful it is—and, of course, it's just as painful for me." Norbridge put a hand to his mouth for a moment before continuing. "The fact is, though, that Gracella tracked down your mother and father and used that evil force of hers to make their car swerve off the road. So Elana says."

Elizabeth felt her stomach drop. During the Christmas past, Norbridge had shared with her some facts he'd uncovered about the death of her parents, Winnie and Ferland Somers; the primary thing was that they'd been killed in a mysterious car accident when Elizabeth was four.

"One detail Elana clarified for me which I'd never guessed," Norbridge continued, "is that Gracella is best able to replenish her own vitality by—well, there's no delicate way to say this—taking the lives of members of the Falls family. I thought she was simply an indiscriminate killer and that she kept up her magical strength by murdering anyone she chose. But it turns out the ideal victim is someone with the blood of her own family." Norbridge closed his eyes and gave a little shudder. "It's awful to even think about it, much less discuss."

Elizabeth put her hands to her face for a moment. She was thinking of her poor parents and the fire and noise of the car crash; the memory of it was indistinct in her mind.

She lowered her hands. "Why didn't I die, too?"

Norbridge held up a finger and allowed a moment of silence to gather. "Maybe because you're the last one or the youngest or some other reason that's not yet clear. But she couldn't destroy you along with your parents. In fact, when she used her powers to try to get rid of all three of you, it nearly caused her own death. At the last minute, she preserved herself by . . ."

"Using the Dredforth Method?" Elizabeth said.

"Exactly. My point is that Gracella's helpers—and I'm positive Selena and her husband were the ringleaders—preserved her body. Elana explained, too, how the family tried to get you to use the power of your necklace to further their schemes." He tapped the side of his head. "We're fortunate you're not only clever but have the resolve to withstand all the attacks that have come our way. You've saved Winterhouse twice now."

Elizabeth, though, felt her mood shifting from sadness to anger: She pictured Gracella, and Selena, too, and the others, engaged in all their plotting and schemes solely for selfish ends—and bringing unhappiness to Winterhouse and the people Elizabeth loved.

"But I couldn't save my parents," she said sharply.

"You were four years old. Gracella was a powerful sorceress."

"I'm the only one who survived." Elizabeth allowed her voice to rise a notch as she stared at Norbridge. "And maybe Gracella's still not really dead and gone."

Norbridge's face became very calm, and his voice softened. "Elizabeth," he whispered.

Something in this made her feel even more agitated, and despite her grandfather's attempt at consolation, her blood began to stir. *The feeling* arose—unbidden, as it still sometimes did, rather than as a thing under her control—and she fixed her wrathful eyes on a book sitting on the small table before them. With a burst of sound and motion, the book whipped off the table and flew toward the wall to Elizabeth's left, smacking against it before dropping to the carpet. Elizabeth hadn't seen this coming and was startled—but she also felt, in some part of herself, pleased. Her power was thrilling. She looked to Norbridge with an expectant, triumphant expression, even though she hadn't intended the thing to happen.

He, however, pointed to her sternly, his eyes narrowed with menace. "Don't!" he said, quietly but fiercely.

Elizabeth was taken aback. "But I—"

"I said don't!" Norbridge said, more loudly. "You need to control that. Always." He remained scowling at her.

The intensity of Norbridge's anger alarmed Elizabeth, even as she realized how satisfying it had felt to give free rein to her power. "Why are you so upset?" she said.

"Because I don't like to see that," Norbridge said sharply, raising his hand. "My sister did those sorts of things when she was your age. I didn't like it when she did it, and I don't like to see it now in you." He extended one finger in exclamation. "She got carried away."

Elizabeth felt a powerful urge to explain that it was impossible for him to understand how satisfying it had felt to have the book crash into the wall; something about this almost made her feel she understood why Gracella had gotten carried away all those years ago.

"You told me she thought no one here at Winterhouse listened to her," Elizabeth said, with a bit more exasperation than she intended. "So maybe she was just . . ." Elizabeth regretted her words instantly, even as her sentence died. Norbridge's scowl deepened, and he looked at her as though he didn't entirely recognize her. Silence hung between them for a moment, and then Norbridge stood and went to where the book lay on the floor. With a slow movement, he leaned down and picked it up before returning it to the table. *The North Sembla Chronicles* was the title on its front, and he laid it down gently.

"I'm going to forget this happened," he said. He sat at his desk and examined some papers, not looking at her. "Please meet me in front of Elana's room at seven thirty." He suddenly seemed occupied with reviewing the pages before him.

After a long silence, Elizabeth stood and departed the room without saying a word.

CHAPTER 6

A SILENT ERRAND IN A
FORBIDDEN ROOM

Elizabeth felt so confused—somehow both ashamed and cross—as she took the stairs down from the thirteenth floor, she couldn't focus on which one thing had flustered her most: the alarming manifestation of her power, the fact that in a few hours she would finally speak with Elana, or the news about her parents. All of them had been confounding, especially after the strangeness of what had happened at the Ripplington Mine.

But did Norbridge have to get so mad at me? she thought. She'd seen him angry before, of course, but this instance had seemed particularly severe.

She continued turning this over in her thoughts—not allowing the advice Leona had once given her ("Is the other person in control of your emotions, or are you?") to intrude on her foul mood. And then she pushed open the door to the third floor and saw, far down the hallway, that Freddy's workshop door was ajar. With an abrupt stop, Elizabeth peered along the corridor and considered what it might mean that a room that had remained locked since New Year's Eve now stood open. The last time she'd been in the workshop was almost three months before, when she and Freddy had discovered an entrance—the fourth and final entrance—into Winterhouse's secret passageways, hidden behind stacks of boxes. It had been through that doorway that Gracella, Selena, and Elana had stolen into the dark passageway as part of their plot.

Now Elizabeth listened for a moment, and then she stepped quietly forward, keeping her eyes on the door. No sound came from within; no ripple of *the feeling* arose inside her. She gave a single light press upon the brass door handle and stepped inside the workshop, which looked almost exactly as she remembered it: a workbench at its center, a wall covered with tools dangling from hooks, pieces of plywood and sawhorses and cabinets here and there. The one thing that was different—dramatically different—was that the wall with the fourth entrance had been bricked over completely. Elizabeth stared in amazement: If someone wanted to get inside the passageway again, it wasn't going to happen here.

She moved to the wall and ran her hand over the rough brickwork, tapping it lightly as if to test its strength. On impulse, she placed an ear against the wall and listened—just as she had listened at the door itself nearly three months before. On that previous occasion, she'd heard a faint humming, the same sound she'd eventually followed to find the odd ice sculpture hidden far beneath Winterhouse and that had allowed her to bring the power of her necklace to life. Now she expected only silence. But when she pressed her ear to the wall, she was startled to hear, faintly, the very same low sound that had arisen just after Christmas. She held her breath and closed her eyes. The humming was so indistinct, it almost couldn't be heard—but it was there.

Elizabeth jerked her head from the wall and peered around the room. A recollection came to her, and before she considered what she was doing, she moved to the hooks where the tools were arranged. On the right side of the panel and closer to the floor than the ceiling, hung a silver skeleton key—the very one Elizabeth had used two Christmases before to steal into Gracella's room. She glanced at the open door, and then she plucked the key from off its hook and departed the workshop. Without breaking stride, she moved down the corridor and took a left at the corner—toward Room 333. A moment later, Elizabeth stood before Gracella's door.

Room 333 was an oddity in the hotel and a place Elizabeth had, until now, avoided since she'd begun living at Winterhouse. It was at the end of a dark hallway that had no other doors along it, as though for some reason a dead-end corridor had been built and then never altered. The bulb in the ceiling outside the door was perpetually a notch or two more dim than any other light in the hotel, and a small sticker beside the lock on the door said NO ADMITTANCE. Everything about Room 333 was foreboding, and there were plenty of times when Elizabeth could hardly believe she'd once worked up the nerve to step inside. Now, all apprehension ignored, she told herself all she wanted to do was see if the Anna Lux book remained where she'd left it.

Elizabeth unlocked the door with the key and stepped inside, flicking on the light switch. Everything looked as she recalled: a bed in one corner with a quilt and blue pillows, a large bureau on the wall beside it, an empty

bookcase, a couple of chairs. All was as plain and simple as she'd found it when she'd been in the room on that only other occasion.

She moved directly to the bureau and slid open the top drawer—and there lay the book, a gray and ordinary hardback, as if it had been waiting for her these many months: *The Secret Instruction of Anna Lux*.

Right where it's always been, Elizabeth thought.

The feeling began to buzz inside her. She snatched up the book, opened to the first chapter, and read the first sentence, words she recalled so well she could have recited them: "There once was a girl so intrigued by magic and spells and all sorts of hidden things, she decided to become a witch."

She wanted to put the book down and leave, but something made her turn to the inside front cover of the book, where she found a neat, handwritten message in black ink: *For Gracella—Someday she will show everyone what they overlooked. Damien Crowley.*

Elizabeth put a hand to her forehead: Someone was approaching. With a quick motion, she put the book back, closed the drawer, and crossed the room. She peered through the doorway, and when she saw no one in the corridor, she turned off the light and exited. It was right as she pulled the door closed that Sampson rounded the corner.

"Elizabeth!" he said. "What are you doing here?" He strode forward warily.

"I . . . I thought I heard something." Elizabeth looked at the door behind her.

Sampson came to her and stopped. He squinted at the door as if he could tell if someone was within simply by focusing his concentration, and then he turned to Elizabeth with a smile and said, "Maybe you heard the storm outside. This room's locked tight."

She smiled hesitantly. "That's gotta be it. The storm."

An uneasy silence came over the corridor.

"Say, did I see the workshop open?" Elizabeth said. The key felt heavy in her pocket, and she realized she would need to figure out a way to return it at the first opportunity.

"You did." Sampson grinned. "Mr. Falls wanted me to . . ." He clamped a hand to his mouth and then, lowering it, said, "Well, you'll see soon enough! My lips are sealed."

Elizabeth laughed lightly, glad to move off of talking about Room 333 or what she was doing here in the hallway.

"I understand, Sampson," she said. "There's always something going on around here."

He nodded his head at her. "That's for sure." With a final glance at Room 333, he said, "But I better get back to work. And you might want to leave this part of the hallway to itself."

"Lead the way," she said. And as she followed Sampson down the corridor and listened to him talk about how festive everything was going to be for Easter, Elizabeth couldn't help thinking, *Damien Crowley left that book for Gracella.* There was a deeper thought, though, one she realized would be more difficult to quiet because it was so similar to words she sometimes told herself: *Someday she will show everyone what they overlooked.*

CHAPTER 7

THE DANGER IS IN THE PAST— OR MAYBE NOT

Winter Hall was, as always, festive and bright, its round tables laid with crisp white spreads and gleaming fine china, its chandeliers glittering like clusters of stars floating near the high ceiling, its enormous windows reflecting so much light and color the vast room seemed nearly endless. The one thing the dining hall was missing on this night was an occupant of each seat. If there was any doubt that mid-March was one of the slowest times of year at the hotel, one peek in Winter Hall during breakfast, lunch, or dinner on this particular Saturday would have confirmed the fact. The fireplace at the front of the hall still blazed with sweet-smelling fir and hemlock, and the tinkling notes of Bach's *Goldberg Variations* still drifted from unseen speakers in all corners, but the room was only half filled.

Elizabeth entered through a rear door and took in the lavish scene. She ate all her meals in this hall when she wasn't at school, but the sight of it—and the thought that the great hotel was her home and she really wasn't returning to Drere—felt ever new to her, ever gladdening. She straightened her sweater and listened as the wind from the fierce storm pressed against the hall's windows. Over the past hour, she'd resolved to put aside any lingering hard feelings toward Norbridge, and she'd decided—at least for now—not to think about how she'd stolen into Gracella's room. There was too much on her mind suddenly, and all she wanted to do was give herself over to a pleasant dinner in Winter Hall.

"Let's get a good seat, shall we, before the place is mobbed?" someone said behind her, and Elizabeth turned to see Leona Springer, Winterhouse's librarian and the person Elizabeth had grown closest to at the hotel. Not only did Leona love books as much as she did, but Elizabeth could also talk to her about nearly anything, even some of the things she was still trying to work through on her own before discussing with Norbridge. Leona seemed always able to come at things from a fresh angle, and Elizabeth both trusted and respected her opinions.

"Hi, Leona," Elizabeth said, hugging her. "Lead the way through this *massive* crowd!"

"Keep an eye on the bun atop my head," Leona said,

"or we might get separated in all the confusion." She broke into a laugh and moved past Elizabeth. "And let's look for our aspiring instructor, Mr. Crowley. He's been napping—er, studying—in my library the last hour or two while I read that great book you recommended, *The Stars Beneath Our Feet*. What a winner!"

"Glad you liked it," Elizabeth said, reflecting once again how nice it was to have a friend like Leona. She spotted Hyrum at a table near the front of the hall, sitting with Professor Egil P. Fowles and the two puzzle men and their wives. "I ran into Hyrum when I was skiing today," Elizabeth said.

"He mentioned that to me," Leona said. She stopped and eyed Elizabeth seriously. "That boy is quite a scholar. Today he tracked down Herbert Munchglick's *Mayhem and Mystery*, as well as *A History of the Peruvian Salt Ponds* by Shannon Okello, Perlowski's sketches from his travels in Uqbar, and he even thumbed through Marshall Falls's old journal. Quite an eclectic survey!" Her eyes widened with delight; she turned to scan ahead. "Look—he's waving to us."

A moment later, Elizabeth and Leona were settling in at the table and exchanging greetings with one and all. Mrs. Rajput and Mrs. Wellington, in their lovely evening dresses and brimming with jewelry, were delighted to find Elizabeth joining the table. Professor Fowles, despite seeing Elizabeth five days a week in the corridors of Havenworth Academy, was as jubilant as if this encounter were a rare reunion.

"Elizabeth, Elizabeth!" he said, dressed, as ever, in his brown tweed suit that looked thick enough to keep him warm even outside the walls of the hotel. "So wonderful to see you!" He took Elizabeth's hand first and then Leona's. "And our lovely Winterhouse librarian, too," he said, before glancing at his watch. "Who opens her doors precisely at nine o'clock in the A.M. daily, aside from Sundays. How very nice to see you both."

Before long, Norbridge joined them (he gave Elizabeth a little wink), and then delicious plates of fish and yams and green beans and double-corn cornbread were served, and all the members of the table (aside from glum Mr. Rajput) gave themselves over to pleasant conversation and laughter. Elizabeth was enjoying the evening so much, she nearly forgot about the incident at the mine or her worries over Elana or how she'd gone to Room 333. With a small pang of guilt, she thought about the puzzle piece hiding in a drawer of her desk.

"I'm not certain everyone is aware," Professor Fowles announced, after the dinner plates had been cleared and the blackberry pie and vanilla bean ice cream were delivered, "that our industrious Mr. Hyrum Crowley . . ." At this point, Egil placed a hand on the younger man's back and beamed at him. "Is diligently pursuing both his teaching certificate and a degree in comparative literature. Hyrum, perhaps you can share with the table your most recent interests?"

Hyrum, still dressed in the striped blue sweater he'd worn beneath his jacket while skiing, wiped his mouth with his napkin and placed his arms on the table. Elizabeth thought, not for the first time, that he had the straightest jawline and the most deliberate way of moving his hands of any person she'd ever known. Everyone at the table looked to him with expectation.

"Thank you, Mr. Fowles," Hyrum said. "Yes, while I'm training at Havenworth, I'm also working on a paper about fairy tales for my degree at the university. The older fairy tales, that is. They're actually much more frightening and, well, bloodier than people imagine." He bugged his eyes out good-naturedly. "It's been very interesting to learn all the terrifying things behind the supposedly nice stories we all know from the movies and picture books."

"A true heir to the chilling legacy of your grandfather," Mr. Rajput said gravely. "His books have caused so many sleepless nights and dreadful nightmares for countless readers—"

"Mr. Rajput," Mr. Wellington said. "Please, sir. You turn things so miserable so rapidly. It can be quite distressing. You are my good and loyal friend, but I would request discretion."

Mrs. Rajput put a hand on her husband's arm. "Dear," she said softly, nodding her head toward Elizabeth. "We don't want to frighten anyone."

"Oh, it's fine," Elizabeth said. "I've read lots of Damien Crowley's books. *Colin Dredmare's Chamber of Despair*, *The Gloom After Midnight*. A bunch of them. Norbridge gave me one when I first came to Winterhouse."

Elizabeth pictured the Anna Lux book in the drawer

in Gracella's room. She'd never asked Norbridge about this, of course, but it had always seemed curious to her that Norbridge had given her a book by Damien Crowley the day after she had happened upon a book by the same author in Gracella's room.

"Damien's work used to be very popular with people here at the hotel," Leona said. "And many other people, too. But he's fallen out of fashion now, I'm afraid. Today's readers find him a little *too macabre*. Schools, libraries— you can hardly find any of his books anymore."

"He grew up in Havenworth, you know," Norbridge said, turning from Elizabeth to Mr. Rajput. "Quite a man. He used to visit Winterhouse often when I was young."

"They don't write them like that nowadays," Egil P. Fowles said. "Unsettling but stylish. He had taste!" Professor Fowles glanced at his plate. "Friendly with that Avery Dimlow fellow, if I recall correctly. The old book-seller in Havenworth."

A chill went through Elizabeth. She visited Avery Dimlow's bookstore often, even though Avery himself was a bit odd; she'd been unaware of his connection to Damien Crowley.

"I barely knew my grandfather," Hyrum said. He glanced at his plate. "My mother used to say the older he got, the stranger he got, too."

"Stranger?" Mrs. Rajput said.

Hyrum glanced around the table with a furtive expression. "I guess he became interested in, well, magic. Real magic. Black magic, they say."

"He was engaged in research, perhaps?" Mr. Wellington said. "For his books?"

With a shrug, Hyrum resumed eating his pie. "I don't really know. We didn't talk about it much in my family. Everyone just sort of always mentioned 'Strange Old Damien.' I haven't read everything of his, but I do know his books got weirder over time. He started putting more magical stuff in them." Hyrum took a bite of his pie and paused to chew. "Personally, I find those later books kind of boring. He had this one called *The Electric Can Opener's Hideous Revenge* that was basically unreadable."

"You know, I met him once," Mrs. Wellington said softly, and everyone at the table looked to her. The wind outside howled and then quieted. "Here. When I was eleven."

An interesting thing about Mrs. Wellington was that she knew a great deal about the history of Winterhouse, having fallen in love with the hotel because of a lengthy stay she and her family had made when she was a girl. It was this fondness for the hotel—and her good memories of befriending both Norbridge and Gracella on that long-ago visit—that had led her and her husband and their friends the Rajputs to visit so often.

"You might recall it, Norbridge," Mrs. Wellington continued. "I think Damien's second book, *The Tower of Shadows and the Insatiable Noose*, had just come out, and he visited for dinner one night." A look of uncertainty came over her face. "Goodness, shall I go on?"

Elizabeth felt another chill go through her; she forked

up a bite of pie and began eating quickly to mask her discomfiture.

"Please do," Professor Fowles said. "You have us curious. In your clutches, absolutely."

Mrs. Wellington glanced about the table, her eyes resting on Hyrum. "Your grandfather found Norbridge's sister, Gracella, very charming, I recall from that evening. Very precocious. She was eleven and he was nearly thirty, of course. But she asked a number of questions at the dinner table, and it was clear he thought she had a remarkable intelligence. He even said, 'Why maybe I'll write a special book for you one day,' and we all laughed. I probably felt a little envious. You know how you can be at that age." She looked to Elizabeth and wagged her head contritely. "Or any age! Anyway, that's the whole story. Not very exciting, I'm afraid." She began fidgeting with one of the glassy earrings she wore. "You've mentioned he used to visit Winterhouse often, Norbridge," she continued. "Do you recall the last time he came?"

"I do," Norbridge said. He'd been listening with something of a shadow over his face, Elizabeth felt. "It was nearly twenty-five years ago, and he came to visit for a night. Very anticlimactic. He seemed tired the entire time. As you can imagine, I was surprised to have his company again. We hadn't seen him in ages, and I'd lost track of him. I actually thought he'd passed away."

"I recall the visit," Egil P. Fowles said. "And, yes, I think it's safe to say we all thought the gentleman had gone to the old haunted house in the sky. Fitting, eh, Norbridge? Given that Crowley often wrote about those who returned from the grave." He looked around the table. "A scarab—a beetle revered by the ancient Egyptians— figures in some of his novels." He looked around the table once more. "The scarab is an ancient symbol of immortality. Of *resurrection*."

Elizabeth was completely alert now. "Do you think he really learned about those things?" she said, with a glance at Norbridge. "Like, real magic?"

Professor Fowles drew his chin in. "I had little personal acquaintance with the gentleman, though I've read up a bit on him. The Egyptologists' Society of Northern South Dakota maintains an engaging website called the Crimson Scarab, on which they make some mention of him." He turned to Hyrum. "Any contributions to our knowledge from you, sir?"

Hyrum dabbed a napkin to his mouth; with an impish expression he said, "I just didn't know Grandpa Damien at all. But, gosh, all this talk about him is starting to creep me out!"

Everyone at the table laughed, and a momentary tension seemed to have passed. Elizabeth noticed, though, that Leona appeared distracted, even as she tried to laugh along with the others. There was something more to the story of Damien Crowley, Elizabeth felt certain.

"You understand we're not letting you leave in this weather," Norbridge said, pointing to Egil and Hyrum.

"The roads are impassable, and so you must stay the night. What fun! Concert at eight, and then a round of hot chocolate for everyone. It will be a night to remember."

"We have a puzzle to attend to," Mr. Wellington said, winking at Mr. Rajput. "Music and levity are all fine, but—"

The ground rumbled.

Everyone—not just at Elizabeth's table, but across the dining room—froze and stared with wide eyes. Winter Hall shook for a good five seconds, and when the rumbling ceased, all the diners sat warily, waiting to see what would happen next.

Norbridge stood. "I believe an exceptionally rare thundersnow event has just occurred!" he called, turning to look at the tables on all sides. "They don't happen often, but when they do they can be startling." He put both hands to his ribs as if prepared to explain more and then he hesitated. "Enjoy your pie, please, and let me go check on something. I shall return shortly."

He leaned down to the others at the table and said, "I keep a seismograph downstairs in a locked closet near the air hockey tables. I want to take a quick gauge of things. Remarkable! Thundersnow! Who would have guessed? This last happened eighteen years ago."

He pivoted and rushed from the hall, the eyes of everyone on him as he disappeared. A murmur of concern overtook the large room.

Professor Fowles looked stunned, and Mr. Rajput

appeared so distraught Elizabeth wondered if he was about to cry. "Thundersnow?" he muttered.

"Can there really be thunder with snow?" Mrs. Rajput said.

"Wouldn't we have seen a flash of lightning first?" Mr. Wellington said.

It was exactly what Elizabeth was thinking. She was distracted, though, because Hyrum was so pale and dazed he looked ready to lose his dinner.

"Are you all right, young man?" Leona asked him.

He flinched and then turned to her. "Fine," he said weakly. He sat up and inhaled; his color returned, and he put a chipper look on his face. "Shaking like that really gets me, I guess." With a shrug of embarrassment, he looked to Elizabeth. "Wanna play some air hockey later?"

Everyone laughed once more, the strange moment passed, and dessert resumed. But Elizabeth couldn't stop thinking she hadn't seen any lightning at the mine earlier in the day when the ground had rumbled there, either.

CHAPTER 8

YEAR ONE HUNDRED FOR THE OLDEST WOMAN AT WINTERHOUSE

When Elizabeth arrived at Elana's room just before seven thirty to find Norbridge waiting for her, she wanted to ask him what he'd discovered about the rumbling that had interrupted dinner. Not only was she curious—she felt, too, discussion of this sort might fully dissipate the tension that had arisen between them earlier that day. Norbridge, though, simply opened his arms to give Elizabeth a hug as she came up to him. The two of them embraced in silence for a moment and then Norbridge, with a gentle glance, opened the door.

Elana's room was lit by a small lamp on an end table beside the bed. Elizabeth had been inside at least a dozen times before to visit Elana, but never had she seen what she saw now: Elana sitting upright beneath her quilts, with her back against two heavy pillows, and her eyes finally open. Not only open—she was reading a book, *From the Mixed-Up Files of Mrs. Basil E. Frankweiler,* and this, almost as much as seeing Elana awake and alert, took her aback.

"I love that book!" Elizabeth said, and then put a hand to her mouth and looked to Norbridge. "Sorry. I didn't mean to be loud."

Elana set the book on her lap with a deliberate motion and regarded Elizabeth with mournful eyes. She looked every bit an old woman. Gone were the lustrous black hair

and dancing eyes and smooth skin that had once made Elizabeth so jealous. Elana's youthful attractions had been replaced by thin white hair and a face so wrinkled and drawn, Elizabeth wondered if Elana had worked up the nerve to look at herself in a mirror. There was nothing wrong with growing old, of course, Elizabeth considered, but to jump from being twelve years old to . . . this. It was unsurprising that Elana's eyes brimmed with weariness.

"I love this book, too," Elana said, her voice as aged as her body.

Norbridge took in a deep breath. "I thought you'd like to have a visitor," he said to Elana. "And Elizabeth has been hoping to see you for weeks now. Maybe the two of you—"

But before Norbridge could finish, Elizabeth rushed to the bed and put her arms around Elana, and they embraced, neither saying a word for nearly two minutes. When Elizabeth finally pulled back, Elana simply looked at her, but still neither spoke.

"Some Flurschen, anyone?" Norbridge said, removing a packet of candy from his pocket. Elizabeth laughed lightly, Elana smiled, and the room settled a bit.

Elizabeth sat on the bed. "I'm so sorry about everything."

"I'm the one who should be apologizing," Elana said. "There were so many times I wanted to warn you about what was going on and what my aunt and my parents were planning."

"You couldn't go against your family," Norbridge said

matter-of-factly. "We understand. Everyone understands. It was an impossible situation, and you shouldn't blame yourself."

"They knew everything about Winterhouse," Elana said. "From all the stories the family told over the years. That's how my parents knew about The Book and the passageways, and that's how Aunt Selena got us to go along with her. All the promises she made. And Gracella frightened all of us. I felt like I couldn't say no."

"Please, you don't have to explain," Norbridge said, idly shifting the bag of candy from hand to hand. "It's unfortunate, everything that happened. And I feel awful about things with your parents and how they've just gone and disappeared. Still, you're not to blame for any of it."

Elana's tired eyes settled on her book. "I know," she said, nearly whispering.

"We're going to do something to help you," Elizabeth said, taking Elana's hand. "I don't know what, but we'll figure it out." She turned to her grandfather. "Right, Norbridge?"

Elana tilted her head and looked to him. "What can you do? I know that no one . . ." She paused and lifted her hands before her; she stared at them as if they didn't belong to her before dropping them back to the bed. "I know there's nothing anyone can do."

"I wouldn't be so sure," Norbridge said. "Both of you understand better than most anyone that there's plenty of magic in the Falls family and this old hotel." He lifted an arm to flex in imitation of a bodybuilder. "Even in these old bones."

He looked from Elana to Elizabeth as they both remained silent. And then, with utter and unforeseen swiftness, he tossed the candies up to the ceiling as he snapped his fingers, and somehow—in some flash when Elizabeth maybe blinked or was blinded by a spark of light—the small package was gone, and in its place were two balloons, one silver and one purple. They hovered at the ceiling as though a child had let them loose to float to the top of the room where they'd become stranded. And then, as if that wasn't enough, the balloons slowly drifted downward and floated right to the two girls, though when Elizabeth reached for the purple one and Elana for the silver, the balloons popped in unison with a sharp crack.

Elizabeth laughed in wonder. "Wow!" she called out.

Elana smiled wanly, but she seemed genuinely pleased. "Well, that was very cool," she said. And Elizabeth laughed again, both because what Norbridge had done was so delightful and because it was nice to know that the true Elana—the one who was twelve—was still inside the old woman who was on the bed; until that moment, she'd seemed completely defeated. Maybe Norbridge really could come up with something to return Elana to normal.

"Have you read any other good books lately?" Elana asked Elizabeth, and with that, the two of them began chatting away as if this was simply an ordinary visit on an ordinary day. After ten minutes, despite Elana's evident fatigue, Elizabeth felt that, if nothing else, Elana had maybe forgotten her unfortunate circumstances for a little while.

"Can you bring me some good books from the library?" Elana said after a time.

"I'll bring a few of my favorites," she said. A flutter of *the feeling* came over her.

"Well, listen, you two," Norbridge said, "I have some things to attend to before the concert. Elizabeth, if you'd like to stay and visit for a bit more, please feel free, but—"

A knock at the door interrupted him; before he could rise or call to whoever was in the hallway, the knob turned and the door was opening. There, to Elizabeth's absolute astonishment, stood Lena Falls—the elderly daughter of the oldest inhabitant of Winterhouse, Norbridge's ninety-nine-year-old cousin, Kiona Falls. Lena's gray hair was combed, her jaw was set firmly, she had on a navy-blue bathrobe, and she looked as though the room belonged to her and she was perplexed to find three people gathered within.

Norbridge stood. He looked unnerved, his face pinched with bafflement. "Lena?" he said, though it wouldn't have mattered what words he'd uttered, because Lena could neither hear nor speak, a condition that had arisen more than sixty years before. As far as Elizabeth knew, Lena had only left her room for Christmas Eve dinners over the past two decades, and she hadn't even done that during the holiday just past. She spent her days in a nearly endless nap, and no one—not even her mother, Kiona—knew what went on in her head or why she'd slipped so far from the rest of the world. She could eat, she was able to stand up and walk; she just simply did not communicate. One thing was certain, though: She hadn't left her room by herself in years.

Norbridge swept his arm past himself to welcome Lena into the room, and she nodded to him as if they were in the habit of running into each other all the time. She dipped her chin to Elizabeth in greeting. And then she made directly for the bed, sat on it, took Elana's hand in both of hers, and stared into her eyes as if her sole reason for coming to Room 423 was to examine the color of Elana's pupils.

The room was completely silent as Lena sat staring.

"Is there something you want to say?" Elana said finally.

"She's unable to speak," Norbridge said. "She can't hear anything, either." And then, in a lower voice: "I'm stunned to see her out and about."

Elizabeth looked to him in confusion. Lena closed her eyes and tipped her head forward. She moved her lips silently for several seconds, and then she let go of Elana's hands, stood, turned, and walked out the door. Just like that, the three were alone again, and the aura of bewilderment that had enveloped them when Lena had been present grew even thicker.

"What was that all about?" Elana said. And after Norbridge explained Lena's condition and how she'd taken to her bed twenty-three years before and seemed almost entirely unaware of the existence of a world outside her head, Elana stared at her quilt and sank into deep thought.

"It was like she wanted to tell me something," Elana said softly.

The feeling came over Elizabeth once more, and by way of alerting Norbridge that all the strangeness of the evening was perhaps not yet over, she gestured with her chin to the door just before another knock sounded at it.

"Come in," Norbridge called. When the door opened, there appeared Sampson standing behind a wheelchair in which sat Kiona Falls with a heavy blanket covering her up to her neck, a pink stocking cap on her head, and a look of incomprehension on her face.

"Was my daughter just in here?" Kiona said. Sampson gave a little grimace behind her, as if he had no idea what was going on and was only doing the old woman's bidding.

"Actually," Norbridge said, "she was. She departed ten minutes ago. First time we've seen her down this way in, oh, more than two decades." He went to Kiona, knelt, and kissed her on both cheeks. "What, exactly, is *up*, as they say nowadays? Please edify us, my dear lady."

Kiona lifted a hand and stiffly turned to glance back at Sampson. "Thank you, sir, for accompanying me to this room. You wheel exquisitely."

Sampson grinned and looked to Norbridge. "Miss Falls requested a little trip down here."

Kiona saluted in Elana's direction. "A hearty good evening to you, Elana dear. Very glad to see you are doing well." She placed a hand over her heart. "It warms me. To my core." With her hand still pressed to her chest, she smiled at Elizabeth. "And my dear second cousin twice removed, Elizabeth, it is a delight to see you, as always." She shook her head in wonderment. "I never get over how much more you resemble your mother with each passing day."

Kiona dropped her hand and shook her head at Norbridge. "I can't account for it, but over the last three days, my daughter has become more . . . *active*. More alive, more awake, more *with it*! She's never been much for signing with her hands, but yesterday she began spelling out something. At first, I thought it was her own name, but then I realized she was working through Elana's. And then it became clear she wanted to see the dear girl." She grimaced. "Or 'dear woman,' perhaps I should say?" She gave Elana a look of uncertainty. "I'm sorry. I don't . . ."

"It's okay," Elana said. She stared at her hands.

Kiona touched her forehead as if to indicate she'd made a careless mistake, and then she continued. "Lena kept spelling the name over and over, and she became more agitated. It kept on this morning, and then when I woke up not long ago, she was gone! Imagine my surprise. She's been sleeping in the bed beside me since August sixteenth twenty-three years ago, and suddenly—" Here, Kiona made a slicing motion before her. "Gone!"

"That is unusual," Norbridge said. "Very unusual." He set his teeth on his lip.

"I figured she must have come here," Kiona said. "Though I have not the slightest idea why. She seems to be in the grip of some obsession. It's the strangest thing."

"She didn't try to spell any other words?" Norbridge said.

Kiona looked to the carpet for a moment before peering

at Norbridge. "Twice she spelled out 'method.' I have no idea what she was getting at."

An uncanny quiet filled the room. Elizabeth felt chilled. *Lena couldn't possibly be referring to the Dredforth Method, could she?* she thought.

Kiona looked to Elana, who tapped her ear and said, "How did it happen?"

"Lena's hearing and speech?" Kiona said. "I wish I knew. She was out skiing one day and didn't come back. She was twenty at the time. When they found her out-side late that night, everything was different. She was in a daze, and she's never recovered. Maybe it was the cold or . . . I don't know. Lena never explained. Many more years passed, and she slowly sank into herself." She shook her head. "Very sad. Very sad for all of us."

"Your birthday is coming up?" Elana said. Norbridge inhaled sharply, but Kiona put a hand out to him and leaned forward.

"It's all right," Kiona said. "I don't mind talking about it. Yes, dear, on June twelfth. My one hundredth birthday. Quite a milestone, particularly around this place."

It was a very peculiar thing, but—as was plain from the family tree on the wall outside Winter Hall—nearly every woman in the Falls family had lived to be one hun-dred years old. Not a year more or a year less, but one hundred exactly. Why this was the case was something no one understood—not Norbridge or Leona or anyone at the hotel. It simply *was*, as much of a fact of life at Winter-house as snow all winter and the aroma of Flurschen in

77

the corridors. Elizabeth had often wondered what went through Kiona's mind as she considered the months ahead: Everyone understands, on some level, what the future holds, but to know with almost complete certainty what your next birthday holds must be discomfiting.

"Are you afraid?" Elana said.

Kiona smiled faintly. "I've had a good life." She winked at Elizabeth. "I've tried to put others before myself, and I have to say, that's been my secret formula for happiness."

The Winterhouse chimes sounded, signaling the concert would begin in ten minutes.

"Just as I planned it," Norbridge said, and everyone began to laugh. "I really better run now. You, too, Elizabeth, if you want to hear the sonata."

"And I'm going to chase down my daughter," Kiona said. She thumped a loose fist on the arm of her wheelchair and turned to Sampson. "Let's fire this thing up, young man."

"Aye-aye, Miss Falls," he said.

Elizabeth gave Elana one last hug. "I'll see you soon. And I'll bring you plenty to read. There's one called *Five Children and It* that you'll love."

Elana gave a thumbs-up that she displayed to the entire room. She seemed glad—though as Elizabeth headed to Grace Hall, she felt certain Elana had been holding back tears.

CHAPTER 9

A SWITCH IN GEARS

By ten thirty that night—after Sunny Chen's concert, after the promised hot chocolate, after helping Mr. Wellington and Mr. Rajput locate four pieces in their puzzle, and even after making a new entry in her journal under "Pros and Cons of Living at Winterhouse" ("Pro #48: meeting friendly and famous musicians")—Elizabeth was sitting at her desk and finishing her email response to Freddy. She told him she agreed there was plenty more to discuss regarding Riley Granger and the Dredforth Method and then she caught him up on everything important she could think of: Elana, the mine, Lena's unexpected appearance, the puzzle men, the rumbling in Winter Hall, and even her classes at Havenworth and the latest books she had read.

I'm really looking forward to having you come for Eaters, she wrote as she came to an end. *I mean Teaser. I mean Easter. Seriously, it will be great to see you in a few days. Your friend—Belize Hat (that's "Elizabeth," in anagram form, in case you're losing your touch!)*

She clicked Send, and then opened her drawer to peer at the blue puzzle piece. *I'll return it soon,* she thought, before closing the drawer and considering the rumbling at dinner. After Sunny Chen's concert, Norbridge informed Elizabeth that his seismograph had registered a shaking equivalent to a very minor earthquake, and he said he recalled the very same thing occurring three times in his memory, all with an absence of lightning on those occasions, too.

"Perhaps it was just natural shifting under the ground," Norbridge told her. "Heat vents or ice balls or something or another. Let's hope that's what occurred when you were at the mine."

It was all very disconcerting to Elizabeth, and as she thought about the many ups and downs of the day, she felt what she most wanted to do was sit on her sofa and let all her cares drift off as she turned the pages of a good book.

She grabbed *Darkness at the End of the Tunnel* from the small table beside her bed, plopped down on the sofa, and began to read.

Elizabeth arose at midnight. She left her room and wandered through the cold and gloomy corridors, eventually finding herself in the library, where everything was tattered and dark. Winterhouse was deserted, with no guests and no staff and no members of the Falls family remaining; everyone had departed, and the enormous hotel was silent and empty.

A voice called as she stood in the dim center of the huge, ruined space: *Elizabeth*. And then her name sounded again, and then once more. Three times in total.

A crimson light appeared from far atop the staircase on the third floor.

I loved this library, too, the voice called. *I loved to spend hours here. Just like you.*

Though she couldn't see anything other than the thin crimson light, Elizabeth stood looking upward, listening for the voice from the darkness far above. She moved to the staircase and put a hand on the banister. A powerful desire to ascend to the top floor came over her as the words she'd heard echoed in her head: *Just like you.*

A small lamp set on a table beside the staircase flickered; Elizabeth felt an unaccountable impulse to point a finger at it and, with a surge of her power, send it crashing to the ground.

Yes, came the voice once more. *I understand. That power. Who wouldn't want to use it?*

Elizabeth extended her finger toward the lamp, experienced the familiar flutter in her stomach, felt herself set to let loose with something fierce and satisfying—something powerful.

Just like you.

She kept her finger pointed straight at the lamp, focusing, concentrating, her vision beginning to blur and a buzzing arising in her head.

Just like you! came the voice once more, and the thrumming noise inside Elizabeth became so loud that she pressed both hands to her ears and—

With a gasp, she jerked her head off the sofa cushion and looked to her clock. Midnight. The nightmare had blinked out.

She's tempting me, Elizabeth thought as she sat and tried to calm herself. *Gracella's tempting me.* She couldn't help thinking, though, how much she'd wanted to see that lamp broken on the carpet.

Elizabeth stood and went to the window and, in the faint light of the hotel's outside lampposts, saw that the snow was falling harder than ever. High white drifts had swelled on the ground, stretching away from Winterhouse and toward the chill darkness of Lake Luna; the black sky was alive with tumbling flakes. Elizabeth's heart was still beating quickly, and she thought for a moment what she ought to do was change into her pajamas, have a glass of water, and get into bed. But then a sensation of restlessness came over her, and as she looked to her door, she found herself turning the knob and stepping into the hallway beyond. She wanted to see someone—anyone at all, for a bit of reassuring company, perhaps, or a few minutes of conversation—and so she headed to the stairwell and walked quickly down to the lobby.

At Christmastime, the Winterhouse lobby would have been a bit lively even at midnight, but on this evening, especially with the storm raging outside and so few guests staying the night, the enormous space was as quiet and dim as Elizabeth's own room. No one was in sight, the chandeliers were dark, and a dull glow from the lampposts standing sentry outside filtered in through the high windows with a spectral dimness. At the clerk's desk was a sign beside the silver call bell that read PLEASE RING IF SERVICE IS REQUIRED. WE ARE AVAILABLE TO MEET YOUR NEEDS.

Elizabeth was about to press a finger to the small button atop the bell when she stopped and looked to the puzzle table. A flicker of curiosity—something like *the feeling*, but only a fraction as insistent—came over her, and she found herself drawn to the spread of pieces. Mr. Wellington and Mr. Rajput had left their customary sign on display, the one they used when they were staying at the hotel: WORK IN PROGRESS; PLEASE DO NOT TOUCH.

The puzzle lay before her.

With a glance at the clerk's desk, Elizabeth pressed both hands to the table and studied the pieces. So much of the picture had been completed, the assemblage was near to matching the illustration of the stone sanctuary depicted on the enormous tin box that had housed the pieces. Elizabeth had thought often about the temple since she'd first seen the puzzle. The thought that Norbridge's grandfather Nestor, along with his friend, the enigmatic

Riley Sweth Granger, had spent half a decade there, apparently studying ancient secrets, seemed both thrilling and scary. She couldn't picture living in such a desolate, distant place.

Once again, within the rim of the puzzle, she ran her finger over the foreign letters—a word for "faith"—above the door of the building. She examined the scattering of wooden shapes lying about; her hand moved directly to a snowy white piece that she drew—without hesitation—to a section of mountain, and she locked it in snugly to an empty space. It was only later that she considered how strange this had been: For the first time, she'd worked on

the puzzle without either Mr. Wellington or Mr. Rajput present.

"Wow!" someone said behind her, and Elizabeth nearly tumbled forward into the table, she was so startled by the voice.

"Yikes!" she called as she turned and saw Hyrum Crowley, still in his blue striped sweater, standing and raising his hands in what looked like surrender. Her shock had shocked him, she realized as she put a hand to her chest. "You scared me!"

"Sorry," he said, his voice full of apology, his hands still lifted to show he'd meant no harm. "You were concentrating so hard, I didn't want to throw you off. I'm really sorry!"

Elizabeth sighed heavily to calm her pulse. "It's okay," she said, even as Hyrum was looking past her to the puzzle. A thought came to her that she hadn't had any bit of premonition of his presence, and this surprised her; maybe her concentration had been so complete as she'd located the puzzle piece, there hadn't been any space for her mind to sense Hyrum's arrival.

"How do you do that?" he said, his voice and expression—the whole cast of his body—full of wonderment as he examined the puzzle. "That's an amazing talent."

"I don't know. Something just comes to me."

Hyrum shook his head, baffled, and continued to study the puzzle. "Well, I'm sure Mr. Rajput and Mr. Wellington appreciate it. At this rate, they might be done by Easter."

"It'll be incredible to watch them finish." Elizabeth

thought again of the piece she'd hidden in her drawer; she glanced past Hyrum into the dark corridor. "You're up pretty late."

Hyrum ran a hand through his black hair. "With that wind blowing, I just couldn't nod off." He looked sheepish. "And then I started reading one of my grandfather's books, and you can forget about falling asleep at that point! I was hoping to grab a little snack or something, so I came down here. But it looks like the shop is all closed up."

"We can ring the bell if you like."

"No, it's okay." He lifted his head to gaze at the ceiling. "It almost looks more majestic here at night with no one around." He sighed in wonder. "Winterhouse."

"I know," Elizabeth said. "It's the best." She paused. "I really like going to school in Havenworth, too. It's way better than the one I used to go to."

"Professor Fowles runs a great school. I'd like to be a full-time teacher there someday."

"I think you're doing a great job so far. Everyone thinks that."

Hyrum shrugged. "I was lucky to get an assignment here. I always wanted to come back to this area, seeing as my family was from here. Or my grandfather was, at least. 'Winterhouse, Winterhouse!' That's all I used to hear from my mother when I was a kid."

"Your dad wasn't from here?"

Hyrum shook his head. "No. And I never had a chance to know him, either. He died about three months before I was born."

Elizabeth wasn't sure what to say. It was one thing to have your parents taken from you at a young age; it seemed another thing entirely—something not only rare but very peculiar—for your father to have not even been alive when you were born.

"I'm sorry," she said. "I didn't mean to bring it up."

"It's okay," Hyrum said. He gave her a reassuring smile, and it was at that moment she decided to return to the topic they'd been discussing earlier in the day.

"Have you ever read a book by your grandfather called *The Secret Instruction of Anna Lux*?" she said.

He tilted his head in surprise. "You know, interesting thing about that book. According to what my mother told me, no copies of it exist anywhere. Grandpa Damien wrote it and then just before it was going to be published, I guess he had second thoughts and told the book publisher to destroy all the copies. No one seems to know why, but my mother once told me he put something in there about some magical ceremony and then decided he didn't want people to know about it." He shrugged. "How did you hear about that book?"

Elizabeth was flustered by this. "Leona mentioned it once."

"I've seen stuff online where collectors ask about it. If a copy turned up, it would be a big deal."

Elizabeth thought of the first sentence in the book: *There once was a girl so intrigued by magic and spells and all sorts of hidden things, she decided to become a witch.*

"Hey, you guys!" someone said. They turned to see

Sampson at the clerk's desk. "I thought I heard something out here."

"You're on duty tonight?" Elizabeth said as Sampson came to them.

"I am," he said, straightening his tiny red hat. "The diligent and dapper desk-front dude on duty during . . ." Sampson's eyes moved left and right as he tried to think of the right words. "The dead of night!"

"Wow, you are one poetic . . ." Hyrum began, losing his way immediately. "Person!" he said, with a snap of his fingers. "Seriously, that was incredible. Especially at this late hour."

"The *witching* hour," Sampson said, in a slow, spooky voice, before breaking into laughter. "It's always good to see friendly faces around this place when I have the night shift."

They caught up for a few minutes, and Elizabeth—despite the moment of surprise when Hyrum had startled her—felt glad she'd come to the lobby. After her nightmare, a friendly conversation with Sampson and Hyrum was exactly what she needed to calm her thoughts.

"Well, if you want a bite to eat," Sampson said to Hyrum finally, "I can take you to the kitchen and we can rustle something up, no problem."

Hyrum held up both palms. "Then let's do it."

"You coming, Elizabeth?" Sampson said.

A part of her wanted to say yes, but another part had the feeling she wanted a moment alone in the lobby, without interruption. She forced a yawn. "I think I'm gonna turn in," she said, and then she gave Hyrum a little frown. "I have a ton of homework to do tomorrow."

"Come on, then," Sampson said. "We'll walk you to the stairs on our way."

Five minutes later, after she was certain the two others were gone, and after she'd retraced her steps and returned to the lobby, Elizabeth stood before the puzzle table and understood just what had been gnawing at her: She wanted to locate another piece to fit in. It was almost as though, because she'd already found one piece without the puzzle men present, she felt less reluctance about finding another. A part of her sensed the minutes ticking by, and she wondered what she would say if Sampson and Hyrum returned and found her there. But the larger part of her felt driven, her thoughts unsettled. And then a piece seemed almost to affix itself to her searching hand, and without thinking about what she was doing, she locked it into a cluster along the bottom of the puzzle. The sensation was so satisfying, she had to keep herself from continuing. But just then she heard voices from the corridor and so she turned and rushed off in the opposite direction and raced up the stairway.

When she reached the third floor, *the feeling* came over her. In complete silence, she tiptoed upon the carpet, her eyes searching the distance ahead, and as she turned the corner to the long hallway that ended at Room 333, there stood Lena Falls in her bathrobe and slippers, motionless before Gracella's door and with her back to Elizabeth.

The fluttering in Elizabeth's stomach went wild, and

a low buzzing sounded in her head. With a hesitant step, she moved forward, toward Lena. But then she heard the swishing of someone coming quickly up the staircase just ahead of her to the left, and she retreated behind the corner she'd just turned and listened.

"Miss Falls?" came a voice.

That's Sampson, Elizabeth thought. She heard his footsteps moving away from where she was hidden, which could only mean he was approaching Lena, so Elizabeth peeked around the corner to watch.

"Miss Falls," Sampson said, stepping up to her slowly and then delicately putting a hand on her arm. "I know you can't hear me, but it's very late, and you should be in bed." He bobbed his head kindly to her. "Please. Let's get you back to your room."

With no hesitancy, Lena turned with him and moved away from Gracella's door. Elizabeth ducked out of sight and then rushed, as silently as she was able, to her room; she didn't want Sampson or Lena to see her as they walked to the elevator.

What is going on with Lena? Elizabeth thought. As she slipped inside Room 301 and closed the door behind her, she heard the voice inside her head once more: *Just like you.*

Elizabeth felt a wave of panic go through her. Without considering what she was doing, she opened her drawer and stared at the puzzle piece lying there.

That power, came the voice again, even more insistent. *Who wouldn't want to use it?*

Elizabeth slid her drawer closed quickly and looked to the window. Snow was pouring down through the black sky. Her room was shadowy and still. She changed into her pajamas in seconds, dived under her covers, and pulled her blankets up over her eyes.

"I will not be afraid," she whispered, but it took her a long while before she fell asleep.

PART TWO

ALAS, THE DANGER INCREASES

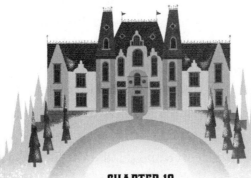

CHAPTER 10

IN THE DIM, LOWERING LIGHT OF AFTERNOON

Five days later—the next-to-last Thursday in March— the Havenworth Academy dismissal bell chimed at exactly two thirty in the afternoon, announcing the start of Easter holiday. Elizabeth offered quick farewells to her friends before presenting handmade *Have a Nice Vacation!* cards to the staff assembled in front of the school: seventeen teachers, Professor Fowles, the two ladies who served lunch, and the custodian, Mr. Willard Fentley. At 2:39, she was hurrying past the town gazebo and hoping she had time to complete a single task—a thing she'd spent all week working up the nerve to attempt—before catching the three-o'clock shuttle back to Winterhouse. And even though she had her mind fixed on the matter at hand,

Elizabeth could barely contain her excitement, not only because she had eleven and a half days of vacation ahead, but because Freddy and his parents would be arriving that afternoon to spend the entire Easter holiday.

As she rushed, and even as she continued thinking about what she was resolved to do, Elizabeth admired her surroundings. Havenworth, with its Bavarian-style buildings and carefully cleared and piled snow (if half of it melted by May Day, that would be a rare warm spring), was decorated with strung lights and glittering banners; the music that lilted from speakers here and there made the atmosphere almost as festive as it had been during December. Elizabeth had grown to love the town, with its gleaming shops and cozy hideaways. Sometimes she almost had to pinch herself when she considered she attended school in such a lovely place, especially when she compared it to the shabby school she'd gone to in Drere. Three months before, she'd yet to set foot in Havenworth, and now she had the good fortune to spend five days a week there.

Two minutes ahead of the schedule she'd drawn up in her head, Elizabeth arrived at her destination two blocks north of Main Street: Harley Dimlow and Sons, Booksellers. Since she'd begun living at Winterhouse, she'd visited the place, which had thousands of books and was generally so hushed and dim it felt a bit like a library itself, at least two dozen times. On this afternoon, cold and overcast, but without snow, Elizabeth was hoping Mr. Avery Dimlow, one of the deceased Harley's sons, wouldn't seem quite as creepy and intimidating as he usually did—because she'd come to his shop to ask him a question.

Elizabeth hitched her backpack high onto her shoulders, took a deep breath, opened the door, and stepped inside. She looked to the clerk's desk, which appeared empty, and waited. Despite the many times she'd been in the bookstore, Avery Dimlow, with his bloodshot and bulging eyes, his thin gray hair, his sallow skin, and the lethargic and deliberate way he moved his body—as though every action risked a tumble or some sharp pain—still scared her a little. He typically sat stooped at a high desk behind a perpetual mini wall of books stacked here and there, and he always seemed to be lurking in the protected and shadowy zone he'd arranged for himself. Behind him was a black recess; before him were the brimming and massive rows of shelves on which sat thousands of books, all beneath a few pale ceiling bulbs and enclosed on three sides by dark oak paneling. The walls were mostly hidden behind bookcases, but on an empty patch near the door were two faded posters, one featuring a picture of the cover of *The House with a Clock in Its Walls* and the other of the circle at Stonehenge with a rising sun shining through a frame of rock pillars.

Elizabeth cleared her throat. All was silent for a moment and then, like a turtle tentatively extending its snout from its shell to make certain nothing hazardous was nearby, Avery Dimlow stretched his head from the murky space where he sat, and a creaking sound echoed. Elizabeth was never sure if this little noise—which arose every time the old man moved—came from somewhere in Avery Dimlow's rusty bones or had something to do with the floorboards or maybe the legs of his chair; it always sounded uncomfortable.

"Good afternoon," the old man whispered, examining Elizabeth through his thick glasses.

"Hello, Mr. Dimlow," Elizabeth said, already extremely edgy. "Good afternoon. Good *Thursday* afternoon. I hope you're doing well here." She never knew what to say to the clerk, especially because he made her so nervous; however, as was her habit with any adult who hadn't proven unkind to her, she was unfailingly polite. It was the words, only, that were difficult in this case. "With all your books," she added, because he hadn't said anything back to her.

The corners of Avery Dimlow's mouth flicked upward almost imperceptibly. On anyone else, this would have been nothing more than a wince, perhaps, or even an indication of displeasure. On Avery Dimlow it was, essentially, a smile.

"All is well," he said, so faintly it was difficult for Elizabeth to hear him, even though she now stood just before his desk.

With that, he lowered his eyes, and Elizabeth thought he was dismissing her. She felt herself forming the words she wanted to say to him, but then he reached for a small, worn paperback sitting off to one side of his desk. He leaned closer to make certain it was the book he wanted and then he gripped it with his bony hand.

"For you," he said, his voice rasping. Avery Dimlow

slid the book across his worn and cluttered desk and steered it directly in front of Elizabeth: *The Next-to-Last Shriek of Uriah Mordred* by Damien Crowley.

Elizabeth gasped. "Where did you get that?"

He peered at the book with his watery eyes and said merely, "It arrived two days ago."

In the three months she'd been coming to his store—after Elizabeth had let Avery know she was a Crowley fan—he'd only been able to find her a single book by the author. The others she'd read by Damien Crowley—seventeen thus far—had come from the Winterhouse library.

"I can't wait to read it," Elizabeth said. She set her backpack down and took out her coin purse. Norbridge had been good about providing her an allowance—she worked several days a week in the library and spent an hour every Saturday morning demonstrating the camera obscura to guests—and Elizabeth had been so careful with her funds she had now saved forty-three dollars.

Avery Dimlow was busy tallying a figure on a pad before him. "The total is three dollars and seventeen cents," he said. He eyeballed the pad momentarily.

Elizabeth counted out this very reasonable sum, presented it to him, and put the book in her pack. The shuttle to Winterhouse would be arriving in a little more than ten minutes—but Elizabeth still wanted to ask her question.

"Sir," she said, her voice catching, "I heard you knew Damien Crowley." She hesitated. "Do you know if he stayed friends with Gracella Falls—Gracella Winters—when he got older?"

Avery Dimlow's eyes widened slightly, enough to show a tiny bit more of the whites and to allow the pouches of his eyebags to droop even more than usual. He put a hand to his chin and examined her over the top of his glasses. "Damien and I were *acquaintances*, you might say," he whispered. "He came to the store often."

"Oh." Elizabeth was too rattled to continue.

"He moved from Havenworth in 1950," Avery said. He gave a single, raspy sigh, and Elizabeth felt certain he was through offering information; this seemed as talkative as Avery Dimlow would get.

"Did you ever see him again?" she said.

Avery leaned forward. "He last stopped in on a visit twenty-three years ago. To show me a copy of a book he'd written. For a friend. I have not seen him since."

A chill went through Elizabeth. She looked to the door of the shop and hoped someone else would enter; she was beginning to feel extremely apprehensive.

"Do you remember what the book was called?" she said. "Or who it was for?"

Avery Dimlow kept his eyes fixed on Elizabeth's for a moment. "*The Secret Instruction of Anna Lux*," he said finally. "For Gracella Winters."

Elizabeth felt her heart leap. "I better go catch my shuttle," she said, her voice shaking as she strapped her backpack on.

"Of course," Avery said, retreating, once again, into the dimness behind his desk.

"I say," came a voice from the rear of the store. Elizabeth

turned to look; she hadn't even considered there might be another customer inside the bookshop.

A tall white-haired man wearing a trim black overcoat and a red-and-blue peaked cap—like an army general—approached from around a bookcase. Beneath the overcoat and just visible was a scarlet shirt and what appeared to be the angled top of a sash on which were affixed gold and silver medals. Elizabeth was not only surprised to realize this man had been in the shop all along, she also felt he looked far too regal to be browsing for books in Avery Dimlow's store.

"I'm hardly one for eavesdropping," the man said, nodding pleasantly at Elizabeth before fixing Avery with a kindly and unflappable look, "but I couldn't help overhearing you mention something about a Damien Crowley book, yes? *The Secret Instruction of Anna Lux?*"

Avery slowly and deliberately pressed a finger to the bridge of his glasses and stared at the man. "Certainly," he said.

Elizabeth felt Avery hadn't exactly answered the man's question, but she was so discomposed by the scene developing before her she merely stood in silence. She needed to leave, but she also wanted to hear what might come next.

"That book is among the rarest of the rare, from what I understand," the man said.

"You are a collector?" Avery Dimlow said.

The man nodded briskly. "The acquisition of books is one of my many pursuits, yes. And I find this connection

to Damien Crowley intriguing." He leaned forward. "I'm curious, sir. Did the author inform you of the contents of the novel, its plot or some such? The gentleman's stories always arouse my interest."

Avery shifted his eyes to Elizabeth before returning his gaze to the man. "I believe," he said, "it was about a girl who discovers the instructions for something Damien called . . . Let me see if I recall. If memory serves, it was something he termed the Dredforth Method."

Elizabeth's skin began to tingle. The white-haired man's face became blank as he continued to stare at Avery, and a deep silence reclaimed the bookstore.

The man cleared his throat and stood straight. "It would certainly be quite a find should that book turn up," he said. He glanced over his shoulder at the shelves behind him and then smiled pleasantly at Elizabeth before giving Avery a salute. "Kudos to you, sir, on this fine shop." With a gesture toward a far wall, he began to move off. "I shall continue my perusals."

"I better go catch the shuttle," Elizabeth said.

Avery dipped his chin in her direction. "Of course."

Elizabeth turned and left, stepping into the bracing chill of the street and then racing for the gazebo.

CHAPTER 11

MORE PICTURES, MORE NAMES

Elizabeth's mind was swirling with thoughts about the Dredforth Method and Avery Dimlow as she rode the shuttle to Winterhouse. But it all blinked out when she entered the lobby and saw, before the front desk and beside a pile of luggage, Norbridge, a man and woman she didn't recognize, and—next to them—Freddy, wearing his blue ski jacket and holding a small bag.

"You're here!" Elizabeth called as she rushed to the group.

They all turned to look, and Freddy's eyes went wide with delight. He dropped his bag, took a broad step to his right, pointed to his feet with both hands, and said, "No, I'm right *here*!"

Elizabeth let go of her backpack, threw her arms around him, and gave him probably the biggest greeting hug she'd ever given anyone.

"Well, wherever you are," she said as she pulled back, "it's great to see you."

"They seem to know each other," Norbridge said with a laugh.

"A little bit!" Freddy said, and he held his fist out to Elizabeth so they could give each other a friendly tap with their knuckles. "Great to see *you!*" he added and then turned to the man and woman beside him. "Elizabeth, this is my mom and dad."

Mr. Knox was very tall and sturdy, and he wore a gray suit under his brown overcoat that matched his just-graying hair and mustache. "Elizabeth, *Elizabeth!*" he said, shaking her hand. "Freddy is always talking about the fabulous Elizabeth Somers! Wonderful to finally meet you."

His wife, a petite lady in a blue dress, blue hat, and blue coat that reached to her knees, offered her hand to Elizabeth and smiled. "You have no idea how overjoyed we are," she said, "that our dear Frederick has found such a kind and intelligent friend here during his most recent stays at this hotel." She placed a hand on her chest.

They seem very nice, Elizabeth thought, before saying, "I'm really glad to meet you both—and really glad you're here." She bobbed her head toward Freddy. "And you too!"

Everyone laughed, and then Freddy said, "You look cold, Elizabeth." Before anyone could comment, he added,

"Cold, hold, held, head, heat!" And then: "Fireplace, here we come!"

Norbridge clapped a hand to his forehead. "Oh, no! It begins already. The word games!" He dropped his hand and wagged a finger at Freddy. "You two are going to drive your parents crazy over the next week and a half, I can see it now."

"It sounds as though there will be plenty to distract us," Mr. Knox said. "Mr. Falls was just telling us about all the events coming up. This sounds like a busy place!"

"On Saturday," Norbridge said, "Sir Reginald Eton-Pailey will deliver a lecture on his exploits in Panama fifty years ago involving a stolen opal and the most expensive bottle of perfume ever made. On Wednesday we have a visit from the world-famous paper folder Aristotle Schliemann, and then we follow that up the next night with a talk by Hediyeh Salafani on her interpretation of the ancient and mysterious Antikythera mechanism. Quite a week ahead! And that doesn't even include our nightly concerts, including a performance by Thrackin O'Malley on his Celtic harp next Monday and a few other surprises as we get closer to Easter."

"It all sounds so wonderful," Mrs. Knox said.

"You were explaining why the hotel has thirteen floors, Mr. Falls?" Freddy's father said.

His wife put a hand on his arm. "Donald, the children want to catch up."

"It's okay," Elizabeth said. "You'll like this story." She

looked at Norbridge with an expression that said, playfully, *Tell it right!*

"Well," Norbridge said, "when my grandfather Nestor Falls built Winterhouse in the 1890s, he wanted to please his wife, my grandmother Lavina, whose mother was from Italy. It turns out that in that country, the dread some people have regarding the number thirteen—"

"Triskaidekaphobia," Elizabeth said. The other four looked to her blankly. "Fear of thirteens," she added.

"Yes," Norbridge said, clearing his throat and leaning toward Elizabeth. "Triscuit-hecka-delphia." He stood tall again. "To continue, in Italy they do not fear the number thirteen. In fact, they extol it! They commend it! Far from being unlucky, it is considered to be lucky in the extreme. *Fare tredici,* they say. That is, 'do thirteen,' as in 'hit the jackpot!'" Norbridge threw his arms wide. "So there you go. Thirteen floors for a very lucky hotel. My grandfather wanted to delight my grandmother, and I'm pleased to say he succeeded. Lucky thirteen!"

"The camera obscura is up on the thirteenth floor," Freddy said to his parents. "The thing I was working on a few months ago."

"Well, we'll have to see *that,*" Mr. Knox said.

"And the library, too," Mrs. Knox said. "It sounds marvelous."

"I work there, Mrs. Knox," Elizabeth said. "I'd be happy to show you around."

Freddy's mother's face blossomed with joy. "That

would be wonderful. I'll be sure to take you up on your kind offer." She put her arms around Freddy's shoulders. "Frederick, your friend is every bit as gracious as you'd indicated."

"Mom!" Freddy said, wriggling his shoulders.

"And that puzzle!" Mr. Knox said, turning to look at Mr. Wellington and Mr. Rajput, who stood together on the far side of the lobby examining pieces. "It's huge!" Mr. Knox said.

Mr. Rajput muttered something to Mr. Wellington, who looked at him with exasperation. "But we agreed," Mr. Wellington said loudly. "Five more pieces. And then you can visit the lavatory, if it's truly necessary. Until then, we must remain here at our work."

Elizabeth, Norbridge, Freddy, and Mr. and Mrs. Knox, along with everyone else in the lobby, became silent and looked toward the puzzle table.

Mr. Wellington turned away from Mr. Rajput and, the expression on his face calming, glanced about. "Most apologetic," he said generally. "I didn't intend to raise my voice so." He looked to Mr. Rajput and gave him a weak pat on the back. "The stress of puzzling, I suppose. It's wearing on us." He offered a jittery little nod. "And now we shall continue."

He and Mr. Rajput resumed studying their puzzle, and everyone in the lobby returned to what they'd been doing before the interruption.

Norbridge smiled at the Knoxes. "Let's get you situated

in your room, shall we?" He snapped his fingers and looked to the bellhops' desk. "We'll get your bags up there right away."

"Frederick," Mrs. Knox said quickly. "Why don't you and your friend catch up? We'll be in our room, and you can join us when you're ready."

"A request, as well," Norbridge said. "Freddy and Elizabeth, can you meet me in Freddy's workshop in forty-five minutes?"

"For sure," Freddy said. He looked to his mother and father. "Remember how I told you Mr. Falls turned one of the rooms into a place where I can work on inventions and things?"

His parents nodded, and Norbridge beamed at them. "Your son's been a huge help here," he said, tapping the side of his head. "Ingenious." He looked back to Elizabeth. "I'll see you in forty-four and a half minutes, then. Go find the fireplace, if you like, and I'll see you soon."

"Nice to meet you, Mr. and Mrs. Knox," Elizabeth said. She and Freddy turned to leave.

"The pleasure is ours," Mrs. Knox said.

"We hope you'll join us for dinner, Elizabeth," Mr. Knox said. "And Freddy, come check in with us in an hour, after you're done meeting with Mr. Falls."

❄

Elizabeth and Freddy reached the enormous dining hall and took seats before the crackling fire; before long, Elizabeth had shared with him everything that had happened since her last catch-up email from the Saturday before: what she'd heard at the bookstore, that Lena had been visiting Elana, that the puzzle men were working twice as hard, and that nothing new had been discovered at the mine even though Norbridge had been sending someone out daily to check. There had been no recurrence of "thundersnow," either—Norbridge had even corrected himself a day after the incident and indicated (after conferring with Jackson) he believed the shaking had been caused by a shift in the permafrost just off Lake Luna, something that sounded a bit odd to Elizabeth but perhaps a bit more plausible than the thundersnow explanation.

One thing she didn't mention to Freddy (aside from the fact that she'd sneaked into Gracella's room again), was that she'd taken the blue puzzle piece from the table in the lobby and hadn't yet been moved to bring it back. Occasionally, she pictured herself returning it just in time for the two men to complete their puzzle. She tried to tell herself she hadn't actually stolen the piece but was more holding on to it to surprise the men right as they came to the end of their work—sometimes she actually believed her own story, even though it didn't feel correct.

"Everything's as normal as ever at Winterhouse," Freddy said when Elizabeth was done.

She laughed lightly. Freddy's expression became serious. "Elana's definitely doing better?" he said.

"Definitely," Elizabeth said. "About a week ago, she finally got more alert."

Freddy looked to the carpet. "Maybe we can go visit her?"

"She's usually resting now until after dinner," Elizabeth said. "But, yeah, either tonight or in the morning we can see her."

Freddy stared into the fire. "So, you like living here still? I mean, you must."

What he'd said was one hundred percent accurate, but Elizabeth didn't want to be too forward with detailing her good fortune. "It's been pretty good so far."

"This is my fifth time at Winterhouse. I'd love it if I could just stay here."

"But your parents are really nice." Based on everything Freddy had shared with her, Elizabeth had thought his mother and father would be, at a minimum, dismissive of Freddy—not cruel or unpleasant like her own aunt and uncle, who, at least until a year or so before had been outright mean to Elizabeth much of the time—but a little bit unkind, nonetheless. Mr. and Mrs. Knox hadn't seemed anywhere near as aloof or arrogant as Elizabeth would have guessed.

"Things have been a little better lately," Freddy said. "My dad's still pretty busy with work, and my mom spends a lot of time buying things and going places, but at least they've been asking me more about how I'm doing. Stuff like that. And we all went to a movie last month."

"It'll be fun to have them here. You can show them around and everything."

"Maybe." Freddy frowned. "I'm still kind of wondering . . . I mean, did they want to come to Winterhouse to be with me or because they wanted to see the hotel? Norbridge talked to them a few months ago, you know. He told them they should come, so maybe that's why they did it."

"Well, at least they're here."

"I guess. It's just . . ." He shook his head. "I don't want to have to check in and stuff like that. In the past, I could always do whatever I wanted here. I hope it's not different this time." He sighed. "Anyway, I want to show you something I found."

He took his phone from his pocket and began scrolling through photographs. Elizabeth, who didn't have a phone, was fascinated by them—though she also told herself that when and if the day came when she herself owned one, she would use it only when absolutely necessary.

"I did searches on the people related to Riley Granger that we've been talking about in email," Freddy said. "And I found something interesting about his cousin Jenora Sweth. She lived in Ithaca in New York State, and she also collected a lot of art. When she died, it all ended up in the museum there. So, I started thinking: Riley Granger was a painter; maybe some of his paintings are in that museum. You can see their stuff online, so I checked into it."

Elizabeth leaned closer and peered at his phone with interest.

"Here, look," Freddy said. He scooted closer and

showed her his screen, on which was a portrait of a woman in a black dress. "*Mrs. Philomena Glorzingis of Geneva.*" Freddy enlarged a portion of the portrait at the bottom right. "Signed by RSG."

Elizabeth studied the picture and saw the signature, which was identical to that on a handful of paintings in the Winterhouse portrait gallery.

"That's cool that you found that," she said, though she was mostly interested in what connection might exist with the paintings at Winterhouse itself. "Is there something more to it?"

"Look at these ones," Freddy said. He displayed three additional portraits: *Mr. Yadier Villarinos of Culebra, Puerto Rico*; *Miss Holmfridur Birna Baldursdottir of Skutustadahreppur, Iceland*; and *Dr. Matthias Peterson-Hansen of West Okoboji, Iowa.*

Each painting, Elizabeth saw, had the RSG signature in the bottom-right corner. Finally, though, she gave a deep shrug and said, "I see what you've found, but what's the big deal?"

"Okay," Freddy said, "here's the one I want you to check out. It's called *Woman with Mirror, Pomegranate, Scarab, and Dented Thimble.*"

He held his phone out, and Elizabeth stared at a painting beneath which was a small plaque that read FROM THE WINTERHOUSE HOTEL. The portrait was of a woman who resembled Nestor's sister-in-law, Morena. She was standing in a dimly lit room, and on a table before her lay an ornate hand mirror, a plump pomegranate, and a silver thimble so bashed in it would have been impossible for a person to fit it onto a finger. Strangest of all, the woman extended her hand toward the viewer, palm upward, and on it lay a golden beetle (a scarab, as Elizabeth had learned it was called) that was either a very beautiful insect or a piece of jewelry—it was impossible to tell. The woman's expression was

inscrutable—blank, as though she was in a daze—and it wasn't clear if she was displaying the beetle or offering it.

A chill went through Elizabeth. The scarab symbol was the very one members of Gracella's family had used to assist Gracella's spirit—it seemed to attract and strengthen her.

"The scarab!" Elizabeth said, astonished. "And that looks like Morena Falls from the painting in the gallery here."

"Definitely," Freddy said. "And the whole thing's so weird." He pulled his phone back and used his thumb and forefinger to enlarge the picture, centering on something in the background of the portrait. "Look at this," he said, holding the phone up.

She peered at the screen, though all she saw was what appeared to be a small placard hanging on the wall behind the woman. "What am I looking for?"

"Look closer at the little sign there," Freddy said.

Elizabeth studied the framed picture on the wall, on which was written these words:

Reflections

My! Within them, *discover.*
Can you?
Place this *inside.*
Things magical *of number.*
    Timét O'Reve
    (R.S.E.)

"*R.S.E.* stands for 'Royal Society of Edinburgh,'" Freddy said. "I looked it up."

Elizabeth stared at him. "What do you think it all means?"

"The sign or the painting?"

"The whole thing," Elizabeth said.

Freddy shook his head. "I don't know. But there's got to be something to this. I mean, we know Riley Granger didn't just do things for nothing. There's a point he's trying to make. Some kind of clue. Maybe he's hiding something in his pictures."

An odd feeling went through Elizabeth. "Say that again," she said.

"Which part?"

"The last part."

"He's hiding something," Freddy said. "In his pictures."

There was some realization so close to becoming distinct in Elizabeth's mind, she almost felt she could touch it. A connection, if she could only recall what it was, seemed within reach.

"Oh, no!" Freddy said. He was staring at his phone, but no longer at the painting. "We're supposed to meet Norbridge in two minutes!" He leapt up. "Come on."

CHAPTER 12

ALL THE GOOD FORTUNE STORED IN THE CRATES

Elizabeth and Freddy reached the workshop just as Norbridge turned the corner of the hallway.

"Right on time," he said, tugging at his bow tie. "Punctuality is next to cleanliness, as I often say."

"I've never heard you say that," Elizabeth said, giving Freddy a sidelong look and a little smile. "And does it even make sense?"

Norbridge stopped before them and then put a hand to his chin in contemplation. "You're right," he said. "Perhaps it was 'partiality is next to friendliness,' or maybe 'plausibility is next to manliness.'" He grinned and waved his hand in the air as if scrubbing away all the nonsense. "No matter! We're here, we're on time, and we're all friends."

Freddy looked to the ceiling and clamped his lips together, lost in concentration. "How about," he said, facing Norbridge, "popularity is next to trendiness?"

The two others looked to Freddy with admiration.

"That's a good one," Elizabeth said.

"I'll second that," Norbridge said. "See? You return to Winterhouse, and your verbal skills shoot way up."

"All I know is it's great to be back here," Freddy said. "I almost feel like I never left."

Norbridge's expression became serious, though kindly still. "And it's wonderful to have your mother and father with us, too."

Freddy gave the tiniest of smiles, and no one spoke for a moment. Norbridge removed a ring of keys from inside his vest and turned the lock on the handle. He nudged the door open and gestured with a hand into the workshop. "Shall we?" he said, and the three of them entered.

Immediately, Freddy, who'd spent so many hours in this room working on his inventions, looked to the bricked-over wall with astonishment. "You covered the door into the passageway!"

Norbridge smiled. "You noticed."

"Wow," Elizabeth said, not wanting to let on that she'd been in the workshop a few days before and had already seen this. "All sealed up."

"No one could get in there now." Freddy pushed at his glasses and surveyed the wall.

"I thought it was wise to do so after what happened on New Year's," Norbridge said.

The memory of that time was particularly unhappy for Freddy, Elizabeth knew, because on that occasion he'd been ambushed by Elana's brother, Rodney, in the corridor near the workshop and then had his key to the room stolen so that Gracella could enter through the door.

"I'm glad," Freddy said. "I wasn't going to say anything, but it would have been kind of creepy to start working on stuff in this room again with that door there behind me all the time."

"Hey, what's all that?" Elizabeth said, pointing to a half dozen wooden crates—each the size of a small hope chest—set beside the worktable.

"That," Norbridge said, moving to them, "is the reason I asked you to meet me here. Well, one of the reasons." He put a hand on the nearest crate as if testing its warmth, and then he examined Elizabeth and Freddy. "You two caught up a bit? Talked things over?"

Elizabeth knew Norbridge well enough to understand he was leading up to something but wanted to get his bearings first.

"We did," she said. "All the regular and unexciting stuff that goes on at Winterhouse." She was trying—without success—to keep a straight face. "You know, us wanting to make Elana twelve again and Lena wandering around after so long. Even all the completely uncreepy stuff out at the mine. Just the usual."

"Well, the Winterhouse staff reporter has filled us in on the basics, I can see," Norbridge said, and Freddy and Elizabeth laughed.

"Truly, Freddy," Norbridge said, "I've appreciated your discretion in not discussing all of the *interesting* things you've seen here." He inclined his head toward Elizabeth. "Including my granddaughter's . . . *abilities*, for lack of a better word."

For a time, Elizabeth had been reluctant to share too much with Freddy about her powers. She'd thought it might alarm him or make him think of her differently. But a point had come during their conversations and email exchanges when it seemed pointless to keep him in the dark. One thing for certain she'd learned during the time she'd known Freddy was that being a friend often meant setting aside her own preferences and instead thinking about things from another person's point of view. Before long, it had seemed obvious that if she and Freddy were going to be true friends, she'd need to answer his questions about some things he'd noticed—her uncanny knack for predicting that someone would arrive, for instance—and she'd need to be forthright with him about the things she was able to do.

Freddy looked slightly confused. "I think if I told anyone, 'Hey, this evil witch lady has been trying to attack the hotel, and—oh yeah—my friend there has these cool powers,' they'd think I was sort of . . ." He made several small circles beside his temple with a finger.

Norbridge laughed, but Elizabeth was still wondering what he was leading up to. "So what did you want to tell us?" she said.

"Part of it," Norbridge said, "is that Freddy and his

parents are only here until a week from Monday. Just after Easter. And I want their vacation . . . In fact, I want the entire upcoming holiday week to be . . . Well, I'm hoping that the two of you . . ."

"You want us to stay out of trouble," Freddy said. "Is that what you mean?"

"The young man has an uncanny sort of genius," Norbridge said, pointing. "I didn't even need to spell it out, and yet he caught my meaning straight off. Bravo, to you, Mr. Knox!"

"We don't mean to get in trouble, Norbridge," Elizabeth said. "It just comes our way."

"Debatable," Norbridge said. "Very debatable. However, in an effort to forestall the arrival of said trouble, and out of a desire to channel Freddy's creative instincts and your love of games, Elizabeth, I'd like to assign the two of you a little project that I think you'll find enjoyable." He leaned to pat the crate beside him. "And it has to do with these containers here."

Elizabeth looked more closely at them. "They look old," she said. "Like the pirates' chests in *Treasure Island*."

Norbridge removed the lid of the one closest to him. "You will notice if you examine these, they have a *Property of Nestor Falls* label on them." He pointed to the side of the lid, and Elizabeth saw exactly what he'd mentioned.

"These belonged to your grandfather?" Freddy said.

"They did," Norbridge said. "Six boxes of mementos, memorabilia, and miscellany from Winterhouse's first decades." He patted the crate. "About three years ago, I started thinking about all the old keepsakes my grandfather had stashed away, and so I got these out from the back of my closet and began rummaging around. I found plenty of interesting things. Old photographs and letters and documents and much more. Kept me busy reminiscing for a good three days, though I haven't been through all of it." Norbridge surveyed the crates proudly, and then he turned to Elizabeth. "That's when I found Nestor's puzzle, too, by the way. In here with the rest. I'd forgotten about that old thing, but that's when I pulled it out and took it down to the lobby for our two friends to work on. Anyway, these boxes are filled with memories from the hotel."

"Do you want us to organize it all for you?" Freddy said.

Norbridge shook his head. "What I was thinking was, wouldn't it be fun if guests who came to Winterhouse and wanted to learn about the hotel could go on a little adventure while doing so? Sort of a scavenger hunt, if you will. I'm envisioning a brochure or something, or maybe a map, and it would have interesting tidbits of information on it and facts about Winterhouse, and guests could follow it here and there as they explore."

Elizabeth was excited by the idea. "Like a guide to the hotel?"

"Yes," Norbridge said. "A guide and a game all in one. We could offer it at the front desk. If guests wanted a little challenge and a fun diversion as they learned about Winterhouse, they'd take the thing and start poking around the hotel. What do you think?"

"I think it's a great idea," Freddy said.

"Me too," Elizabeth said, nodding. "We can make a really cool handout full of clues."

"For instance," Norbridge said, even more animated suddenly, "maybe you have something like, *On the second-floor landing, you can see Nestor's bust. If you knock it over and break it, the thing will turn to dust.*" He gave a little scowl. "I'm sure you can do much better than that, but you get the idea. *Grace Hall is better than a face fall*, or *We make Flurschen, it tastes good to every person.*" He scowled once more. "You can see why I'm wanting to enlist the two of you. And it doesn't have to rhyme, either. That's just, you know, a possibility."

Elizabeth gave him a thumbs-up. "We can handle this, Norbridge. Just leave it to us. By Easter, we'll have a great brochure for you."

Freddy eyed the crates. "I'm sure we'll get a lot of cool ideas here in this stuff."

"Just go through everything and use what you need," Norbridge said. "Talk to me or Leona or anyone around the hotel if you need help or more information. Have fun with it."

"This will definitely keep us busy," Elizabeth said.

"Say, I have another idea, too!" Norbridge said, his face bright with enthusiasm. "Come Saturday morning, Freddy leads the camera obscura demonstration, and we make sure to have a full house there, including Mr. and Mrs. Knox. It will be the hit of the day."

Freddy lifted a hand and swiveled his index finger

upright in a sluggish little circle. "Woo-hoo," he said with no enthusiasm.

"I think it's a great idea," Elizabeth said. "In fact, I'm temporarily quitting my job as camera obscura operator and turning it back over to you. The demo is yours on Saturday."

Freddy closed his eyes for a moment and then opened them. "Demo," he said. "Mode."

"Dome," Elizabeth said with a triumphant lift of her chin.

"It never stops," Norbridge said, shaking his head.

"I just remembered," Freddy said. "My dad wanted me to check in. I better get going."

"We'll look forward to seeing the entire Knox family at dinner, then," Norbridge said.

Freddy smiled thinly and tipped his head toward Elizabeth. "Alter," he said. "I mean, later." And with that, he slipped out the door.

"It was a pleasure meeting his parents," Norbridge said to Elizabeth, staring in the direction of Freddy's departure before turning to her. "You're glad to have him back visiting again, aren't you?"

"Very glad. And I think we're going to have fun working on your project." Elizabeth studied Nestor's crates. "I can't wait to go through everything."

"The history," Norbridge said. "So much of interest."

As Elizabeth examined one of the labels with Nestor's name on it, she considered something Norbridge had said earlier. "These boxes have been in your room all these years?"

"Packed away. I'd almost forgotten about them."

"What made you get them out?"

He looked perplexed. "I can't say I know for sure. Just one of those things."

"Three years ago?"

"About, yes. Why?"

Elizabeth couldn't explain why this detail stood out to her, but something in the timing of it seemed noteworthy to her—she just couldn't figure out why.

"Just curious, I guess," she said. She was thinking that the first time she'd experienced *the feeling* had been roughly three years before.

She placed a hand on the crate beside her and had a strong desire to open it and begin searching within—but she was also eager to look at the book she'd bought from Avery Dimlow, and she wanted to take a rest before dinner. She envisioned a full evening with Freddy starting in Winter Hall and continuing with the choir concert afterward, and then maybe even a swim in the downstairs pool after that. If she was lucky, too, perhaps she could spend a bit of time before she went to bed assisting Mr. Wellington and Mr. Rajput with the puzzle.

"I suppose I'm always wanting to learn more about Winterhouse," Elizabeth said.

Norbridge arched his eyebrows. "So I've noticed," he said. "But I'd better get back to the lobby. We have plenty more guests on their way."

CHAPTER 13

WONDER AND OMENS

The following morning, Elizabeth and Freddy began making their way through the crates in the workshop. They came across so many interesting things, however, they wondered if they'd ever be able to start on their actual work. Among the things they found were a photo album from a 1928 "Winterhouse Summer Fruits Gala" that showed hotel guests dressed up like pineapples, bananas, and papayas; a bundle of letters and postcards that Donald Falls had sent to members of the family during his world travels across forty years (Elizabeth found herself most interested in stamps from countries that no longer existed: Basutoland, Neutral Moresnet, Rhodesia); newspaper clippings—some in English and some in other languages—from the 1920s about Winterhouse with headings such as FAMED HOTEL SECURES REPUTATION AS HAVEN OF THE VERY RICH, THE VERY FAMOUS, AND THE VERY PECULIAR and WINTERHOUSE—THE HOTEL THAT OTHER HOTELS ENVY and FALLS FAMILY FINDS FAME AND FORTUNE WITH FROSTY FLAIR, FESTIVE FUNCTIONS, AND FABULOUS FLUR-SCHEN. They arranged various items into piles—photos here, newspapers there, letters over there, and so on—and were having so much fun with their discoveries, they very nearly didn't notice that ten thirty was drawing near.

"Hey," Freddy said, handing Elizabeth a photograph of the library from 1935, "see how your favorite place used to look?"

Elizabeth examined the picture, which showed the Winterhouse library's broad staircase just behind the enormous card catalog.

"It looks pretty much the same," she said.

"Exactly," Freddy said. "And I bet if we came back in fifty years, it would *still* look the same! I love that. Like it's always going to be here. And someday *you'll* be running the library."

Elizabeth smiled weakly as she returned the photograph to Freddy. "Thanks."

"Don't get too overjoyed, now." Freddy hesitated. "Is something wrong? I thought you'd like to see that picture."

"I do. Definitely, I do. It's just, I don't know if I'm going to be taking over the library."

Freddy lowered his eyebrows. "Isn't that what Leona told us?"

"What I mean is, Norbridge hasn't ever said it himself, but I think the plan is . . . or, I guess I should say his hope is that I'll take over the entire hotel. That I'll run Winterhouse."

Freddy's eyes went wide. "That would be incredible! The whole place—yours? What could be better?"

But even as Freddy said the words, Elizabeth didn't think that a future where she oversaw Winterhouse would be the best she could imagine. It seemed overwhelming.

"I don't know the first thing about running a hotel," Elizabeth said.

"Well, no one does when they're our age," Freddy said. "But you can learn. I think it would be great to run this place."

"Then why don't you do it?" she said, teasing him, but only partially.

"I bet I could," Freddy said. "But I'm not a Falls." He raised a finger into the air dramatically. "However, if you paid me a decent salary and made my workshop twice as big, I'd be your right-hand man!" He closed his eyes momentarily before announcing, "Right. Girth!"

Elizabeth was glad to be distracted from thinking about a time when Norbridge wouldn't be around. Something in the old photograph, too, had made her think of Gracella and how she'd spent so many days in the Winterhouse library herself years ago. As she followed this thought, Elizabeth considered how, at times, she preferred to consider a future where she didn't have to be responsible for anything or anyone. Maybe a life where she learned more about her powers—where she developed her powers—would be more interesting than running a hotel.

Just like you, she thought—the words from her nightmare kept returning to her.

"I'll think about your offer," Elizabeth said. "But I'd have to interview you first."

Freddy closed his eyes once more. "Oh, no," Elizabeth said. "Here comes another one."

"First," Freddy said, his eyes popping wide open. "Rifts!"

"Stop!"

"Pots, post, tops, spot, opts!" Freddy said. "But those are simple."

Elizabeth squinted at him, her lips tightening. "Simple!" she said. "Impels!"

"Well done," Freddy said. "And now we can call a truce!"

"Cuter!" Elizabeth said, and they both exploded in laughter.

When they were about to quit to go visit Elana, Elizabeth found a small square envelope on which was written *For*

Milton, My Dear Nephew—In Appreciation for Your Work on the Camera Obscura. From Your Uncle Nestor.

"Whoa!" Elizabeth said. "Look at this. A letter from Nestor Falls."

Freddy scooted close to her as she lifted the envelope's flap. But instead of the expected letter, all that was inside was a notecard on which was the following:

```
owded a poor crowded a poor crowded a poor crowded a poor crowded a poor crowde
hief a handkerchief a handkerchief a handkerchief a handkerchief a handkerchief
g i toy away egg i toy away egg i toy away egg i toy away egg i toy away egg i
playhouse city playhouse city playhouse city playhouse city playhouse city pla
a a lonely sin a a lonely sin a a lonely sin a a lonely sin a a lonely sin a a
cracker ah firecracker ah firecracker ah firecracker ah firecracker ah firecrac
linen this ray line this ray line this ray line this gray line this gray line
pe you camera ape you camera ape yo camera cape yo camera cape yo camera cape y
ught hip does ought hip does ought hi does fought hi does fought hi does fought
alley ah amaze alley ah amaze alley a amaze valley a amaze valley a amaze vall
r i a i a me nor i a i a me nor i a i a me nor i a i a me nor i a i a me nor i
b bravo east web bravo east web bravo east web bravo east we bravo beast we bra
rds to ate towards to ate towards to ate towards to ate toward to rate toward t
ught you ow thought you ow thought you ow thought you ow though you low though
ne a dab magazine a dab magazine a dab magazine a dab magazine a dab magazine a
top a yo plate top a yo plate top a yo plate top a yo plate top a yo plate top
amp a loose a lamp a loose a lamp a loose a lamp a loose a lamp a loose a lamp
m aid leg so him aid leg so him aid leg so him aid leg so him aid leg so him ai
a handkerchief a handkerchief a handkerchief a handkerchief a handkerchief a ha
ndwriting ow handwriting ow handwriting ow handwriting ow handwriting ow handwr
ing to handwriting to handwriting to handwriting to handwriting to handwriting
entlemen kiss gentlemen kiss gentlemen kiss gentlemen kiss gentlemen kiss gentl
ion ill ox station ill ox station ill ox station ill ox station ill ox station
```

"That's bizarre," Freddy said. "Look at this, too." He moved to one of the boxes he'd been looking through earlier.

"What is it?" Elizabeth asked.

"Those words." Freddy turned over the lid of the crate to which he'd returned. "I saw the same kind of thing here. Look."

On the underside of the lid, which he held up for Elizabeth to see, was printed the following on a piece of paper that had been glued firmly in place:

```
ss a dug princess a dug princess a dug princess a dug princess a dug princess a
bay bluebird a bay bluebird a bay bluebird a bay bluebird a bay bluebird a bay
i lay fist let i lay fist let i lay fist let i lay fist let i lay fist let i la
freedom bat um freedom bat um freedom bat um freedom bat um freedom bat um fre
master a schoolmaster a schoolmaster a schoolmaster a schoolmaster a schoolmast
oy tablecloth toy tablecloth toy tablecloth toy tablecloth toy tablecloth toy t
er in look either in look either i look neither i look neither i look neither i
an bet beneath an bet beneath an be beneath fan be beneath fan be beneath fan b
umble if this rumble if this rumble i this crumble i this crumble i this crumbl
ink week cover ink week cover ink wee cover wink wee cover wink wee cover wink
rous lady dangerous lady dangerous lady dangerous lady dangerous lady dangerous
d notes rain lad notes rain lad notes rain lad notes rain la notes drain la not
der to round rider to round rider to round rider to round ride to around ride t
eamy find on creamy find on creamy find on creamy find on cream find son cream
t with me bright with me bright with me bright with me bright with me bright wi
an by try hunt an by try hunt an by try hunt an by try hunt an by try hunt an b
ne id upset stone id upset stone id upset stone id upset stone id upset stone i
ming aim i swimming aim i swimming aim i swimming aim i swimming aim i swimming
lt ivy lake quilt ivy lake quilt ivy lake quilt ivy lake quilt ivy lake quilt i
its everything its everything its everything its everything its everything its
aner i sack cleaner i sack cleaner i sack cleaner i sack cleaner i sack cleaner
plaything i of plaything i of plaything i of plaything i of plaything i of play
arelessness a carelessness a carelessness a carelessness a carelessness a carel
```

"That's strange," Elizabeth said. "I wonder what they're all about."

"Norbridge must have seen these. We can ask him."

Freddy returned the lid to the crate and came to look at Elizabeth's note once more. "They're just a bunch of random words."

Elizabeth ran a finger inside the envelope to make certain she'd removed everything from it. "Or maybe there's a secret message hidden—"

"Don't go there!" Freddy said, interrupting her. "Don't go there. We already have one secret message in Riley Granger's painting. Don't add another."

"We'll make this one second in line," Elizabeth said, tucking the notecard back into the envelope and then sliding it inside her notebook. She pointed to the crate. "And that one's third."

"You're really enjoying this, aren't you?" Freddy said

with a roll of his eyes. He checked his watch. "Hey, we need to get to Elana's room."

"After you." Elizabeth stood and gestured toward the door.

"You sure it's going to be all right to see her?"

"It'll be all right," Elizabeth said.

As Freddy headed out the door, Elizabeth hesitated momentarily before moving to the wall that had been covered. Just as she had a few days before, she put an ear against the brickwork and, sure enough, from somewhere far distant, heard a faint humming sound. The sound was lulling, soothing—something in it took her back to her thoughts from a few minutes before about Winterhouse and the years ahead.

"You all right?" Freddy said, staring at her from the corridor.

Her thoughts blinked out, and Elizabeth backed away from the wall.

"I'm fine," she said, smiling at Freddy as she headed for the door. "Lead the way."

CHAPTER 14

THE ATTEMPT TO UNRAVEL AN ALLURING CLUE

As Elizabeth and Freddy approached Elana's room, Mrs. Trumble—one of the nicest people at Winterhouse, and one who'd worked there for nearly fifty years—was exiting and had an anxious cast to her face.

"Hi, Mrs. Trumble," Elizabeth said. The older lady looked up and instantly attempted a smile, though it was far weaker than her typical jolly expression.

"Hello, dear," Mrs. Trumble said. "And welcome, young Mr. Knox. Glad to have you back with us." She came to an awkward halt. "The two of you are heading outside, perhaps? Some sledding on this beautiful morning?"

Elizabeth gestured toward the door. "We were hoping to visit Elana."

"We wanted to say hi," Freddy said.

Mrs. Trumble shook her head slowly; no one spoke for a moment.

"Has something happened?" Elizabeth said. Elana had remained stable—listless and sad, but lucid—since Elizabeth had first visited her. She'd taken it for granted that Elana's condition was, if not set to improve markedly, at least not declining, but now she realized her assumptions might be incorrect.

"She's very tired, I'm afraid," Mrs. Trumble said. "The exhaustion seems to be overtaking her, and she's barely able to stay awake. It's come on so sudden."

Elizabeth turned to Freddy with dismay. "I just talked to her a couple of days ago, and she was fine. I mean, as fine as she can be. She's been doing pretty well all week." Elizabeth glanced at the closed door. "We couldn't see her for just a minute or two, Mrs. Trumble? Maybe she'd like the visit. Especially from Freddy."

"Yeah," Freddy said. "If it's okay. We'll just say hi."

Mrs. Trumble lowered her brow in consternation but then attempted her smile once more. "I suppose it couldn't do any harm. But we'll have to keep it short. The doctor from Havenworth who's been looking in on her is due soon."

She opened the door and ushered Elizabeth and Freddy inside. The room was as it had been on the five occasions Elizabeth had visited since the night she and Norbridge had come together. The pile of books on the bedside table had been rearranged since two days before, and Elizabeth took this as a good sign: Elana had been reading—*The Whiz Mob and the Grenadine Kid* lay closest to her—though now she was sound asleep.

Elizabeth glanced at Freddy, who had a look of disbelief on his face. This was the first time he'd seen Elana since the disaster had befallen her, and he seemed shocked into something both sad and deeply unsettled.

"Elana, dear," Mrs. Trumble said softly. "Your friends are here to see you."

Elana stirred. Her eyes opened with a sluggish movement. "Elizabeth?" she said, adjusting her head just barely to look at her. And as she did, her lips curled into a weak smile. "And Freddy?" She sat up slowly, her motions labored and deliberate.

"Hi, Elana," Elizabeth said, moving closer to the bed. She rested a hand on the silver and indigo quilt and nodded toward Freddy. "Yeah, look who tagged along with me." Elana seemed more tired than any of the previous occasions she'd visited, Elizabeth thought.

"Hey, Elana," Freddy said as he moved beside Elizabeth. His voice was low and serious, as if he had no idea what to say now that the fact of Elana's condition was apparent to him.

"You came back," Elana said feebly, casting her pale eyes on Freddy. "I'm glad."

The room went silent. It seemed as though Elana had expended a great deal of energy in just sitting up and uttering a few words.

"Perhaps we should allow her to rest," Mrs. Trumble whispered from behind Elizabeth.

"I'm fine," Elana said. She coughed, three raspy exhalations. "Really."

"It's okay if you want to sleep," Elizabeth said. She looked to Freddy. "We just wanted to stop by for a few minutes."

"Lena came again this morning," Elana said, her voice stronger. "She spelled 'help' with her fingers." Elana slowly slid her hand from under the quilt and reached for Elizabeth's.

"Maybe she wants to help you?" Elizabeth said.

Elana grew silent once more and closed her eyes. She continued to hold Elizabeth's hand, but after a moment it seemed she had fallen asleep.

"Perhaps it's best we leave her be," Mrs. Trumble said quietly.

Elana opened her eyes and moved them anxiously from Elizabeth to Freddy. "I'm okay, really," she said. "I just feel a little tired today. That's all."

"I'm here for over a week, Elana," Freddy said. "So we can come again anytime, okay?"

Elana said nothing. But then, with the slightest tug, she pulled on Elizabeth's hand, drawing her closer to her.

"You okay?" Elizabeth said softly, but Elana's grip tightened, and she drew Elizabeth nearer, so much so that after a moment, the two girls' faces were nearly touching.

"There's something else hidden here in Winterhouse," Elana whispered. "I want you to know that. There's something else here, but I don't know what it is."

Elizabeth stared at Elana's wan and wrinkled skin, her wisps of gray hair, and she felt frightened. "Is that something your parents told you?"

Elana nodded. "If she has any power left at all," she whispered, "she'll use people—she'll control people—to help her get it. Whatever it is that's still here in Winterhouse."

"Sh-she?" Elizabeth said, stammering the word. "Do you mean . . ."

Elana squeezed Elizabeth's hand. "Gracella," she said, her voice barely audible. "She'll do anything. Anything. She'll get people to help her somehow. Even if they don't know it."

"Dear," Mrs. Trumble said, this time with urgency in her voice, "you must get some rest. By order of Mr. Falls." She put a hand on Elizabeth's shoulder and moved her gently away from Elana, who let go of Elizabeth's hand.

Elana closed her eyes. "Thanks for coming," she said. "Both of you."

"We wanted to see you," Freddy said.

"Yeah," Elizabeth said. "And we'll be back soon."

Freddy put a hand on Elizabeth's arm to encourage her to depart, and without a word, that's just what they did.

"That's really sad," Freddy said, once they were in the corridor by themselves. He looked as though he'd just been witness to an accident or received some awful news about a loved one.

The two of them stood in silence, not wanting to dwell on Elana's condition.

"And she said there's something else hidden in Winter-house," Freddy said. "She said she was sure of it. I just wish we knew what it was."

"And if it's the last one." Elizabeth closed her eyes and sighed; it all felt too much. She thought of the puzzle piece in her drawer. "Let's go outside, Freddy. I could use some fresh air."

CHAPTER 15

THE SUPERB ROOM OF PORTRAITS

Following a head-clearing hour outside and then lunch—during which Elizabeth learned Norbridge had departed Winterhouse on an errand and was not expected back until after dinner—the two kids resumed work on their project. They decided, however, to leave the workshop for a while as they took a survey of the hotel and settled on the best spots to highlight.

They moved from floor to floor, taking notes as they went and thinking about the various locations they hoped guests might enjoy visiting or learning about. It was difficult, though, for the two of them to consider the possibilities with fresh eyes, because they'd been in every corner of Winterhouse so many times: the Tower at the top of the hotel with its magnificent views; the famous candy kitchen where Flurschen was made and shipped all over the world; the hall of dioramas on the second floor, with its models of famous places across the globe; spacious Grace Hall with its delicate maroon curtains and superb acoustics; the small theater where movies were shown; the artifacts and display cases on each floor that held so many unique treasures Norbridge and others in his family had collected over the years.

"I haven't seen this before," Freddy said as they made a stop on the ninth floor at a new case. Inside was an aged baseball that looked a bit like a lopsided potato. Its former white color had long since faded to a burnished gray, and its red yarn was badly frayed. Beneath it a plaque read HOMERUN BALL HIT BY NORMAN THOMAS "TURKEY" STEARNES OF THE DETROIT STARS AGAINST THE NASHVILLE GIANTS—JULY 17, 1928. *HE BASHED IT.*

"Norbridge is a big baseball fan," Elizabeth said. "He told me a famous pitcher named Smokey Joe Williams visited Winterhouse in 1946 and taught him how to throw a curveball."

Freddy regarded the display case approvingly. "Impressive. Turkey Stearnes."

"Hi, you two," Jackson said, rounding the corner. Elizabeth and Freddy greeted him as Jackson gestured to the case. "Lovely new acquisition, isn't it?"

"Really nice," Freddy said. "Have you guys gotten any other cool stuff lately?"

"We have," Jackson said, "though nothing on public view yet. There's a beautiful didgeridoo we've received from an old friend of ours in Australia named Maroochi Koori Kelly, but it's eleven feet long, and so we're attempting to come up with a proper way of displaying it. We also recently procured a set of nunchucks used by the martial artist Bruce Lee while filming an episode of *The Green Hornet*, as well as the actual spoon Crown Prince Namgyal Zhalgno used to hack his way out of a collapsed spur of the Khewra Salt Mine in 1922." Jackson smiled proudly. "Look for them soon in a Winterhouse hallway near you," he added in a melodramatic voice, and Elizabeth and Freddy laughed.

Elizabeth made a mental note to add these latest acquisitions to the list in her notebook entitled "Items on Display in the Corridors of Winterhouse." Some of her other recent lists included "Most-Interesting-Sounding Hometowns of Winterhouse Guests" (Walla Walla, Flin Flon, Belchertown, and Tuba City were the latest additions), "Colleges I Might Want to Attend Someday," "Origami Animals I Can Make," "Least-Favorite Lunches at School" (the sole entry was "Sloppy Joes"), "Names of Characters I Will Use in Books I Plan to Write" (Florena Zamensky and Udabello Kiyonga currently topped her list), and "Things People Say When They Want You to Ask Them Something Without Seeming Like They Want You To" ("It's nothing, really," topped her list; next was "It'll probably bore you.").

"Do you know how Lena's doing?" Elizabeth said to Jackson. "We were visiting Elana this morning, and she said Lena had come by to see her."

Jackson sighed. "It has proven very difficult to convince Lena to remain in her room. It seems that every other time we turn around, she's off wandering around the place."

"I have a question," Freddy said. The way he announced this sounded so unusual, both Elizabeth and Jackson turned to him with interest. "Does anyone know who Lena's father was?"

It was a strange fact that on the Falls' family tree on the wall outside of Winter Hall, the space next to Kiona's name—where Lena's father should have been indicated—simply said NOT SPECIFIED, which seemed both very formal and very odd.

"The incidents surrounding Lena's birth predate my time at Winterhouse," Jackson said.

"So, no one knows who Lena's father was?" Elizabeth said.

Jackson paused. "They say that when Kiona was preparing to leave Winterhouse for her university studies, she met a young man at the hotel and lost her head over him. And then she was gone. Two years later, she returned with a young daughter—Lena—and informed the family she'd been married but it was now over." He shrugged. It seemed his story was done.

"But, still, does anyone know who Lena's father was?" Elizabeth said.

Jackson put a hand to his chin. "I do not," he said pleasantly. He stood up straight and clicked his heels. "I must be off. Miss Somers. Mr. Knox. Good afternoon. Enjoy your roaming!"

And after he passed them and proceeded down the hallway, Freddy simply stared at Elizabeth for a moment, and then said, "The Falls family is very . . . *different*."

After two more hours of poking around, Elizabeth and Freddy had nearly finished their list of spots to feature in their brochure and decided to make one last stop in one of their favorite rooms in the hotel: the portrait gallery, where paintings of dozens of members of the Falls family from more than one hundred years lined the walls. It was just as they entered the long hall that Freddy's phone buzzed in his pocket. He looked upward as though his disbelief might be calmed by something he could locate on the ceiling.

"Incredible," he muttered, removing his phone and looking at the text on it. "It's my dad. Somehow at home they never want me around, but now that they're here, all of a sudden they need to check on me all the time." He turned the phone to show Elizabeth. "'*I need to see you*,'" Freddy read in a low voice, mimicking his father and even puckering his mouth and eyebrows as he did so. "Why? For what?" He sighed. "I don't get it."

"Maybe they just want to spend time with you," Elizabeth said, trying to find something positive to say, even though she could see her friend was frustrated. "That's a good thing, right?"

"Easy for you to say." His expression was very serious. "You can do whatever you want. I'll be fourteen in a few months, and my parents either ignore me or treat me like a kid."

Elizabeth was nearing thirteen herself and, although she rarely thought about Freddy being a year older than she was, she sometimes wondered if that one year might begin to matter more as the months and years progressed. Freddy definitely seemed to have matured—and even become a bit more irritable, Elizabeth thought—over the three months since she'd seen him last.

"Well," she said, thinking of the sort of advice Leona might give her, "you have to kind of be patient with things, you know."

He gave her a look of bafflement. "Patient? What are you talking about?"

Elizabeth was taken aback. "Just kind of mentioning . . . Oh, I don't know. Trying to help a little, I guess." She found herself hoping the week ahead would be a good time for her and Freddy. Something seemed to have shifted slightly between them, and she wasn't sure if it was because his parents were at Winterhouse or some other reason.

Freddy displayed his phone again. "I don't like having them on my back all the time. Anyway, I better go see what's up. I'll see you at dinner?"

"In, nerd," Elizabeth said.

Freddy laughed—genuinely, and this made her feel better. "Not bad," he said, turning and heading toward the door.

As Elizabeth watched him walk away, something flared inside her, like a sharp pain arising unexpectedly. She found herself lifting her arm and pointing to a broom set beside the door through which Freddy was about to depart. With a jerk, the broom angled off the wall and smacked onto the floor as though it had been cast down. The whole thing happened so quickly, Elizabeth was almost unable to register that she had caused it—but a pleasant sensation of accomplishment swelled through her. She felt glad to have created this little disturbance.

"Whoa!" Freddy said, jumping a step to one side. He glanced at the broom and then back at Elizabeth with a look that combined amazement with uncertainty.

"Sorry!" Elizabeth said, trying to make her voice sound as light as possible, as if she'd accidentally dropped a fork at the dinner table. "I guess I wanted you to stay."

Freddy pointed to her, though Elizabeth wasn't certain if he was indicating he appreciated her little prank or was disturbed by it.

"You should be careful with that," Freddy said.

"It was just a little joke, Freddy."

He studied the broom for a moment and then looked back to Elizabeth. "I know. But still, maybe you shouldn't play around like that." With a quick lift of his phone in her direction—confirmation that he needed to go see his father—Freddy turned, picked up the broom, replaced it beside the door, and departed.

It was just a joke, Elizabeth thought, but something about the incident no longer seemed so amusing. She glanced at the paintings on the wall nearest her, and then she moved across the room to where the painting of her mother—at age thirteen—was displayed.

"I wish you were here," Elizabeth said softly, placing a hand to the pendant at her neck as she studied her mother's portrait. "You and Dad. All of us, here at Winterhouse." She glanced down toward her necklace and gripped it tightly, trying not to think about the look of disappointment she'd seen on Freddy's face.

After one final moment before her mother's painting, Elizabeth left the gallery.

Five minutes later, Elizabeth strode into the lobby. And although she wanted to talk to Norbridge about the strange notes she and Freddy had found in the crates, she knew it would have to wait until he returned later that evening. For now, she decided to help Mr. Wellington and Mr. Rajput.

The two men didn't notice her enter, primarily because they were so focused on their work, but also because a group of nine people had gathered before them to watch. Elizabeth drew closer. One of the onlookers said, "That piece over to your left might fit there near the top."

"Please!" Mr. Wellington said, glancing up from the puzzle. "We appreciate your interest and your attempts at assistance, but my comrade and I require absolute silence in order to make headway. It's imperative that we approach our work with the proper measure of concentration."

"Imagine we are at billiards," Mr. Rajput said, surveying the group before him, "and that any disruption of our focus might result in grave miscalculation, leading to abject failure, in turn plunging us into a spiral of despair. We beg your indulgence and request you not provide input as we toil away." He sighed. "The strain is harrowing enough as it is."

Mr. Rajput's face brightened just barely—an expression that, on most other people would seem something like anxiety—as he spotted Elizabeth. "And as it turns out," he said, "our co-puzzler has just arrived, and so the need for utter silence must now intensify."

"Miss Somers," Mr. Wellington said. "You are joining us!"

"I didn't know so many people were getting interested in the puzzle," Elizabeth said, nodding to the audience as she made her way past them. "Pretty cool."

"They're getting so close," one man said. "We wanted to cheer them on."

Mr. Wellington dipped his head in acknowledgment, lifting a hand as though providing his fans some small notice of his appreciation. "We're pleased to see the interest in our work," he said, and then he leaned toward Elizabeth. "But we still have a bit of a road ahead of us."

"Well, let's jump in," Elizabeth said, and she moved to the table.

Within an hour, she had found seven pieces, matching

the output of Mr. Wellington and Mr. Rajput for the entire afternoon before she'd arrived. The people watching came and went. During a particularly dramatic moment when Elizabeth located two pieces in quick succession, a crowd of five gasped and then clapped lightly as though they'd witnessed an expert long putt on a golf course; Mr. Rajput scowled dramatically in all directions to quiet them.

"I've been wondering," Elizabeth said, after several minutes of silence when the small crowd had departed, "what got the two of you so interested in working on this puzzle."

"The puzzle?" Mr. Wellington said, so deeply lost in concentration it was as if the words made no sense to him. He shook his head and examined the table before him. "Well, we . . . we . . ."

"Mr. Falls presented it to us nearly three years ago," Mr. Rajput said. "I would say it aroused our interest immediately. The challenge. The pursuit. The hunt."

"Mrs. Wellington was very keen on the effort from the start," Mr. Wellington said, warming to the subject. "My wife's encouragement has been invigorating."

Mr. Rajput regarded Elizabeth. "Why do you ask?"

"I guess I've just never seen two people so focused on a puzzle before," she said, scanning the pieces before her. "And I've never seen such a huge puzzle."

"But can you imagine," Mr. Wellington said, closing his eyes and looking, for all the world, like a man who'd returned home after years of wandering, "that moment when we settle the final piece within its borders? It will be, perhaps, the supreme accomplishment of my life."

No one spoke. Mr. Rajput licked his lips; Elizabeth idly stirred at a pile of pieces and then picked up one that was pure blue; Mr. Wellington opened his eyes.

"Yes," Mr. Rajput said, gesturing to the puzzle, "and now we can return our focus to the necessary endeavor."

"Hey, look," Elizabeth said pressing the piece into the spread of the sky. "Here's where this one goes." She felt enormously guilty as she thought about the piece hidden in her drawer.

"Extraordinary!" Mr. Wellington said.

"Rare talent," Mr. Rajput said wearily. "Very rare."

Dinner in Winter Hall passed pleasantly, though Norbridge remained absent. Jackson delivered the after-dinner speech and then nearly everyone attended the concert of the Winterhouse choir—which comprised eight kitchen staff, six of the guest-room cleaners, the three "Powder Masters" from the candy kitchen, two of the women who tied bows on the Flurschen packaging, various bellhops, custodians, and maintenance workers, and, finally, Mr. Obrastoff, the elderly gentleman who kept the ski trails groomed so nicely. By eight forty-five, Elizabeth and Freddy were taking a swim in the pool on the lower floor of the hotel.

It wasn't until Elizabeth returned to her room to wind down for the night that her peace was disturbed. As she closed the door behind her, Elizabeth had one of the oddest sensations of *the feeling* she'd ever experienced: Something anxious and fraught arose within her, some fluttering variation on the intensity she typically felt and, along with it, a low buzzing sound. For a moment Elizabeth had the unaccountable certainty that someone was in her room, though this notion fled almost as immediately as it had arisen. She glanced all around and then headed directly for her window and looked out. The night was dark, but in the low light cast by the lamps that lined the path to Lake Luna, Elizabeth could vaguely make out the stone bridge that led off into the western forest. An almost imperceptible haze of crimson seemed to surround it, like a hovering red fog.

Elizabeth pressed her face closer to the glass windowpane and stared at the bridge.

Just like you, she thought.

Her hand flew to the pendant at her neck, and she squeezed her fist about it. The buzzing quieted. She drew away from the window.

By the time she'd changed and settled herself in bed, Elizabeth had nearly convinced herself she would—the very next morning—tell Norbridge she'd been in Gracella's room twice.

Nearly.

CHAPTER 16

MERRY SONGS, AN AWFUL DIN, NERVOUS EXPLANATIONS

At six thirty the following evening, Elizabeth, dressed in a green velveteen dress Jackson had once given her, was at the largest dinner table she'd ever joined, something specially arranged by Norbridge. In order, starting at Elizabeth's left, were Freddy (who wore a nice blue shirt and had his hair slicked neatly), Mr. and Mrs. Knox, the puzzle men and their wives, Hyrum Crowley, Egil P. Fowles, Norbridge, and Leona. Twelve people in total—though one seat was still empty—and everyone was wearing their formal best and in good spirits. Elizabeth and Freddy had spent much of the day working on their brochure (the camera obscura demonstration had to be postponed because of cloudy weather), though Elizabeth had taken a couple of hours off to work on the puzzle and help in the library. Norbridge had returned late the night before, and Elizabeth hadn't seen him until just now.

With the boisterous crowd in Winter Hall, it felt to Elizabeth that the holiday season was finally beginning; there was, suddenly, the aura in the hotel of things picking up. It was like that feeling when you're in class on a day in November or December, say, and the week is dragging, and everything has been slow and predictable, and then the first snowflakes of winter drift down from the gray sky, and thoughts of snowmen and sledding and skating cause a thrill to ripple through the room—everyone becomes more animated and senses some new charge in the air, some rising energy. It was like that, and Elizabeth felt overjoyed to still have more than a week of vacation, with her best friend beside her and a table of interesting people before her.

As everyone settled in, a white-haired man approached the table. He wore a regal-looking scarlet shirt and a sash dotted with medals and patches. As he came to Norbridge and shook his hand, Elizabeth realized, with great surprise, this was the very same man she'd seen two days before at Avery Dimlow's shop.

"One and all," Norbridge said, grandly, "please meet Sir Reginald Eton-Pailey, tonight's esteemed speaker and the man about to fill our remaining empty seat."

The white-haired man smiled so brightly it appeared he'd never been more overjoyed to meet a group of dinner guests.

"I am *exceedingly* delighted to be here!" Sir Reginald said. He gestured about the hall as if admiring the walls of a golden temple. "Here, in this magnificent ballroom in this extraordinary hotel and in the presence of such distinguished company." He clasped his hands and scanned the table. "It is my pleasure to meet each one of you."

His gaze reached Elizabeth, and his eyes widened. "The young lady from the bookstore!"

"You've met?" Norbridge said.

"We saw each other at Mr. Dimlow's shop on Thursday," Elizabeth said.

"Well, that is an outstanding bit of chance," Norbridge said. "Sir Reginald, please meet my granddaughter, Elizabeth. And Elizabeth, this is Sir Reginald Eton-Pailey."

"Pleased to meet you, sir," she said, shaking his firm hand.

Reginald began beaming as if he'd learned he'd won a lifetime supply of Flurschen. "The pleasure is all mine! Particularly because it's clear you love books just as much as I do." He turned to Norbridge. "Why, the young lady was conversing with the proprietor of the bookshop like a seasoned bibliophile. Most remarkable!"

Norbridge winked at Elizabeth. "She is remarkable. And sharp as a tack."

"And who are the rest of these outstanding individuals?" Reginald said. A round of introductions ensued as Elizabeth reflected on how unusually interested Sir Reginald had been in the Anna Lux book when she'd first seen him.

Dinner—which was a prime rib beef roast, roasted garlic mashed potatoes, and browned butter green beans with pecans—progressed with lively conversation. The Wellingtons and Rajputs explained how glad they were to be back at Winterhouse, and the two men announced they were optimistic about completing their puzzle before Easter; Hyrum indicated he hoped to spend a lot of time at the hotel over the holiday to work on his term paper; and Professor Fowles described the alarm clock his wife had bought him as an early Easter gift.

Sir Reginald, however, did most of the talking, relating so many stories about his journeys in various corners of the globe, it was exhausting to listen to him. He was an extremely interesting man—his father was from Guildford in Surrey, and his mother was a native Ugandan, something Leona found delightful because it turned out her family and Reginald's mother's had lived within five miles of each other in Kampala—and seemed to have traveled everywhere, from Outer Mongolia to Cape Horn, and from the Sahara Desert to the remote Yukon. He was also quite a collector of books, and his stories of acquiring rare volumes in dusty shops in such places as Marrakesh and Jaipur and Valparaiso delighted not only Elizabeth and Leona, but everyone else at the table, as well.

"What has been one of the most interesting or amusing things you have ever come across in your travels?"

Norbridge asked Reginald, just as the Bundt cake and sorbet arrived for dessert.

Sir Reginald, with eyes so penetrating and dark he seemed to have the restless energy of someone half his age, set his teeth on his bottom lip and considered. "Once I was in southern India," he said finally, "at the tip of the country in a place called Kanyakumari, and I stayed with a family that spoke their words backward half the time. It was uncanny! The whole lot of them—mother, father, and their nine children—would speak the regular way, you know, as we all do, a portion of the time. But then they would suddenly switch to pronouncing everything backward. Remarkable! So I requested a more formal demonstration. I would ask them, 'Say the words to "Happy Birthday" in reverse,' and they would do it, right on the spot. Starting with the first word flipped around, and then the second word flipped around, and so on, all by sound not just the letters. 'Eeppah aidthrib oot ooy! Eeppah aidthrib oot ooy!' I don't know what caused them to do it or why they continued it, but it was extraordinary."

"Perhaps they had memorized a few things just to impress you," Mrs. Rajput said.

Reginald lifted both hands dramatically to dismiss the charge. "Not at all. Why, I could pass half the night simply lobbing words or sentences at them. 'Constantinople,' I would say. Or 'Ticonderoga,' or 'flabbergasting.' Or 'I come to bury Caesar, not to praise him.' Or 'How much wood would a woodchuck chuck if a woodchuck could chuck wood?' and straight off they would twist the words around one by one. And by sound, please note! Which is not easy. You take the words 'taco time,' for instance. Someone who just wanted to look at the letters might say 'oh, cat, emit,' but to reverse it with the sounds, you would say 'oh, cot, might,' which is exactly what this fascinating reversing family did. You've never seen or heard anything like it." He gave a wink to no one in particular. "The backward speakers—they were truly unique."

"Well, that's the darndest thing," Mr. Knox said. He looked transfixed, as though Sir Reginald had explained how he'd been kidnapped by extraterrestrials. "They must have been geniuses!" He looked to Freddy. "You take my boy, here, though. He's pretty good with words himself. What's that thing you always do, Frederick? With mixing up the letters and all that?"

"Anagrams," Freddy said. "It's where you rearrange the letters of a word or a bunch of words and turn them into something else."

"Yeah, amagrans," Mr. Knox said.

"Anagrams!" Freddy said, raising his voice slightly.

"A delightful form of wordplay," Reginald said. "I've experimented with the form often myself. Best one I've ever made of my name is 'legionnaire adeptly,' of which I'm very proud. Also 'delaying peritoneal,' which sounds like a diagnosis your doctor might offer to encourage you to eat more vegetables." He looked to Freddy with a grin. "And you? Any favorites?"

"Actually, Elizabeth and I do them all the time," Freddy said. "She's just as good as I am. Probably better."

"We like to do names," Elizabeth said.

"Anyone at this table?" Professor Fowles said.

"Well," Elizabeth said, looking to Norbridge, "for my grandfather, you can turn 'Norbridge Falls' into 'folding barrels.'"

Leona began to laugh. "Somehow that seems to fit just right!"

Freddy looked to her. "We've also done your name, Leona." Her laughing stopped. "'Leaping snorer,'" Freddy said, and now it was Norbridge's turn to laugh.

"You know," Hyrum said abruptly, "I was poking

around the hotel today, and I came across something interesting." He'd been relatively quiet throughout the meal. Elizabeth had been surprised to see him at Winterhouse, given that school had just gone on holiday two days before and she'd assumed he would head back to Bruma for the break.

"What was that?" Norbridge said. The lightheartedness that had held at the table a moment before began to dissipate; the circle of diners was waiting to hear what would come next from Hyrum.

"A sealed room," Hyrum said. "Number 333. It's the only one I've seen here that says NO ADMITTANCE on it."

Elizabeth held her breath; everyone at the table was leaning in, rapt with interest.

Norbridge peered at Hyrum for a moment. "My sister's room," he said. "Gracella. Been sealed for many years, and sealed it shall remain." He glanced around the table and chuckled, as if hoping to change the darkening mood that was descending; a few of the others laughed along with him, though not very enthusiastically.

"You know," Hyrum said, "the last time I saw my grandfather, he said something I didn't understand. But it makes sense now, I guess." All eyes were on the young teacher; everyone was still. "He was in the nursing home, and well, frankly, the things he said didn't really add up. At one point he kept saying, 'Anna Lux. Three, three, three. Anna Lux. Three, three, three.' I thought he was just babbling, but maybe he really meant something. About Room 333."

No one said a word. Everyone was expecting Hyrum to continue, but as he moved his eyes across the faces before him, some hesitation came over him and he went silent. It was as if he suddenly wondered if perhaps he'd said too much.

"The Anna Lux book?" Mr. Wellington said. "That one by Damien Crowley they say doesn't actually exist? My wife investigated it a bit once."

"I understand there might be an edition somewhere," Sir Reginald said. "As it turns out, the local book dealer in Havenworth was mentioning that fact the other day. That a copy might exist. Quite a find, if it ever appears."

Elizabeth replayed the conversation with Avery Dimlow in her mind; she was wondering just what, exactly, Reginald might have heard.

"A book that doesn't exist, but which might actually exist!" Mr. Knox said. "That is the sort of thing that fires the imagination." He stretched his chin over his plate and eyed the group furtively. "You wonder what the locked room—333—has to do with this." He sat back and gave an inscrutable smile, as though wanting to be mischievous, and then he winked at Norbridge.

"Nothing mysterious, my good man," Norbridge said. "I've been all through that room, and there's nothing in there. No books by Damien Crowley. In fact, no books at all." He raised his eyebrows as though the entire matter had been resolved. "Sorry to disappoint."

The atmosphere at the table, though, had altered irreversibly, and everyone had become fidgety and distracted. Elizabeth had to keep herself from shivering; she felt accused of something, and although no one was looking at her, she somehow felt the attention of the entire table was set to turn toward her. She thought of what she'd read in the Anna Lux book: *For Gracella—Someday she will show everyone what they overlooked. Damien Crowley.*

It is easy to be overlooked, she thought. A flutter went through her, and she had the strangest feeling that she understood—exactly—how Gracella had felt all those years ago.

"Maybe we should get to our puzzle," Mr. Wellington said somberly to Mr. Rajput.

"Is the library open now?" Mrs. Knox said to Leona, though she didn't sound very eager.

"A quick game of Ping-Pong before the lecture?" Mr. Knox said to Professor Fowles, as if asking if he wanted a cup of water.

"Wait, one and all," Norbridge said. "Please, finish your coffee and tea while I address the throng here in the dining hall, and then you can go about your business. I want to put in a little plug for Sir Reginald's lecture tonight, so allow me a moment or two of public address."

And with that, Norbridge rose and strode to the lectern at the front of the hall. He raised he hands to quiet the crowd and began to speak.

"A most joyous Saturday evening to all of you," he began, and Freddy turned to Elizabeth and sighed, even giving a playful roll of his eyes.

"Frederick!" Mr. Knox said sternly under his breath. "Be respectful."

"We've heard him give his speeches a million times," Freddy said.

His father tilted his head, narrowed his eyes at Freddy, and then looked to Norbridge.

"I hope you enjoyed the meal, my friends," Norbridge said, "and welcome to Winterhouse—that's if tonight is the start of your stay with us. If tonight isn't your first night here, we're overjoyed you're here for more than one night, and you are, of course, welcome to remain for as many nights as you desire, and we hope all those nights are happy nights for you."

"Night, night, night," Leona said, just loudly enough for Norbridge to hear. He scowled at her, and everyone at Elizabeth's table laughed.

"And happy days, too!" Norbridge said, scanning the crowd in Winter Hall.

Elizabeth couldn't help thinking, as her grandfather spoke, that Hyrum's words had cast a sobering spell on the assembled group and that everyone had now been made aware of some connection, however tenuous, between the Anna Lux book and Room 333. Elizabeth picked at her cake and thought through everything that had been mentioned.

"And so," Norbridge said, winding down his brief address, "if you will indulge me, I would like to dust off—so to speak—a little tune I enjoy sharing with our guests as the month of March nears its conclusion. It seems fitting, too, to offer this jingle tonight, because it is sung to the tune of 'Happy Birthday,' and that venerable favorite was just mentioned in conversation at my table not twenty minutes ago." Norbridge looked down at the lectern, adjusted his bow tie, cleared his throat, and then raised his chin and began to sing:

Happy springtime to you,
The sky's not yet blue.
The snow is still white, though,
And the lake's frozen through.

Way up here we love cold
And our cake without mold.
We like our hot chocolate
With cream that's not old.

With some Flurschen for all,
You might stay till fall.
In summer we play Kubb,
KanJam, and spikeball.

Yes, our inn's so much fun.
Stay awhile, everyone,
But be sure to bring long johns
'Cuz you might not see sun.

Well, my tune went too long,
And I sang one verse wrong,
But my heart's in the right place,
And soooo ennnnnds myyyy sooooong!

At that, Norbridge lifted his arms in triumph, and the audience clapped politely—and very lightly—as he glanced around.

"Big hit, that number," Leona stage-whispered in Norbridge's direction. He looked to her, and she put a hand to her mouth and tried to look embarrassed. Elizabeth wanted to laugh, but *the feeling* started to come over her— dully and indistinctly. She glanced around anxiously.

"Well," Norbridge said, addressing the hall, "some people like that tune, and some people don't. There's no accounting for taste these days. What I'm certain you will enjoy is the address to be given this evening at seven thirty in Grace Hall by Sir Reginald Eton-Pailey, a gentle- man with whom I've just had the pleasure, over dinner, of coming to know a bit more than I had before I had the pleasure of getting to know him." Norbridge put a hand to his head and then flicked his fingers as if to clear his thoughts. "What I mean to say is that Sir Eton-Pailey has led such a fascinating life and has such a capacious cata- log of captivating yarns to share, you will not want to miss his presentation. I know I will be there and am looking forward to . . ."

Norbridge stopped and his face went blank. Elizabeth glanced at the ceiling—the chandeliers were trembling gently. The floor of the hall began to vibrate, and the guests seated at the tables as well as the waitstaff lining the walls began looking in all directions and examining the ground beneath them. A rumbling sound arose from some hidden place beneath the hotel or outside of it and all around. It was like the noise of waves building for an enormous swell or the moment after a spark of lightning has flashed and an avalanche of thunder is about to tumble from the sky. And then a slow-rolling, rattling boom let out, and the floor and the chandeliers and the glasses on the table all shook as the crowd gasped or even, a few of them, let out shouts.

"Please, remain seated!" Norbridge called over the noise. He held up his hands, scanned the corners of the room as if wanting to keep the hall from cracking apart, and then the noise stopped. Like that, everything went silent, and the room was still.

Norbridge lowered his hands, looked in all directions warily but slowly, as if uncertain if there might be more to come.

"I recognize that was unsettling," he said as the buzz among the diners stilled. "But it is completely normal. Completely. I have lived at Winterhouse for over seventy years, and I assure you that this jostling is an inconvenient, occasional, but entirely harmless occurrence I've experienced many times before. Even just last week." He glanced at Leona. "Though before that was some years ago. You see, we have a deep, complicated strata of permafrost here beneath us extending off of the lake, and as we move out of particularly cold winters, we get this sort of settling. Not to worry!" Norbridge scratched his head. "I guess the ice spirits are trying to tell me to stop singing after dinner!" The diners laughed lightly, and Norbridge looked to

Mrs. Trumble, who was standing beside the kitchen door with a look of alarm. "I suppose what I am trying to say is: If there are any cookies in the kitchen, let's bring them out for everyone to enjoy!"

He snapped his fingers, and a moment later a line of servers entered with plates of cookies as the crowd in Winter Hall began to settle slightly. Everyone was, clearly, very uneasy.

"Permafrost?" Mr. Rajput said derisively, the first person at the table to speak. "I've never heard of such a thing. Last time he said it was so-called thundersnow. Why, I wouldn't be surprised if the entire structure collapses and we find ourselves crushed beneath—"

"Sir!" Mr. Wellington said loudly. "Enough! Mr. Falls has just elucidated the elaborate science behind the event, and I for one accept his explanation." He looked to Sir Reginald. "And you, sir? Any comment?"

"I'm no meteorologist," Reginald said, "though I once was conscripted to deliver the evening weather report for a cable news channel in Utrecht for three weeks when their regular gentleman took ill with Vlah's Disorder, a very rare and unpleasant fungal illness. But I've never heard of permafrost shifts causing the sort of quaking we just now experienced."

Mr. Knox had begun eating a cookie and was shaking his head. "Permafrost doesn't do that," he said, his mouth full. "It does not do that. I recall that time when we were in Siberia . . ." He turned to his wife. "With the Finklemanns.

You remember? Someone on that trip explained that the permafrost stays, well, permanently frosted." He glanced around. "I suppose."

Norbridge approached the table as though nothing unusual had happened. "That was fun! Always love those." He looked to Leona. "Like the old days around here, eh? The old days."

"So old I still don't know that I remember them," she said. "You should go check that seismograph thingy of yours, Mr. Proprietor."

Norbridge looked at her dryly. "The librarians are taking over." He stood straight and addressed the table. "I certainly don't think there is any cause for alarm. In any event, I hope to see you all at the evening's lecture."

With a flash of his eyes at Leona, he turned and headed for the rear exit of the hall.

Within two minutes, the adults at the table were offering farewells and making their departures. Freddy's parents clarified with him that they would be going to their room and would see him at the lecture; the puzzle men were heading to the lobby; Egil and Hyrum were leaving for the library with Leona; and Mrs. Wellington and Mrs. Rajput were off to view the new diorama of the London Bridge Norbridge had added to the collection on the second floor.

"Ne-ee-maid Eelwork," Freddy said to Elizabeth once they were alone at the table. "That's 'Damien Crowley' pronounced backward."

Elizabeth closed her eyes and put both hands to her temples as if to indicate a headache was settling. "Oh, no! Now you're going to be saying everything backward."

Freddy crossed his arms proudly. "Stath tire," he said. "Er, that's right! You looked like you were very interested in the conversation about that book, by the way."

Elizabeth's expression became instantly serious. "I never told you this, Freddy, but remember when I used your master key the Christmas before last? I went into Gracella's room, and I found the Anna Lux book in her cabinet. The one everyone was talking about."

Freddy stared at her in amazement. "That book was *there*?"

"It was. Or, I should say, it is. I checked again a few days ago."

"You went back?"

She nodded.

"And it's the book that has instructions for the Dredforth Method?"

Elizabeth nodded again, this time somberly. Neither of them spoke for a moment.

"And now everyone knows the book might be in Gracella's room," Freddy said.

"Exactly," Elizabeth said. "And I'm starting to come up with a plan."

"Why do I think you're already about to break Norbridge's *stay out of trouble* warning?"

"Maybe when the coast is clear sometime tomorrow,

you and I can get the book. That way we can be sure no one else does. Just in case Gracella is trying to work her magic on someone to help her come back."

"That is totally insane!"

"No one will find out."

"But my parents are here! I don't want to get in trouble."

"Pleh eem," Elizabeth said.

Freddy sighed and then went quiet for a moment. "You really have a way with words."

"So, it's a deal."

CHAPTER 17

ONE MORE VERSE TO SHARE

Sir Reginald Eton-Pailey's talk was every bit as fascinating and entertaining as Norbridge had promised, a thing Elizabeth was pleased to discover as she and Freddy sat in the back row of the packed hall and listened to him speak. As the minutes of Sir Reginald's address drifted by pleasurably and he related one incident after the next—the daring recovery in Tajikistan of a jade sea horse figurine (valued at seventeen million dollars and stolen from the nizam of Hyderabad), six weeks stranded in the swamp forests of Borneo with only a machete and two boxes of Tootsie Rolls, the time he composed a State of the Union speech for President Lyndon Johnson as they barbecued pork ribs at a ranch outside of Austin—Elizabeth felt she could have sat until midnight just listening to him talk. When he neared the end of his address, though, and described how he'd tracked a stolen opal to a famous elephant trainer's mansion in Panama, she found herself particularly riveted because he began to talk about word puzzles.

"It was there," Sir Reginald said, "that I first heard someone utter the sentence 'A man, a plan, a canal—Panama!' And that is when I became fascinated by palindromes." The sentence appeared on the screen behind him, and Elizabeth peered at it. Freddy nudged her and then turned to her with an expression on his face that said, *This is about to get even better.*

"A palindrome," Sir Reginald continued, "is, typically, a word or phrase that reads the same backward or forward. Take the word 'noon,' for instance, or 'civic' or 'radar.' You'll easily note that they spell exactly the same thing whether begun at the front or the back. Palindromic sentences or phrases are much more difficult, as you can imagine, but deliver much greater delight—though you generally have to discount spaces and whatnot. There are famous ones, such as 'Madam, I'm Adam,' or 'Never odd or even,' or 'Step on no pets,' or the Panama one I mentioned, which is very well known."

All appeared on the screen behind Reginald, and Elizabeth recognized instantly that each sentence could be reversed and, with a bit of mental recalibration of spaces or punctuation, read exactly the same as it had been if taken from the front side in the standard fashion.

"I became obsessed with palindromes from then on," Sir Reginald continued. "And if you will indulge me for a moment, I will share a few of my favorites."

The screen behind him displayed ten sentences that he read aloud.

Eva, can I pose as Aesop in a cave?
I saw desserts; I'd no lemons, alas no melon. Distressed was I.
Live not on evil.
Ten animals I slam in a net.
Never a foot too far, even.
Niagara, O roar again!
No, set a maple here, help a mate, son.
A dog! A panic in a pagoda!
Red roses run no risk, sir, on nurse's order.
Too far away, no mere clay or royal ceremony, a war afoot.

Sir Reginald Eton-Pailey continued to detail his love of palindromes, and Elizabeth found herself so excited by the possibilities in this sort of wordplay, it took her a moment to realize Freddy was looking at her.

"What?" she whispered to him.

He looked as though he was working through a difficult problem, and Elizabeth was expecting him to utter some clever palindrome he'd just thought up. Instead, though, he leaned closer to her and whispered, "This makes me think about something in that painting of Morena."

Elizabeth looked to him with bewilderment.

"After this is over," Freddy said, "let's take a look at that picture again."

The final fifteen minutes of Sir Reginald's talk were just as interesting as the preceding seventy-five, but now Elizabeth's mind was swirling with speculation about just what it was that Freddy had connected to the painting of Morena. When the talk concluded and the last bit of applause from the crowd had died away and the audience was dispersing, Elizabeth and Freddy remained in their seats and Freddy took out his phone. With a few quick pecks and swipes, he brought the portrait up, and the two of them examined it.

"Let me zoom in on the poem on the wall," Freddy said. And once he had, he and Elizabeth studied the lines intently.

Reflections

My! Within them, *discover.*
Can you?
Place this *inside.*
Things magical *of number.*
      Timét O'Reve
      (R.S.E.)

Elizabeth read the words three times through, but nothing new came to her. "What do you see?" she said, because Freddy was peering at the words as though trying to make sure they didn't start scampering around on his screen.

He looked up at her with a grin. "I think I just figured something out. All that talk about backward things and reversing words."

Elizabeth studied the poem again. "I don't see any palindromes in there."

"There aren't any palindromes, but you can do some reversing. In fact, the name of the writer is a clue to that. Look at it more closely, without all the punctuation and everything. And forget about the R.S.E. thing standing for an organization. Just look at the letters."

It took a moment of adjusting her natural instincts for scanning the words, but once she did, Elizabeth suddenly realized the name wasn't really a name at all.

"It says 'time to reverse'!" Elizabeth blurted out.

Freddy nodded. "And if you reverse the words in the little poem, they say '*Number of magical things inside this place? You can discover them within my reflections.*'"

Elizabeth's mouth dropped open. "This painting used to be here in Winterhouse. And it was painted by Riley Granger, and in it is a message that is telling us how we figure out how many magical objects are in the hotel!"

Freddy was shaking his head in wonder. "Riley Granger really loved puzzles."

"So what does he mean by 'reflections'?" Elizabeth said, but then she turned to Freddy and seemed to answer her own question: "His paintings!"

"That has to be it. There's something to discover in his paintings, is what he's saying."

"Somehow we can figure out how many magical objects are in Winterhouse by looking at Riley Granger's paintings," Elizabeth said. Her thoughts were going in all directions, but everything seemed an immediate dead end. "We've looked at his paintings in the portrait gallery so many times, though. We would have noticed something by now."

Freddy frowned. "Maybe he means something else?"

"Well, at least we figured it out, right? We should tell Norbridge."

"Tell me what?" someone said, and the two kids turned around to see Norbridge entering through the doorway behind them.

"I didn't hear you," Elizabeth said, half startled and half delighted to see her grandfather.

Norbridge pointed to his boots. "I'm trying to perfect my 'spy-stepping,' as Sir Reginald put it. That tale about the time he walked across a castle floor covered with dried rice cakes and didn't make a sound? All to warn the Princess of Brunei of a threat to her life? It sounded . . . unbelievable." He pinched his lips together as if to keep himself from saying more. "Regardless, it was a magnificent presentation. But there's something you wanted to tell me?"

"Norbridge," Freddy said, "look at this." He took out his phone and, over the back of his seat, displayed the portrait of Morena as he and Elizabeth explained what they'd discovered, including the reverse message in the painting. Throughout, Norbridge's brow dropped lower and lower, and his expression of interest deepened.

"I've never seen that painting," he said. "It must have left Winterhouse before my time, or else I've completely forgotten about it." He peered at Freddy's phone once more. "But that little backward poem you've uncracked! There's definitely something there."

"It has to be a clue," Elizabeth said. "And if we could figure it out, we'd know for sure if there were other objects at Winterhouse, right? I mean, if we knew there were only two things—The Book and my necklace—then we wouldn't have to worry about anything else."

"But if there's, like, ten things . . ." Freddy said, putting a hand to his forehead as if an awful headache had settled in. "That would be bad." He glanced at the clock on the wall behind Norbridge. "I better get going, though. My mom and dad told me they wanted me back in our room after the lecture."

"Your parents want to spend time with you," Norbridge said. "That's wonderful."

Elizabeth looked away; Freddy didn't answer.

"Say, we have chocolate-chip pancakes on the menu tomorrow for breakfast," Norbridge said to Freddy. "Your favorite."

Freddy smiled. "I knew I was glad I came back. Okay, I'll see you both in the morning."

Elizabeth held her fist out, and they tapped knuckles. "See you at breakfast," she said.

Norbridge touched his temple. "And give some thought to that painting. I certainly will be."

"Sounds like a good plan," Freddy said as he left the hall.

"He seems . . . a little uncertain about having his parents here," Norbridge said.

"I think he's mostly glad," Elizabeth said. "He's just getting used to it."

"Is that how it was for you when you started living here? You had to get used to it?"

"I think I got used to it in about five minutes."

Norbridge laughed. "Glad to hear it." He leaned closer to Elizabeth and gave her a hug that she returned. "I think I got used to you being here in about four minutes."

"You win," she said.

"I need to make the rounds," Norbridge said. "Perhaps you should get some rest? Tomorrow's bound to be another busy day."

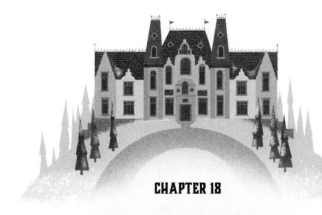

CHAPTER 18

SOMETHING AMISS IN GRACELLA'S ROOM

Half an hour later, Elizabeth was in her pajamas and on her bed, finally able to resume reading *The Next-to-Last Shriek of Uriah Mordred*. By ten forty-five—finding the book so gripping that all thought of turning in early had disappeared—Elizabeth had made her way to page 213 and was about to force herself to stop reading, when she heard someone's voice in the corridor outside her room. She set the book down and moved quickly to the peephole, looking through it just in time to see Professor Fowles and Hyrum walking past and engaged in conversation.

They must be heading back to Havenworth now, Elizabeth thought, though it seemed odd that the two of them had remained at the hotel so late.

Elizabeth turned away and went to her window. The night was clear and quiet, and the frozen expanse of Lake Luna appeared peaceful beneath the quarter moon. She pulled the curtain closed, sat before her laptop, and began looking up information on permafrost and earthquakes, though she found little of interest. After several minutes, she slid open her drawer, removed the small puzzle piece, and set it on her desk beside her computer.

I should return this, she thought.

Another voice sounded in the corridor, and with an unaccountable tremor of concern, Elizabeth turned from her desk and peered at the book she'd left on her bed. She allowed her thoughts to settle and her vision to become soft; a flutter arose in her stomach, and all became deathly still. The book began to tremble where it lay and then, as if impelled by some internal force, it leapt off the quilt, made a high arc in the air, and landed directly in her waiting hands. She let out her breath and clutched the book to her chest.

Is there really something about the Dredforth Method in the Anna Lux book? she thought. *Did Damien Crowley put some magical secrets in there?*

Elizabeth closed her laptop, set the Uriah Mordred book on her desk, returned the puzzle piece to the drawer, and climbed into bed. The light on her nightstand remained on because she was feeling more than a little anxious and wasn't sure she wanted the room to be dark. And as she tried to make her thoughts calm so that she could fall asleep, Elizabeth continued to be bothered by the thought that everyone at the dinner table that evening was now aware of the possibility that the Anna Lux book was in Room 333.

I don't think any of them would actually try to get into Gracella's room, though, Elizabeth told herself as she drifted off. She kept repeating it to herself, over and over—primarily to convince herself it was true.

⁂

Another nightmare—or, rather, a snippet of one—awakened her. It was a single scene, a single moment: Elizabeth approached the reference room on the third floor of the Winterhouse library and, although she'd thought she was all alone, when she entered, Gracella stood before her bathed in crimson light. It seemed she'd been waiting for Elizabeth to arrive. With utter calm, she stared at Elizabeth and said, "Of course you want to develop your powers. And no one should keep you from that." Gracella took a step forward. "I can help you."

Elizabeth sat up with a gasp and looked around her room. All was silent; everything was as she'd left it. She looked at her clock: 11:48. With a toss of her blankets, she slid out of bed, pulled on her robe, put her key in her pocket, and stepped into the corridor. She hadn't yet considered where she was heading, but as she moved to the stairs, she heard voices—agitated voices—from around the corner and down the corridor. And as she rounded the turn and saw what was before her, she was more astonished than she'd been at anything else the entire day: Sir

183

Reginald Eton-Pailey, Freddy's parents, the Wellingtons, the Rajputs, Hyrum, and Egil were all clustered in the hallway outside of Room 333, and Mr. Knox was berating Reginald.

"It sure looked like you were closing the door to Gracella's room!" Mr. Knox said. He glanced behind him. "We saw it. My wife and I. You can hardly deny it!"

"I most certainly was not closing the door!" Sir Reginald said angrily. He thrust an arm in the direction of the knob. "I was merely fiddling with the handle because I was certain I had heard a noise within." He glared at Professor Fowles. "And that was right after I noticed this gentleman skulking away from the room with his assistant."

"Skulking we were not!" Professor Fowles said indignantly. Elizabeth stood just outside the circle; no one seemed yet to have noticed her.

"Young Hyrum and I were departing the hotel," Professor Fowles said, "when we heard a banging noise up here and came to see what was going on." He turned to Mr. Wellington. "And, frankly, that was right when we saw you and Mr. Rajput rushing down the hallway."

"Because we were following them!" Mr. Wellington said, his voice booming as he pointed to Mr. and Mrs. Knox. "And I find it very curious—*very curious*, indeed—that the two of you would be up and about at this hour, particularly after you learned that a certain *very* valuable book by a certain *very* strange author just might be hidden in this *very* locked room."

"I find the entire episode extremely disconcerting," Mr. Rajput said, in a voice a notch quieter and a notch slower than any that had preceded his. "Extremely."

"Ladies and gentlemen," came a familiar voice from behind Elizabeth. Norbridge approached with Jackson and a young bellhop named Gustavo Lapointe. "The excitement of the day continues here in this dim hallway and at this late hour. Just what, exactly, is the occasion?"

Everyone began talking at once, and chaos claimed the corridor. Norbridge gave Elizabeth a quick nod and then raised his hands high over his head.

"One at a time," he said. "One at a time, please. Let's sort this through."

What ensued was a series of explanations of how there had been some rounds of cards and tea and perhaps another beverage or two in the café adjacent to Winter Hall after the evening's lecture, and that everyone present in the corridor now had been gathered there together before slipping off in ones or twos. All had ended roughly an hour before, and yet now, somehow, everyone had been drawn to the vicinity of Room 333 and was certain others had designs on entering the room. Norbridge asked a question or two throughout, but mostly he just listened as each person in turn explained himself or herself and cast aspersions—and, generally, wrathful glances—at one or another of the company in the hallway. Elizabeth found the whole thing not only astonishing but upsetting: All of these people, whom she knew and had every reason to

like, seemed now at odds with others in the group, and she foresaw a gloomy week ahead as they avoided one another or, worse, quarreled.

"My opinion," Norbridge said, after everyone had spoken, "is that the excitement of a return to this hotel, the oddity of the permafrost event, and the exhilaration of Sir Reginald's address has combined to make all of us a bit . . . loopy might be the word. Toss in the peculiar revelation of the alleged contents of Room 333, and we're all on edge, no doubt." Norbridge stroked his beard and lowered his eyebrows. He looked angry, and a new mood descended on the corridor, something that indicated Norbridge would abide no additional nonsense. "But it is after midnight, you are all at risk of disturbing the other guests at my hotel, and I must have you return to your rooms. More so, I expect you'll give yourselves over to pleasant dreams and be in a better position tomorrow to forgive and forget the discord of the night—and resume friendships."

Complete silence held; everyone remained motionless.

Norbridge snapped his fingers. "In other words," he said, "good evening, one and all."

With low murmurs and downcast heads, the nine now-somber disputants glanced around once more, warily, and then they all moved slowly toward the stairwell or down the hall. Norbridge gave a small motion of his head to Jackson and Gustavo, who trailed the others and disappeared. Norbridge and Elizabeth found themselves alone.

"Remind me again why you're here," Norbridge said,

closing his eyes momentarily and pressing a hand to his forehead as if to relieve a headache. "After midnight. Wrong end of the floor. Et cetera, et cetera, and more confusion and whatnot."

"I had another nightmare about Gracella," Elizabeth said. "And then I heard voices and I came down here to see what was going on."

"Another typical evening for you." Norbridge sighed.

"What if there's something going on? The earthquake and the book everyone was talking about at dinner? And everyone being here tonight outside Gracella's room?"

The hallway became deathly silent once again as Norbridge stared at Elizabeth.

"I need to tell you something," Elizabeth said softly.

Norbridge didn't speak, and she continued. "Not this past Christmas, but the one before, on the night before I left—I don't know why I did it, but I snuck into Gracella's room. It's something I never told you about."

Norbridge's expression remained unchanged. Ever since that night when Elizabeth had first found the Anna Lux book in the bureau, she'd wondered if Norbridge had known what she'd done. If he had, he'd never betrayed any knowledge of it, though he must have been upset that she'd disappointed him. Now, seeing him so unfazed by her revelation, she felt more certain than ever that he had, somehow, known that she'd been in Gracella's room.

"Go on, please," Norbridge said.

"I guess I was just curious or something. But right when I went in, I heard a noise from inside one of the drawers in her bureau, and I opened it. The Anna Lux book was in there. I took a look at it for just a second and then put it back. The whole thing scared me. I even thought I saw a crimson flash right when I was closing the door."

Norbridge waited for a moment to speak. "Is there anything more you want to tell me?"

Elizabeth had been hoping to avoid this, but she knew she needed to reveal everything. "I went back into her room a few days ago. Right after you and I had that argument in your office. I think I was mad—I don't know. There was a key in the workshop, and, well, the main thing is the book was still there. I took a quick peek and left right away."

Norbridge shut his eyes and took a deep breath. "I'm glad you told me about this," he said, exhaling slowly. "The fact is, I'm well aware that the book is in Gracella's room."

Elizabeth stared at Norbridge, uncertain if she'd heard correctly.

"This may not make complete sense to you, but Damien Crowley brought that book to us over twenty years ago, and I left it in Gracella's room. It was his wish, and I respected it."

It took a moment for Elizabeth to get the words out of her mouth: "But why?"

"As much hatred as Gracella has directed toward me, I've always tried to find some way to not return it. Call me idealistic or maybe even foolish, but I always thought maybe, just maybe, I could help Gracella return to the good side if I showed her some compassion. Some understanding. I suppose I thought leaving the book there might demonstrate that spirit of understanding to her—if she even had it in her to realize it."

One part of Elizabeth couldn't grasp what Norbridge was telling her. Gracella had tried to destroy Winterhouse and Norbridge both, and yet he was explaining that he still hoped there was something good inside her, something he could reach. It didn't seem possible. Another part of Elizabeth, though, felt it all made perfect sense: Norbridge hoped to save someone he'd loved, someone who'd perhaps been misjudged simply because her interests had landed on things others at Winterhouse couldn't understand. Perhaps—*perhaps*—Gracella deserved sympathy.

"But what if he left the book just in case Gracella ever needed it?" Elizabeth said. "Or if someone who was helping her needed it? Like, in case she died. Then someone could get the book, follow the instructions in it, and bring her back. Freddy even found something about the Dredforth Method that said the right spell has to be done on the third full moon after a person's death. That would be a week from tonight." Elizabeth nodded to the door. "Don't you think we should at least check on the book? Or take it out of the room and put it in a safer place?"

Norbridge studied Elizabeth for a moment before reaching into his pocket to bring out his ring of keys and unlocking the door. He turned the handle, flicked on the light switch, and entered the room. "Let's take a look," he said, and she followed.

All appeared exactly as it had when Elizabeth had been in the room a few days before. She stood by the door and watched her grandfather step gently toward the bureau without saying a word. He turned to her as if to confirm she recalled in which drawer she'd found the book. She pointed to the bureau. "Top one," she said.

Norbridge slid it open—but nothing was within.

Elizabeth's mouth dropped open. "It was in there. I saw it just a few days ago."

Norbridge opened the remaining drawers in turn and examined each. "Nothing," he muttered, his voice tinged with a desperation Elizabeth had never heard. "Nothing at all." He turned to look at her. "You definitely saw the book when you were in here?"

"I took it out and opened it up. I even read the first line. It was about a girl who was interested in magic, and then she decided to become a witch."

The ground rumbled beneath them, a fraction as violently as it had during dinner, but it rumbled nonetheless.

"And we see where that sort of interest can lead," Norbridge said with a scowl; he seemed to be talking to himself. He turned back to the bureau and put his hands on its top. "There's nothing here now."

"It had to have happened after dinner," Elizabeth said, "after everyone found out about the connection between the book and this room."

"If you're correct"—Norbridge turned back to her— "someone in the hotel right now has stolen the book."

"But who would have done it?" Elizabeth said.

"I don't know." He shook his head. "Let's hope there's a simple explanation, though. It could be one of those book collectors."

Elizabeth stared at Norbridge as the ground rumbled once again.

"Or someone who wants Gracella back in Winterhouse," she said. "Before the next full moon."

PART THREE

THE WINDS HOWL AS THE DARKNESS GROWS

CHAPTER 19

NAMES OF SUSPECTS TO LENGTHEN THE LIST

Breakfast was a somber affair, where the various parties sat at separate tables—Mr. Knox on one side of the room, the Wellingtons and Rajputs together across the way, Sir Reginald by himself off to an opposite side—and cast wary glances around the dining hall. The sky beyond the windows was cloudy and dim. Elizabeth, who took a seat at a table with a family visiting from Nebraska, looked in vain for Freddy and his mother as she ate her pancakes and scrambled eggs. Norbridge and Leona were nowhere to be seen; Hyrum and Professor Fowles had returned to Havenworth late the night before.

It wasn't until Elizabeth was nearly done with her meal that Mrs. Knox and Freddy arrived and joined Mr. Knox near the back of the vast room. Elizabeth caught Freddy's eye as he and his parents ate in silence, and he flashed her an *I'll see you after breakfast* look as he munched away. When he finally stood to leave, he spoke a quick word to his mother and father, made a gesture to Elizabeth, and a moment later, the two kids were departing through the rear doors of Winter Hall.

"Last night was crazy," Elizabeth said as they entered the corridor.

"My parents told me." Freddy was shaking his head as if he still hadn't absorbed the strangeness of it all. "What happened?"

Elizabeth shared everything as they walked to the workshop—the scene outside Room 333 and then how she and Norbridge had inspected the room to find the Anna Lux book missing.

"It's gone?" Freddy said as they entered the workshop and moved to the crates. "You guys looked everywhere?"

"Everywhere."

"All I know is my parents left to go to the café about an hour after I got back to our room last night. I guess they noticed the Wellingtons and the Rajputs walking by and looking funny, so they followed them. At least, that's what my mom and dad told me at breakfast."

"Everyone said they saw someone else acting funny or trying to open Gracella's door," Elizabeth said, "but as far as I can tell, no one saw anything for sure."

Freddy was peering into the crate he'd opened, but he stopped and squinted at Elizabeth. "But wait a minute. If you saw the book in there a week ago, then it could have been taken anytime between then and last night, right?"

Elizabeth shrugged. "I guess. But, I mean, it had to have happened last night. Before that, no one else would have even known to look in Room 333. It had to be someone who was at our table for dinner and heard what Hyrum said."

"But who?"

With a tap on the side of her head, Elizabeth said, "I made a list." She pulled her small notebook from the pocket of her sweater and displayed it. "Right here."

"I should have known," Freddy said, smiling in spite of himself. "You and your . . ." He looked to the ceiling for inspiration. "Koobtone."

"You're actually getting pretty good at talking . . . drowkab," Elizabeth said.

She thumbed to the most recent list she'd created— "People Who Sat at the Dinner Table the Night the Anna Lux Book Turned Up Missing"—and read the heading to Freddy. Beneath it she'd written thirteen names, crossing off her own, Norbridge's, Leona's, and Freddy's. She was tempted to cross off Mr. and Mrs. Knox, too, but she hadn't done so yet. Beside the remaining names, she'd made a note about each individual's possible motivation for taking the book.

"Okay," Freddy said, "so what have you come up with?"

"Basically, the reason Sir Reginald might have stolen the book is because he's a collector. The Wellingtons or the Rajputs might have done it because they're interested in anything having to do with Winterhouse, Mrs. Wellington especially. She's always been interested in stories about Gracella."

"*Maybe* on any of them," Freddy said. "But it's a stretch. What about Professor Fowles?"

"I can't picture him doing it, but he *is* a big fan of books by Damien Crowley."

"Enough to steal one? From his friend Norbridge?" Freddy shook his head. "I don't think so. Same with Hyrum. He wouldn't have done it."

"I agree." Elizabeth had resisted thinking of Hyrum or Professor Fowles as suspects, but she was trying to be systematic in her investigation. "But he is Damien's grandson. Maybe he wants the book because it kind of belongs to the family?"

"I don't know," Freddy said doubtfully, tilting his head. "And please don't tell me you think my parents have something to do with any of this."

"No, but I can't just cross them off. I mean, anyone at the table might have done it, right?"

"Including Norbridge and Leona? Or me?" Freddy bugged his eyes out. "Or you?"

Elizabeth sighed. "I see your point. But you know what they say: It's always the person you least suspect who ends up being the one who did it."

"Who's *they*?" Freddy held his hands out with palms up. "And when did *they* say it?"

"It's just an expression!" Elizabeth said. "Still, the book is gone, and someone's responsible. I'm just not sure who the most likely culprit is."

"Yes," Freddy said, with a look on his face that indicated he was about to choose his words very carefully, "it's tough to know who's in the *top spot*."

Freddy put so much emphasis on his final two words, Elizabeth began trying to figure out what he was getting at—and then it came to her. "Nice!" she said. "You made a palindrome."

Freddy grinned. *"I did, did I?"* He grinned even harder. "And there's another one!"

"Okay, okay! You're good at those! I admit it."

"Wow," Freddy said. "That's one more!"

"Enough!" Elizabeth said, and they both began laughing even harder.

Freddy and Elizabeth spent the time before lunch going through the crates, and then—after Elizabeth joined Mr. Wellington and Mr. Rajput at the puzzle table for an hour—they met back at the workshop. As they continued their work, they compiled a list of locations and landmarks to spotlight for their brochure, settling on twenty-seven in total, which seemed like the right number to allow for a thorough introduction to Winterhouse. The famous spots—the candy kitchen and Grace Hall, for instance—were easy. It was more fun to settle on some of the lesser-known sights (a paintbrush from the artist Frida Kahlo in a display case on the sixth floor, an unopened pack of Juicy Fruit Chewing Gum from 1898 on the twelfth floor, the wall in the back of the theater where actors such as

Buster Keaton and Grace Kelly had left their autographs) and then use some of the charming articles and photos in Nestor's crates to add background for their write-ups.

"This is like a homework assignment you don't mind doing," Freddy said, typing on his laptop while Elizabeth sifted through papers. The afternoon was growing late.

"Cruw-moh," Elizabeth said. "That's 'homework' backward."

Freddy looked away in momentary concentration. "Doog boj," he said, and as Elizabeth laughed, he pointed to his laptop screen. "Hey, listen to this. What do you think?"

When you visit the fabulous candy kitchen on the second floor, you'll notice the trays of Flurschen sitting in front of the doors to the kitchen waiting for you— no one can resist nibbling on a piece or two or three of these delectable treats before touring the kitchen itself. That's because Flurschen is the most delicious candy you'll ever eat, made from walnuts, apricots, powdered sugar, and a few secret ingredients. Nestor Falls himself perfected the recipe back in 1909. He'd eaten candy like it during his days in Turkey, and he thought the guests at his hotel might like his version of it. Flurschen is now famous throughout the world, and people have been known to go to great lengths to make sure they have enough. In fact, in 1932, Sheikh Ahmad Al-Jaber Al-Sabah of Kuwait ordered five thousand boxes of Flurschen for a royal wedding.

And in 1968, the Apollo 8 astronauts took a box of Flurschen in their space capsule and let the pieces of candy float around so they could grab one when it went by. Nestor's niece Serena loved Flurschen so much, she used to wear a hat that had pieces on it, and she also ate five pieces with each meal, every single day. Step into the candy kitchen to learn more— and enjoy the Flurschen!

"I think it sounds pretty good," Elizabeth said. "But maybe it's too long?"

"But we're talking about Flurschen!" Freddy said. "You can never say too much."

"Still. The whole brochure's only supposed to be a couple of pages."

"We can write small?" Freddy said, and then, after a moment, "Hey, we should visit Elana after dinner tonight, don't you think?"

"For sure. I hope she's doing better." Elizabeth glanced at the clock. "I'll probably go help Mr. Wellington and Mr. Rajput in a little while, too."

Freddy raised his eyebrows. "You're kind of spending a lot of time on that puzzle."

"Well, it's so close to being done. I mean, the work is really starting to move a lot faster. Don't you think it would be cool if the puzzle was done by Easter?"

"I guess. But do you really like spending time with those two? They always seem grumpy lately. Like they can't stop working on it."

"They can get kind of moody, but it's still fun. I just want to help them finish the puzzle." *Like they can't stop working on it.* Elizabeth had been thinking the exact same thing herself.

"I hope it wraps up soon," Freddy said.

"Hey, look at this," Elizabeth said, removing a book from the crate she'd been digging through. It had a textured olive-colored cover with no illustrations, and although the spine was frayed, the book felt sturdy and trim. Elizabeth held it up so that Freddy could see the title, which was written in old-fashioned block letters: *Artifice, Ruse, and Subterfuge at the Card Table: A Treatise on the Science and Art of Manipulating Cards* by S. W. Erdnase.

"Looks interesting," Freddy said. "And old."

Elizabeth thumbed through the book to find page after page of descriptions of card tricks, along with plenty of drawings of pairs of hands engaged in handling or displaying cards.

"It's all about magic tricks," she said, before leafing to the front couple of pages. "From 1902. This *is* old." Her eyes landed on a pen-written note on the inside front cover: "Property of Nathaniel Falls—magician in training! 1913."

"Hey," Elizabeth said, reading the inscription aloud. "This was Norbridge's father's!"

"He would have been about our age in 1913," Freddy said, returning his attention to his laptop.

Elizabeth gently riffled the pages of the book and was about to set it aside when a small piece of paper slipped from the back inside cover and fluttered to the floor. She picked it up and, setting the book down, read the message written on the page:

Dear Rowena,

I'd like to discuss Gracella soon. Now that she is thirteen years old, I find I have concerns about her that are increasing. Although she is an intelligent, curious girl, and—like myself—a lover of books, she seems, more and more, to be withdrawing from the family. You and Nathaniel have been wonderful parents, and Norbridge and Mickelson are loving brothers, but still I worry about her. She confides in me at times, often mentioning she's not certain a life here at Winter-house is what she desires. Of course, I hope her feel-ings change in this regard, but I also hope we can all look for ways to help her find direction. The poor girl seems so unhappy—I want the best for her.

With love and concern,

Lavina

Elizabeth read the note to herself twice before she real-ized a deep silence had come over the room. She looked up. Freddy was staring at her.

"You okay?" he said. "You look like you just found out you're heading back to live with your aunt and uncle again."

"This note," Elizabeth said, limply holding up the paper. "It was in the book."

"What's it say?"

Elizabeth stared at the paper. "I'll read it to you."

When she finished, Freddy sat in silence for a moment before speaking. "I wonder how that note ended up in the book." He paused. "It's really strange to think about Gracella being a kid. I mean, now that we know all the things she's done."

A ripple of exasperation went through Elizabeth, not at Freddy but at something she couldn't put into words, a thought that Gracella hadn't needed to take the path she'd ended up traveling.

"Maybe she could have had a different kind of life," Elizabeth said. "Not turned out to be so evil."

Freddy's face scrunched up, and he pressed at his glasses. "Maybe. But still . . ."

"I mean, if people had listened to her more, maybe," Elizabeth said. "I don't know." She glanced at the note again. "Maybe if she'd had some other kind of chance to—"

"Elizabeth," Freddy said, dropping his mouth open to emphasize how dumbfounded he was by her words. "You're talking about Gracella. She was a sorceress! I mean, she killed people with her black magic, including your parents!"

"I know!" Elizabeth said. And without any warning, *the feeling* overtook her, and—as if to dispel the force of it—she pointed to the lid of the crate beside her. With a flick of her fingers, the lid leapt off the floor, zoomed toward the far wall, and then smacked into it with a sharp crack before dropping to the carpet.

Elizabeth gasped and then became still. "I know," she repeated, the words coming from her meekly. She turned to Freddy, who was staring at her with an uncertain look on his face.

"Elizabeth?" he said warily.

She put a hand to her necklace. "I'm sorry."

"Okay," Freddy said. He shifted his eyes to the lid Elizabeth had sent flying. "But I think you need to be real careful doing that kind of stuff. Seriously."

Elizabeth moved her hand to her eyes for a moment to calm herself. When she dropped it, she tried her best to put a smile on her face. "You're right. And I really am sorry. That note just made me feel funny, but I know you're right."

"Maybe we can just keep working on our brochure?" Freddy said. "We do have a deadline, you know."

"That sounds good." Elizabeth picked up the S. W. Erdnase book and placed the note back inside. She wondered if Norbridge had ever seen it. "Let's get back to work."

The room was silent once more, and Elizabeth looked to Freddy; he was examining her.

"You sure you're all right?" he said.

She sighed. All she wanted was to put the previous few minutes behind them. "I'm fine. Really. Come on, let's keep working."

And although, over the next half hour, Elizabeth focused most of her attention on writing a paragraph with Freddy about the dioramas on the third floor, she couldn't help thinking that, once again, it had felt very good—very satisfying—to use her power to send that lid crashing into the wall.

I wonder if Gracella felt the same way, Elizabeth thought, but she did her best to dismiss this idea from her head.

CHAPTER 20

KNOBS, CURATORS, AND SMOKE

When she awoke the next morning, Elizabeth glanced out her window before she showered and noticed Hyrum heading into the forest on his skis along the west side of Lake Luna. It seemed a bit early for a morning out on the trail, but she guessed he was wanting to get some exercise in before resuming work on his research paper. She made a mental note to visit him in the library later that day when she went to assist Leona.

At nine thirty, Elizabeth and Freddy were in the camera obscura room on the thirteenth floor. They were, finally, set to begin their demonstration after a few days of cloudy weather. It was Freddy who (at Norbridge's urging the Christmas before) had restored the camera obscura—a device consisting of a box on the roof, a reflecting mirror, pulleys, and a large round screen on which images from outside were projected. It had once been a major attraction at Winterhouse, and now, with Freddy's work and Elizabeth's weekly demonstrations, it was returning to its former status.

A crowd of over thirty people, including Freddy's parents and Sir Reginald (who stood far away from the Knoxes), were gathered on the wooden platform at whose center was the large white screen. An air of expectancy ran through the assembly as Freddy tested the pulleys and he and Elizabeth conferred beside the control panel with its array of knobs and levers.

"Everything's worked just fine since Christmas," Elizabeth told him. "I usually just do what you did when you gave the first demo right after New Year's Day—I explain a little bit about how this thing works and then spend most of the time showing views all around."

"You must have had a really good teacher," Freddy said, giving the front of his plaid shirt two quick little tugs by way of mock self-congratulation.

"But I've taken it to a whole new level," Elizabeth said.

"'Level' is a palindrome, you know," Freddy said, and then he turned to the audience.

"Good morning, ladies and gentlemen!" he said, brushing his hair from his eyes and adjusting his glasses. "And welcome to the world-famous Winterhouse attraction, our camera obscura! Today I'll tell you just what this legendary mechanism is and how it works and what its history is, and then we'll use this mechanism to see what things look like outside the hotel. Because that's what this mechanism does—it brings the sights from out there . . ." He pointed to the ceiling and then gestured to the white disc around which everyone stood. "And slaps them down right here, because that's the amazingness of this mechanism."

"Son," Mr. Knox said, "you're overusing that word. 'Mechanism.'"

"Donald," Mrs. Knox said to her husband under her breath. "Don't interrupt Frederick."

Freddy gave Elizabeth a split-second *I told you it would be "fun" to have my parents here* look, and then continued. "As I was saying, this *thing* lets us see what's out there."

"You might even say," Sir Reginald Eton-Pailey said, "it allows us to *see beyond*." He gave the final two words of his sentence a slow and dramatic enunciation.

"Yes," Freddy said, not missing a beat, "you could say that, because that's what Milton Falls, who built this *thing* in 1934, said right here." Freddy gestured to a metal plate affixed to the knob-and-lever-cluttered control panel beside him, on which was inscribed the words THIS DEVICE ALLOWS ONE TO SEE BEYOND.—MILTON FALLS, 1934.

"And we don't know what it means any more than you do," Elizabeth said.

"I believe," Sir Reginald said, "that's a bit of an inside joke for those enamored of stereograms. *See beyond*. That's the motto of the International Stereogram Society."

"Stereograms?" someone in the audience said.

"Yes," Reginald said. "Have you ever seen those Magic

Eye books? Where you relax your eyes and an image pops out? That's a stereogram. They do them with computers and such nowadays, but decades ago, they made them out of lines of words. You'd cross your eyes as you looked at the sentences, and some hidden words would leap out at you."

Elizabeth was listening raptly. She turned to Freddy, who stared back at her with a knowing expression. "Those notes from Nestor," he whispered to her.

She nodded quickly, and, with excitement, removed her notebook from her pocket, drew out the notecard she'd placed within, and held it out to Sir Reginald.

"Like this?" she said.

```
owded a poor crowded a poor crowded a poor crowded a poor crowded a poor crowde
hief a handkerchief a handkerchief a handkerchief a handkerchief a handkerchief
g i toy away egg i toy away egg i toy away egg i toy away egg i toy away egg i
playhouse city playhouse city playhouse city playhouse city playhouse city pla
a a lonely sin a a lonely sin a a lonely sin a a lonely sin a a lonely sin a a
cracker ah firecracker ah firecracker ah firecracker ah firecracker ah firecrac
linen this ray linen this ray line this gray line this gray line this gray line
pe you camera ape you camera ape yo camera cape yo camera cape yo camera cape y
ught hip does ought hip does ought hi does fought hi does fought hi does fought
alley ah amaze alley ah amaze alley a amaze valley a amaze valley a amaze vall
r i a i a me nor i a i a me nor i a i a me nor i a i a me nor i a i a me nor i
b bravo east web bravo east web bravo east web bravo east we bravo beast we bra
rds to ate towards to ate towards to ate towards to ate toward to rate toward t
ught you ow thought you ow thought you ow thought you ow though you low though
ne a dab magazine a dab magazine a dab magazine a dab magazine a dab magazine a
top a yo plate top a yo plate top a yo plate top a yo plate top a yo plate top
amp a loose a lamp a loose a lamp a loose a lamp a loose a lamp a loose a lamp
m aid leg so him aid leg so him aid leg so him aid leg so him aid leg so him ai
a handkerchief a handkerchief a handkerchief a handkerchief a handkerchief a ha
ndwriting ow handwriting ow handwriting ow handwriting ow handwriting ow handwr
ing to handwriting to handwriting to handwriting to handwriting to handwriting
entlemen kiss gentlemen kiss gentlemen kiss gentlemen kiss gentlemen kiss gentl
ion ill ox station ill ox station ill ox station ill ox station ill ox station
```

Reginald took the notecard, put on his reading glasses, and examined the words. "I'm incurring a bit of eyestrain even as I try to resolve the image," he said, staring at the card. "But with some effort I can see there is a hidden message in here. You allow your vision to relax so that the words overlap—make 'poor' overlap with 'poor' in the first line, for instance—and then some of the words in the middle of the note seem to lift away from the others." He looked up. "It says, 'This camera does amaze,' and in another section it says, 'Bravo to you.' That's very nice. Must have been a note of gratitude to Milton Falls for creating this camera obscura."

"That's just what it is," Freddy said. "From Nestor Falls himself. We found that notecard, but we couldn't figure out what it was all about."

"A stereogram," Sir Reginald said, handing the card to Elizabeth. "Look for yourself."

After a bit of adjustment with focus and concentration, she, too, saw the words—everything was a jumble, and then the words of the message seemed to hover above the page. "That's amazing," she said, handing it to Freddy, who stared at the words himself and then gave Elizabeth a look as if to say, *We are about to solve the next clue.*

"Pass it around," someone said, and the notecard began to circulate.

"I'm afraid I've already hijacked the demonstration," Sir Reginald said. "I promise complete silence from this point on as the curators of this device lead us onward." He clamped a hand to his mouth, and the people around him laughed.

"Thank you," Freddy said. "Elizabeth usually does these demos, by the way. I'm just sort of filling in today while she rests her vocal cords. But continuing—a lot of scientists think something like the camera obscura was used by people thousands of years ago . . ."

Freddy moved into his explanation. Elizabeth was distracted as she thought about the stereogram message she'd read and the other one waiting in the workshop. However, she did her best to stay focused; it wouldn't be long before she and Freddy would be figuring out what Nestor had written beneath the lid of the crate. Finally, Freddy pulled on the rope, and the white surface of the disc burst to life with a tableau of Lake Luna and the distant mountains. Although the same view could be had simply by stepping outside or peering through a convenient window in the hotel, something about having the image arrayed like a living map seemed enchanting beyond description. Everyone oohed and aahed and began pointing out details here and there as Freddy explained what they were seeing and then zoomed in or out or shifted the box with his ropes in order to offer a new vista.

"Absolutely incredible!" Mr. Knox kept saying to no one in particular. "My boy's a genius. An absolute genius."

Elizabeth, pleased to see what a success the display was, tried not to smile too hard at Freddy, who was doing his best to ignore his father. The group hung on Freddy's every word as he progressed through different views, showing everyone the various sights. After about fifteen minutes of this, a woman in the crowd, her voice tinged with concern, said, "Is that smoke?"

At first, Elizabeth thought the woman was referring

to something in the room itself, but then she saw she was pointing to the image on the screen.

"It does look like smoke," someone else said. "Way back in the trees there."

Elizabeth looked more carefully, and then Freddy gave a quick tug on the pulleys, and the scene enlarged. There, along the west side of Lake Luna and far in the distance, a plume of black smoke was rising over the trees.

"That's strange," Elizabeth said to Freddy. "I wonder what that's from?"

"There's not much over there," he said quietly, and then his eyes went wide. "Except . . ."

Elizabeth caught his meaning right away: A couple of miles along the lake trail stood the old cabin Norbridge's father, Nathaniel, had made for the teenage Gracella years before. To Elizabeth, the cabin was an evil place where, it seemed, Gracella had been able to restore herself the Christmas before last and embark on her assault on Winterhouse.

"What's out that way?" Sir Reginald said. "You were saying?"

"Just an old skiing hut," Elizabeth said quickly, though she was certain Sir Reginald had noticed her alarm. She glanced at the screen once more and then looked at Sir Reginald; he was staring at the screen as if lost in contemplation.

"That's a lot of smoke," someone in the crowd said.

"I think we'll be safe over this way," Freddy said, trying to make light of things. "Maybe some snowshoer let his breakfast campfire get too big." With a glance at Elizabeth, he adjusted the ropes and moved to a new view. "But if you look here," he said, "you'll notice you can see Bruma Pass in the distance."

Elizabeth put a thin smile on her lips and made her way around the edge of the platform and to the staircase. A minute later she was hurrying to the lobby, hoping to find someone she could ask about the smoke—which, she felt certain, was coming from Gracella's cabin.

CHAPTER 21

A PUSH AT REDEMPTION

As Elizabeth raced into the lobby, a small crowd around the puzzle table turned to look.

"Sorry!" Elizabeth called as she came to a stop and felt the eyes of a dozen people on her. She'd disturbed the deep quiet Mr. Wellington and Mr. Rajput had clearly established.

"Here to assist, Miss Somers?" Mr. Wellington said, looking up with interest.

"I can't right now," she said. "Has anyone seen Norbridge?"

Mr. Rajput lifted a hand and pointed toward the clerk's desk, though it wasn't clear if he was answering her question or dismissing her.

"Thank you," Elizabeth called. Even in the middle of her agitation, she couldn't help thinking how remarkable it was that crowds continued to gather around the puzzle table. "I'll try to come by later," she added quickly.

"Hello, Elizabeth," Jackson said, stepping out of the door behind the clerk's desk as she approached.

"Is Norbridge around, Jackson?" she said. "I need to talk to him—or you, maybe. We were doing the demo upstairs, and there's smoke coming from out near Gracella's cabin."

Jackson's face became somber. "Actually, it is from the cabin itself. There was a fire there, but it seems to be under control now."

"The cabin was on fire?"

"Norbridge and a few of the others are out there. We just heard from them."

Elizabeth stared, not knowing what to say. "Are they . . . Is there something . . ."

"Your grandfather is on his way. I'm guessing he'll be skiing up to the hotel any minute now."

After getting her parka from her room, Elizabeth waited on the small stone bridge that spanned the creek just west of Winterhouse. Almost as soon as she arrived, Norbridge, in his wool hat and jacket and moving steadily along the lakeshore trail on his old-fashioned wooden skis, emerged from the stand of snow-clad hemlocks. Elizabeth watched him approach with deliberate glides, and as he looked up to see her, she waved to him.

"Elizabeth," Norbridge called. "Good morning." She couldn't be sure if his openmouthed expression indicated surprise that she was there or simple exhaustion from skiing.

"I saw the smoke," she said as he drew near. "From Gracella's cabin. Freddy and I were doing the camera obscura demonstration, and we saw the smoke."

With two final swishing glides and a punctuating exhalation, Norbridge came to a stop on the bridge. Silence resumed. Frozen Lake Luna was before them, and beyond its wide and empty plain, the far mountains rose like immense white sails against the cloud-streaked sky.

"The damage isn't total," Norbridge said, his face taking on a worried cast, "but it's pretty bad. Someone was at the cabin, and they started a fire. I can't even begin to guess why."

"Do you think someone did it on purpose?" Elizabeth said.

Norbridge studied her for a moment. "I don't know what to make of it." He exhaled, a quick sigh of both fatigue and concern. "I'm worried, I confess."

Elizabeth glanced toward the stand of trees into which the ski trail disappeared. "Maybe it's a good thing, though?" she said, thinking of all the evil that had arisen out of the cabin. "Now Gracella can't go back there, just in case . . ."

Norbridge gave a small squint of confusion. "I don't know."

Elizabeth glanced westward once more. "But if

Gracella's spirit somehow survived, it might go there first. Like before." She paused. "Right?"

"My sister is under the ground far beneath us, and I hope that's where she remains." Norbridge turned and looked back. The plume of smoke was still rising in the distance.

"I saw Hyrum heading out that way skiing this morning," Elizabeth said.

"He's been in the habit of taking early-morning exercise ever since he came to teach at Havenworth." He peered at Winterhouse. "But I'll talk to him. Maybe he saw something."

The conversation was oddly stilted, Elizabeth felt; it seemed there was something Norbridge wasn't revealing. "Why didn't you ever destroy the cabin?" she said abruptly.

Norbridge glanced back at the ski trail again and then scanned Lake Luna. "It was my sister's," he said softly. "The one place she could go when she was young to relieve her confused feelings, to be alone with her thoughts."

"But . . ." Elizabeth began, before faltering. One part of her wanted to blurt out, *You mean, her thoughts about black magic and destroying Winterhouse and the whole family?* But another part of her felt she understood exactly why Gracella wanted a place to herself, a place to sort through who she wanted to be and what path she wanted to follow.

Norbridge wiped the sweat from his forehead with the back of his hand and removed his stocking hat. "I know this may sound odd, but even with all that Gracella's done, I still have some affection for her. I still have a sliver of hope for her, a desire for her redemption. If she's gone, there's nothing that can be done. But if her spirit is still out there somewhere, then I hope it can find peace. I don't want to see her punished or miserable. I want to see her free of the evil she's created for herself. I don't know if that's possible, but that's my hope."

The silence resumed; Elizabeth studied her grand-father's face for a moment before speaking. "I found a note in one of the crates from your grandmother to your mother where she says sort of the same thing you're saying. I'll show it to you." Elizabeth paused. "Still, don't you hate Gracella sometimes?"

"To me, it doesn't make sense to return hatred with hatred." Norbridge gestured to Winterhouse, and they began to move to it. As they did, Elizabeth told him nearly everything of what she'd seen or heard over the past few days—the stereogram notes from Nestor, what Elana had said about Lena, what Jackson had shared about Kiona—and he listened with deep interest.

"Also, when Freddy and I were visiting Elana," Elizabeth said, "she said she thought Gracella might try to control someone in order to bring herself back to life. Maybe that's what she's up to. Maybe someone went out to the cabin to help her again."

"I'll start by talking to Hyrum," Norbridge said as they stopped just beyond the roundabout in front of the lobby. "We'll figure out what's going on."

"And we still don't know who took the Anna Lux book," Elizabeth said.

"So many things to consider." Norbridge stroked his beard for a moment. "By the way, I've seen that notecard and the words under the lid. Never knew what that was all about, but we should definitely pay a visit to the workshop." He glanced through the glass doors of the lobby. "I want you to know I spent the day over in Bruma until late last night with a specialist, trying to think through what might be done to help Elana."

"A specialist?"

"In how best to assist someone who's showing Elana's degree of decline. I've not dealt with this before here at Winterhouse. The people who grow old here usually maintain their health until nearly the end."

"You think she's dying?"

"I'm sorry to say I think she may be. She's unusually weak, even though she's broken out of her long sleep. It's just . . . the way things are. I don't know what can be done about it, but I'm trying to confer with some good doctors. It may be out of our hands."

"There has to be something we can do," Elizabeth said. "It's not even her fault. She's not really an old woman. She's the same age as me!"

Norbridge put his head down as a breeze sighed gently. "I wish I knew what to say."

A wave of helplessness arose in Elizabeth, a feeling rimmed with anger; Elana seemed beyond hope. "I understand what you're saying about Gracella, Norbridge, but I hate her for everything she's done," Elizabeth said, though it was an oddly mixed emotion she had even as she spoke the words—it was as though she wanted to convince herself of her feelings. "Why did she have to kill my parents? And hurt Elana like that?"

"Elizabeth," Norbridge said, his voice low, "that anger doesn't help. Not you, not your parents, and not Elana. It simply doesn't help."

"But what if the person deserves it?" Elizabeth said. "What if the person has done things so terrible, she deserves whatever she gets?"

Norbridge stared at Elizabeth; his eyes narrowed. A light snow was falling, and the two of them seemed all alone and far away, although they were standing only a few yards beyond the entrance of the hotel.

"It hurts me to say this," Norbridge said, "but I think you should reconsider that thought. Because the person who runs Winterhouse someday must learn to open her heart even to people who don't seem to deserve it."

The feeling flickered within Elizabeth. "What if that person's not sure she wants to run Winterhouse?" she said.

Norbridge's eyes tightened; he looked as though he'd risen to give his evening speech after dinner and found Winter Hall deserted. Elizabeth felt her intensity shredding as a deep sadness began to replace it.

"I just mean," she said haltingly, "there are things I feel like I want to do sometimes, and I don't think anyone understands that."

Norbridge continued to stare at her, though he widened his eyes just slightly in what looked to Elizabeth like something verging on alarm.

"I've heard those words before," he said. And before he continued, Elizabeth had already guessed what he would say next: "From my sister."

"Elizabeth!" came a voice from the front doors. She turned; Freddy was rushing at them and waving his hands frantically.

"We were just coming in," she said, though she kept hearing the words *from my sister.*

"I looked at the note under the lid of the crate!" Freddy came up to them.

"What did it say?" Elizabeth said.

"You have to come to the workshop and see for yourself," Freddy said. "There's something from Riley Granger! Come on, I'll show you!"

CHAPTER 22

FINDING A MESSAGE IN AN UNEXPECTED PLACE

Freddy could barely contain his excitement as he led Elizabeth and Norbridge up the main staircase. "You won't believe what I found," he said, glancing backward.

"Slow down, please!" Norbridge said. "I'm already worn out from skiing." He put a hand on the banister and paused to catch his breath as Freddy and Elizabeth, too, came to a stop.

"There's really something from Riley Granger?" Elizabeth asked Freddy. Not only was she excited to learn what he'd discovered, she was glad to have ended the conversation with Norbridge—she felt she'd said too much and also hadn't fully clarified her thoughts to herself.

"In one of the crates," Freddy said. He was shifting

from leg to leg, eager to press on. "Actually, not *in* one of the crates. Hidden inside the lid! I figured out what Nestor wrote." He scooped at the air to encourage the others to resume walking. "Come on—I'll show you."

Once they reached the workshop, Freddy made directly for the crate he and Elizabeth had puzzled over the day before. He removed the lid and displayed its underside.

"Look at the words here," Freddy said.

```
ss a dug princess a dug princess a dug princess a dug princess a dug princess a
bay bluebird a bay bluebird a bay bluebird a bay bluebird a bay bluebird a bay
i lay fist let i lay fist let i lay fist let i lay fist let i lay fist let i la
freedom bat um freedom bat um freedom bat um freedom bat um freedom bat um fre
master a schoolmaster a schoolmaster a schoolmaster a schoolmaster a schoolmast
oy tablecloth toy tablecloth toy tablecloth toy tablecloth toy tablecloth toy t
er in look either in look either i look neither i look neither i look neither i
an bet beneath an bet beneath an be beneath fan be beneath fan be beneath fan b
umble if this rumble if this rumble i this crumble i this crumble i this crumbl
ink week cover ink week cover ink wee cover wink wee cover wink wee cover wink
rous lady dangerous lady dangerous lady dangerous lady dangerous lady dangerous
d notes rain lad notes rain lad notes rain lad notes rain la notes drain la not
der to round rider to round rider to round rider to round ride to around ride t
eamy find on creamy find on creamy find on creamy find on cream find son cream
t with me bright with me bright with me bright with me bright with me bright wi
an by try hunt an by try hunt an by try hunt an by try hunt an by try hunt an b
ne id upset stone id upset stone id upset stone id upset stone id upset stone i
ming aim i swimming aim i swimming aim i swimming aim i swimming aim i swimming
lt ivy lake quilt ivy lake quilt ivy lake quilt ivy lake quilt ivy lake quilt i
its everything its everything its everything its everything its everything its
aner i sack cleaner i sack cleaner i sack cleaner i sack cleaner i sack cleaner
plaything i of plaything i of plaything i of plaything i of plaything i of play
arelessness a carelessness a carelessness a carelessness a carelessness a carel
```

The two others leaned over the lid and stared at Nestor's lines. Within seconds, and after allowing her vision to soften enough that the letters began to overlap, Elizabeth saw two sets of words hovering above the others.

"I see it!" Elizabeth said. "It says 'look beneath this cover'! And 'notes to find'!"

"I don't see a thing," Norbridge said, squinting at the words.

"It's just like one of those Magic Eye designs," Freddy said. "Just go kind of cross-eyed."

"I can't ever make those things work," Norbridge said, widening his eyes and then scrunching up his nose and squinting again. "Everyone always says they see sharks and ponies and things in those pictures, but I can't for the life of me see anything beyond a bunch of zigzaggy colors that leave me with a headache."

"Not everyone can see them, I guess," Elizabeth said. "But now we know what Nestor was hiding in these notes." She looked to Freddy. "But what does 'look beneath this cover, notes to find' mean?"

"There's a small compartment here at the top of the lid," Freddy said. "It looks like reinforcement for the wood, but it actually hides a little space inside." With a slide of a one ruler-width piece of wood, and then a twist of it to the right, a small panel was displayed.

"Voilà!" Freddy said. "Secret compartment right there."

A shallow drawer lay inside the lid, and within it were a dozen or so letters addressed to Nestor Falls—as well as a handful for Nathaniel. In the upper left corner of one of the envelopes for Nestor was written, in ornate cursive, "Riley S. Granger," with no return address noted.

"Absolutely mind-boggling," Norbridge said. "And to think this box has been in my closet for years, and I never realized. Nestor must have wanted to keep these secret." He looked twice at the letters. "And my father, too." He shook his head. "Strange."

"Look at some of these other letters," Freddy said, pointing to three envelopes. *Theodore Roosevelt, White House*, read the return address on one; *Mark Twain* read another, with an address in Connecticut; and *Grigori Rasputin* read a third, with no return address indicated.

"Wow," Elizabeth said. "These letters! They should be in a museum."

Norbridge was gazing at them with rapt interest. "This is quite a discovery you've made, Freddy." He gestured toward the one from Riley Granger. "Have you looked at this yet?"

"No, sir," Freddy said. "That's why I wanted to find you. And Elizabeth."

With a delicate scoop, Norbridge gathered up the letters in the compartment and held them up to the kids. "Let's go to the library. Leona needs to be with us when we read Riley Granger's letter."

When, ten minutes later, the four of them were seated in Leona's office—cluttered with books and paintings and thick file folders, and fragrant with the rose tea Leona enjoyed—everyone was at a pitch of excitement and curiosity. Norbridge had set Riley's letter on the table around which they sat, and they were all staring at it like artists analyzing a model before beginning to sketch. The other letters, as interesting and historic as they most likely were, remained inside Norbridge's breast pocket, because, for the moment, there was only one they all wanted to see.

"You go ahead, Norbridge," Leona said, gesturing to the Granger letter. "It's for you to see what's inside." She'd already set the little sign on her checkout desk for when she didn't want to be disturbed or was unavailable (THE LIBRARIAN HAS BEEN CALLED AWAY OR HAS FALLEN ASLEEP IN THE BACK ROOM. SHE WILL RETURN SOON. THANK YOU.) and put her parakeet, Miles, in his cage.

Norbridge's head was tipped downward, and he was staring at the letter as if to make certain it didn't disappear. He shifted his eyes to the three others in turn. Without a word, he turned the envelope on end, allowed a single piece of yellowed paper to slide onto the table, and then he delicately unfolded it and read aloud:

Summer Solstice—1899

Nestor,

As it has been almost one year since I departed Winterhouse, and in the hope that the disagreements that arose between us—and that caused our regrettable falling-out—might be better understood, I find myself writing to you. First, I wish to apologize for the arguments we had during my final months at your hotel; I also wish to explain a bit of the "legacy," if you will, I have left at Winterhouse. I do this in honor of the friendship we had and in memory of the years we spent in the monastery at Lord of the Peaks.

We both recognize we differ in our understanding of life and our approach to it. You think that there is a definite good and evil in this world and that we can know for sure the difference between the two and then live our lives accordingly. I believe things are always changing—even what we call "good" or "evil"—and so we must keep our eyes open and make wise choices. Can we always and forever say that one thing is good and another is evil? Who knows? Maybe we live in a universe that doesn't care about our human needs and desires. Which is why I feel we must be vigilant to protect the things we care for and the people we love. I believe in the necessity of faith just as much as you do, but I also believe our approach to life must change over time.

By way of illustrating my point, I have built what might be called "games" into your hotel to ensure that you and those who come after you do not become negligent. I have hidden within Winterhouse several items, each imbued with some of the magic from our monastery. In time, each will grow in power and will come to the attention of various members of the family—perhaps within a decade, perhaps in a century or more. These items will eventually be discovered—in fact, an especially dedicated or talented member of your family might discover them all. And, upon discovery, the finder must decide what to do with each item in question: use it to increase the individual's own power or let it remain unused. The former option will allow for immense power to accrue to the person in question; the latter option will "defuse" the item and make it no more potent than a lump of clay or a piece of rock. The point is: A choice must be made. Furthermore, the final item is of exceptional strength and interest: Like the fairy tales of old, it will grant its finder three wishes, and so I have made it particularly difficult of discovery.

How many items have I hidden in Winterhouse? Search and you will find. I will not divulge the number in this letter, though I have indicated the number in plain sight somewhere in your hotel. Consider that your first riddle. Also, I retained some of the so-called "magical ink" we received at the monastery, and I may have used some of it to embellish an engaging book I've created. Furthermore, I've used some of the marble found near our monastery to create an ornamental *little . . . Well, I won't say more. I've started you on the path, and perhaps you or your children or their children will work through my clues and claim power for themselves. Or maybe they won't. Who knows? Because there's nothing certain in this world, my old friend—which is, ultimately, the point of my game.*

Yours,
Riley Sweth Granger

Norbridge turned the page over as if there might be something there that he hadn't noticed. And then he laid the letter flat on the table and continued to stare at it.

"That's the whole thing?" Leona said, her face taut with disbelief. "I don't think that man could have been more mysterious or unclear if he'd tried. That letter is about as confusing as anything else he's done—and he's done plenty already to confound us."

"But he does say he put the number in plain sight," Elizabeth said. "And that palindrome poem from Morena's painting said we could figure out the number by looking at his reflections. That's why Freddy and I think Riley Granger must have hidden a clue to the number in one of his paintings. That would definitely be in plain sight, right?"

Leona knit her brow. "She has a point."

"And even if we don't know the number," Freddy said, "we know there has to be at least one more item, right? Even Elana told us that."

"We also know the Anna Lux book was stolen from Gracella's room," Elizabeth said.

"Meaning what, dear?" Leona asked. "These bits of information go in all directions."

"Meaning," Norbridge said, "if I may, that Elizabeth thinks someone here at the hotel is trying to help Gracella, and that part of that 'help' includes using the information Damien Crowley left in that book about the Dredforth Method. Furthermore, the discovery of a third item might advance the effort, too, and increase Gracella's power. Do I have that correct, Elizabeth?"

"You do," she said. His demeanor was so serious and his thoughts seemed to be working so much in alignment with her own, Elizabeth felt that perhaps the awkwardness of their conversation outside the hotel was on its way to smoothing over.

"Let's just all try to figure out what Riley Granger meant when he said the number was in plain sight," Norbridge said. "Maybe if we give that some thought, in a day or two, the answer will come to us." He put a hand on the letter. "I actually find this missive very illuminating, because we finally have some insight into Granger's motivations, which is something I never before understood to this level. We know why he did what he did. We just don't know the actual details." He tapped his temple. "But I think we can figure it out."

Leona raised her glasses from the thin chain around her neck, put them on, and then looked to Elizabeth and

Freddy. "I do, too," she said. "I have every hope the mystery will start to straighten out soon."

Norbridge scooped up the letter, put it in his pocket, and stood. "I'm going to have a little chat with Hyrum about his skiing trip this morning, and then I intend to review this letter and the others very carefully. And then . . ." He checked his watch and held it up toward Elizabeth as if asking her to mind the time. "I'll stop by the workshop to see what sort of progress you two are making. I want to see that note from Lavina you mentioned, too, Elizabeth."

"It seems our little party is breaking up," Leona said.

"We'll get back to work, Norbridge," Freddy said, standing as well. "And if we find anything else in those crates, we'll let you know." He looked to Elizabeth. "You coming?"

Elizabeth was gazing at a Maxfield Parrish print on Leona's wall of a woman gazing into a blue sky strewn with puffy clouds. *"Plain sight,"* she said. "I know I can figure this out if I just put my mind to it."

"I don't doubt that," Leona said.

"I'll go further," Norbridge said. "Elizabeth and Freddy, I'd say we're counting on it."

CHAPTER 23

A SMILE STARTS TO FADE

The day concluded without incident—Elizabeth and Freddy visited Elana and then worked on their brochure, though Elizabeth took breaks to help with the puzzle and even spent two hours shelving books for Leona. Although the Knoxes were not talking to Sir Reginald Eton-Pailey (who had extended his stay till Easter to, as he put it, "restore my vital energies via extended exposure to this region's pure, high-altitudinal oxygen"), who in turn was not talking to Professor Fowles (who appeared each day precisely at noon for lunch) or Hyrum (who came to Winterhouse daily to work on his research paper), who in turn were not talking to the Wellingtons or the Rajputs, the general mood at Winterhouse was pleasant.

The renowned Celtic harpist Thrackin O'Malley had delivered a splendid recital on Monday evening and had even left Leona an autographed copy of his memoir, *My Unbroken Harp: How Music Brought Me Fame, Fortune, and Nine Daughters with Red Hair*; no new storms had rolled through; and Winterhouse itself was filling up with guests eager to celebrate Easter at the grand hotel. The slightest hint of spring even seemed to be in the air, despite the still-freezing temperatures.

At four thirty on Tuesday afternoon, while Freddy remained in the workshop, Elizabeth headed to the library to assist Leona before dinner and found it more deserted than she would have guessed. Leona was behind the front desk and filing checkout cards when Elizabeth arrived; Miles was sitting on her shoulder, motionless until he noticed her come toward them.

"Summer's here!" he said. "Summer's here!"

"Shh!" Leona said to him, stroking the back of his head with a finger. "And, yes, our lovely assistant is here. And to be accurate, my dear bird, you ought to say 'spring's here!'"

"Hello, Leona," Elizabeth said, reaching a finger to Miles. "And hello to you, little guy."

"You have quite a contender for his affections," Leona said, looking meaningfully at Elizabeth over her glasses and then turning toward the maze of bookcases beyond the card catalog at the center of the enormous first floor. "The young schoolteacher Mr. Crowley is here again, engaged in his research, and I swear our Miles goes positively bonkers when that gentleman comes in. If I'd let him, he'd remain perched on Hyrum's shoulder the whole time."

"Well," Elizabeth said, "that's a good sign. Miles has good taste." She gestured to the stack of cards before Leona. "Maybe I can take over for you here, and you can have a break."

"I can see there's been no lapse in your manners despite the hours you've been spending with that Knox boy," Leona said playfully. "But, actually, I'm almost done here. Perhaps you can do a round of the floors and collect the items that need shelving? That would be an enormous help." Leona winked. "And if you visit with Mr. Crowley, I won't dock your pay."

Elizabeth was already moving to the shelving cart. "I'm on it." She leaned toward Miles again. "And you, little bird, please ask your owner to have some tea ready for me when I return."

"Summer's here!" Miles cawed.

"Why don't you take him with you?" Leona said. "Give him some air."

Elizabeth laughed as she extended a hand to Miles. The bird hopped onto her finger, and she lifted him to her shoulder, where he sat as if finally discovering a comfortable perch.

"Traitor," Leona said to the bird through a mischievous grin.

"We'll be back soon," Elizabeth said, and she moved off with the cart.

Ten minutes later, Elizabeth rounded a bookcase and found Freddy's parents examining a shelf.

"Elizabeth!" Mrs. Knox said with delight. "Wonderful to see you."

She and her husband approached Elizabeth's cart and began praising the Winterhouse library as Miles bobbed on Elizabeth's shoulder.

"And to think you live here!" Mr. Knox said, looking up to the vaulted glass dome high above at the center of the ceiling. "Wonderful place."

"Can you recommend any good books?" Mrs. Knox said. "Something you've read lately that you enjoyed?"

"*The Secret Keepers* is great," Elizabeth said. "And the Book Scavenger series, too."

Before anyone could speak, Miles fluttered on Elizabeth's shoulder and started to bob up and down. Elizabeth looked to him, as did the two adults. The bird came to a stop, turned to face forward very deliberately, and then, in turn, glanced at the two pairs of eyes staring at him.

"Gracella!" Miles cawed. "Gracella! Gracella!"

Elizabeth gasped.

"Norbridge's sister?" Mrs. Knox said, dumbfounded.

"The bird could only have said that name if . . ." Mr. Knox began.

"He'd heard it before," Elizabeth said, finishing the sentence. She was staring at Miles, who had returned to his regular, placid self and was now sitting calmly on her shoulder.

"Those birds are very intelligent," Mr. Knox said, his voice clipped and rapid. "Very sharp. He must have picked that up somewhere and then—bam!—just came out with it now."

Elizabeth felt rattled by what she'd heard. She couldn't imagine where Miles had heard Gracella's name—and, it seemed, heard it clearly enough to call it out so distinctly.

"I better keep going," Elizabeth said, backing her cart into the aisle.

"Of course," Mrs. Knox said. "We're holding you up from your work."

"See you at dinner, perhaps?" Mr. Knox said.

"I'll be there," Elizabeth said as she turned the corner quickly.

Within five minutes, her head still spinning, Elizabeth found Hyrum at a corner desk of the first floor, books piled all around him. She noticed some of the titles as she was approaching: *The Egyptian Book of the Dead*, *A Primer on Western Magic*, and *The Afterlife: What's in It for You?*

Elizabeth didn't want to startle Hyrum, but the wheels of her cart squeaked just enough to cause him to turn around with a little start.

"Oh, hi, Elizabeth!" he said. "Gosh, I was concentrating so hard, I didn't even hear you." With a quick motion, he closed the book he was reading and placed it facedown on the desk. Miles began ruffling and flapping on Elizabeth's shoulder and then leapt clumsily in an attempt to fly toward Hyrum, who caught the bird and cupped him gently in his hands.

"He likes you!" Elizabeth said.

Hyrum was stroking Miles's head and looking at him with admiration. "This little guy is super nice. And very friendly."

"I'm helping Leona for a bit and picking up books here and there. You're welcome to watch Miles, if you like. And if you have anything you want me to put back on the shelves . . ."

"Oh, no, but thank you." Hyrum smiled a little awkwardly as he set Miles on his shoulder; Elizabeth had the distinct feeling he was surprised by her presence.

"You're interested in magic," she said, nodding to the books in his stack.

"Research. I've got so much studying to do for my paper. At Havenworth I might be your teacher, but at the university I'm just a regular student like you. I'm so busy all the time."

"Did you always want to be a teacher?"

"Well, when I was little, I wanted to be a fireman. And then it was a soccer player, a lion tamer, and the guy who gives people money on one of those TV shows. But by the time I got to high school, I knew I wanted to be a teacher. I just thought it would be great to teach kids, the way some of my favorite teachers taught me." He shrugged. "I guess you could say it started to feel like I was meant to do it. But why do you ask?"

Elizabeth was very taken with Hyrum's response; she'd never considered before that there might be something a person was "meant to do."

"Just curious," she said. "Sometimes I think about what I want to do when I get older."

Hyrum held both hands out with his palms upward and glanced all about him as if to say *And isn't life here at Winterhouse what your future holds?*

"I guess I'm still trying to figure out how a person knows what she's supposed to do," Elizabeth said. "I mean, what if you make the wrong choice?"

"I think you'll know when the time comes. Just have a little faith."

Elizabeth put a hand to her pendant and let Hyrum's words sink in. She glanced at the book he'd placed facedown on his desk. "Is that one for research, too?" she said, pointing to it.

"Ah," he said slowly. "Okay, I guess my little secret has to come out sooner or later." He picked up the book and opened it to the page where he had left his bookmark, but before Elizabeth could read what was there, he closed it once again. "Personal."

"A journal!" she said. "Sorry, I didn't mean to be nosy. I keep one, too."

"Mine is mostly poetry. I love to write poems." He turned the book over to show her its front, and there in neat print were the words "Hyrum Crowley—Reflections."

A jolt went through Elizabeth. "Reflections?"

Hyrum smiled. "I like the sound of that word. So instead of calling them poems, I thought I would call them my reflections. It makes me feel more like I'm experimenting."

"I know what you mean," Elizabeth said, though her mind was beginning to race.

Miles began bobbing on Hyrum's shoulder. The bird rose up and down and started flexing his wings before jerking his head and cawing, once again, "Gracella!"

Elizabeth looked to the bird, stunned anew. Hyrum, too, was staring at Miles.

"Did he really just say that name?" Hyrum said.

Miles turned to him and resumed bobbing. "Gracella!" the bird cawed. "Gracella!"

Elizabeth felt her stomach drop. She reached out a hand to Miles. "I can take him back."

"You okay?" Hyrum said.

"I don't know why he's saying her name." The bird jumped onto Elizabeth's finger.

"Me neither." Hyrum squinted and stared at the books on his desk for a moment before looking back at Elizabeth. He eyed Miles as if seeing him for the first time. "That's really odd."

A tense silence seemed to hold as Elizabeth waited for Hyrum to say something more. Finally, he smiled faintly and gave a small shrug. "I guess I better get more work done."

"Good luck," Elizabeth said quickly. She set Miles on

her shoulder, clamped both hands on the cart, and began to wheel it away. "Maybe I'll see you at dinner."

"I hope so," Hyrum said.

Elizabeth turned the corner of the bookcase beside them and moved down the row, feeling so anxious it was as if she expected Avery Dimlow to appear.

"That was quick," Leona said as Elizabeth approached her.

"Did you hear what Miles said?" Elizabeth asked, and when Leona shook her head, Elizabeth explained.

"That's never come out of him before," Leona said, examining Miles warily. "He must have heard someone say that name."

"But who?" Elizabeth swiveled her head slowly to glance in the direction she'd come. "He said it in front of the Knoxes and Hyrum. Maybe he heard it from one of them."

"Doesn't seem likely," Leona said softly. "But you never know."

"Have any of the other people who were at the table with us that night come in here? Maybe one of them was talking about Gracella."

"Professor Fowles, of course," Leona said. "And Sir Reginald Speakin'-Falsely . . . er, Eton-Pailey. But it's not as if Miles has been within earshot of them." She scratched the bun atop her head. "Puzzler. A real puzzler. Though I'll continue to reflect on it."

"That word again," Elizabeth said. She snapped her

fingers and widened her eyes. "I'll finish the reshelving after dinner, okay, Leona? I think I might have figured something out." She turned and rushed for the door.

"What in Nestor Falls's name have you discovered?" Leona said.

"A reflection, Leona!" Elizabeth said, but by then she was racing into the hallway.

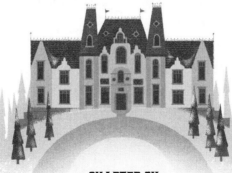

HIDDEN WORDS AND RANDOM COMMENTS

The eight-line poem on the wall above the entrance to Winter Hall had vexed Elizabeth from the first time she'd read it. There had always been something nagging at her mind when she studied the words; it reminded her of the way she felt when she was working on a crossword puzzle or trying to make sense of a coded message, the feeling that there was something to figure out or discover. Norbridge had once informed her that Riley Granger was the poem's author, and this fact had only added to the overall curiousness of the thing.

She stood in the broad and empty hallway outside of Winter Hall and stared up at the poem written in ornate letters there:

The peaks rise high, the north reels on, and mist
   obscures the sky
Where as one hid—denied the night!—the days of
   fall pass by
In winter's tempo we remain, but when fair spring
   returns
Soon summer's knit 'em, sky and storm, and scented
   heaven burns
October ear and April eye catch distant zephyr's song
The airy cloud does wet hilltop—the ancient night is
   long
First light, gong rang, erased the dark, the endless
   river crossed
The pages, pendant, picture all—where faith is never
   lost!

Elizabeth began to feel a flutter inside her, and her vision narrowed and fixed on the words. Some swell of intuition and certainty arose within her; the dining hall and the murals and the family tree—everything other than the poem itself—seemed miles away. She felt she was alone in some soundless, distant place where there was only her and the words gleaming above. Like lights flashing in sequence—some sort of beacon—letters stood out here and there across the lines of the poem, and Elizabeth understood just what, exactly, Riley Granger had hidden in his poem. Or, rather, his *reflections*.

She stood in place, lost in concentration for a good ten minutes, and she worked through the lines of the poem

The peaks rise high, the north reels on, and mist obscures the sky
Where as one hid—denied the night!—the days of fall pass by
In winter's tempo we remain, but when fair spring returns
Soon summer's knit 'em, sky and storm, and scented heaven burns
October ear and April eye catch distant zephyr's song
The airy cloud does wet hilltop—the ancient night so long
First light, gong rang, erased the dark, the endless river crossed
The pages, pendant, picture all—where faith is never lost!

over and over again until she was certain she'd solved the mystery of it. A feeling of deep satisfaction came over her, a private moment of contentment that she was, absolutely, coming closer to solving the final secret of Winterhouse.

I know how many items there are and what the last one is, she thought. *Without a doubt.*

Half an hour later, she had assembled Norbridge, Freddy, and Leona in front of the wall and was set to reveal to them what she'd discovered.

"The number is written in that poem?" Freddy said as he squinted at the lines. "I don't see anything in there about numbers or magical objects."

Elizabeth was studying the poem intently. "Yep, I'll show you. First, though, Norbridge, do you know anything about this poem besides what you've already told us?"

"I wish I had more details to share," Norbridge said. "Riley Granger wrote the thing and painted it up there—that's about all I know of its history. But clearly there's something more to the poem than meets the eye." He gazed at Elizabeth. "And we're waiting to hear what it is."

"Yes, dear," Leona said. "The suspense is . . . Well, it's not killing us, but it's making us deeply anxious at this point. Spill the beans, dear girl."

Elizabeth pointed to the poem. "You see where it says 'north reels' in the first line? The word 'three' is inside the others, starting at the end of 'north' and finishing in 'reels.'"

"You're right," Norbridge said, with a tone of quiet amazement. He held up a hand. "And I see where you're going. In the second line the word 'hidden' is between 'hid' and 'denied.'"

"And in the third line," Freddy said with excitement, "I see the word 'power' if you look at the words 'tempo we remain'!"

"'Knit 'em sky' has the word 'items' inside it," Elizabeth said.

"'April eye' has 'Riley,' in it," Leona said.

"And 'Sweth Granger' is in the next two lines!" Freddy said. "Look! There's 'does wet hilltop,' and 'gong rang erased'! Whoa! That is incredible!"

"The last line?" Leona said, looking perplexed. "I see 'real' and 'this,' but I don't see the connection there."

"Maybe those are just coincidental," Elizabeth said. "Because in the last line I think he really is telling us what the items are—'pages, pendant, picture.' That makes sense to me. The pages of The Book, the pendant on my necklace . . ."

"And a picture?" Freddy said. He frowned. "Wait a minute. We're back to where we started. Looking for a picture."

Elizabeth shrugged. "I don't know what that part means. But we do know one thing now for sure." She pointed up to the poem. "*Three hidden power items. Riley Sweth Granger. Pages, pendant, picture.* It's all right there in the poem. In plain sight. Three items."

"That's such a cool way of hiding a message," Freddy said, gaping at the poem.

"I just hope we can solve everything by Saturday night," Elizabeth said. "I'm positive whoever stole the Anna Lux book wants to work the Dredforth Method by then."

Norbridge was staring at the lines with amazement. "After all these years. We might not know exactly what to be on the lookout for, but we know the third item truly is the last thing. A picture. The third and final object in Winterhouse."

"Bravo, my dear," Leona said. "Now all we have to do is figure out which picture our friend Riley Granger is talking about, and we can sleep tight."

"A picture?" came a voice from behind them.

Elizabeth, Freddy, Norbridge, and Leona all turned at the same time to see Hyrum standing there and looking up at the poem on the wall.

"Greetings, sir," Leona said. "All done with your research for the day?"

"A guy can only spend so much time reading about Egyptian mummies and pentagrams," Hyrum said, rolling his eyes. "But what were you saying about some sort of final object from Riley Granger?" He gestured toward the words high above.

Norbridge approached Hyrum as Freddy and Elizabeth waved hello. "Yes," Norbridge said, "we were just admiring the writing up there and discussing the paintings my grandfather's friend Mr. Granger made of the first members of the Falls family. As you've seen, of course, down in the portrait gallery. Just wondering which painting might have been his last."

"Ah," Hyrum said. "I get it. The painter." He pointed to the family tree high above. "You know, I was actually wondering about Cassandra Falls a few days ago. It says up there she was born in 1920, but then there's nothing else about her. Do you know her story?"

"Cassandra left to join a convent when she was twenty-two," Norbridge said. "In Nova Scotia, according to family lore. But, sadly, we lost track of her many years ago."

"I've looked into the matter a bit," Leona said. "Halifax is where the trail goes cold. There was some gossip that she'd actually eloped, but we don't know anything about her after the late 1940s."

"Halifax?" Hyrum said. "That's where my grand-mother's from."

"Your grandmother . . ." Leona began.

"Grandma Sandra," Hyrum said. "Damien's wife. She died before I was born, but I know she was from Halifax."

Leona gestured to the family tree. "That's quite a coincidence. Sandra. Halifax."

Elizabeth felt something odd had just happened, but she realized both Norbridge and Leona were intent on steering all conversation away from anything curious.

"Hey, Freddy," Hyrum said, a note of concern in his voice. "You okay?"

Everyone turned to Freddy, who stood with his eyes closed. It looked as though he'd fallen asleep standing up.

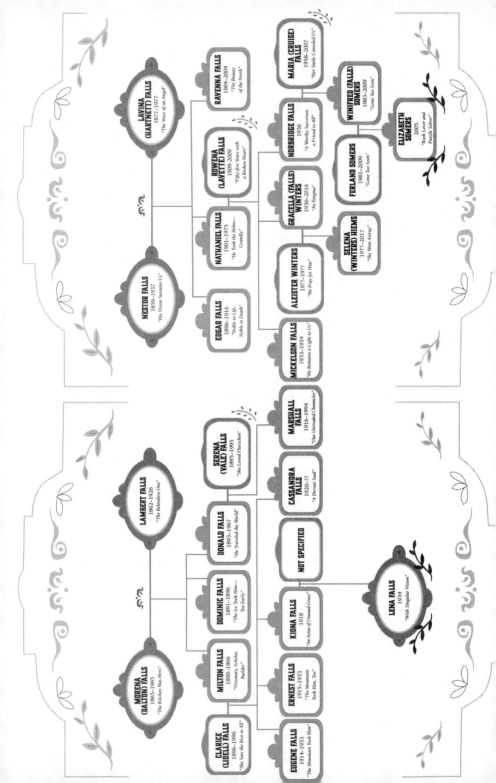

LAVINA (HARTNETT) FALLS
1877–1977
"The Voice of an Angel"

NESTOR FALLS
1850–1937
"His Vision Sustains Us"

RAVENNA FALLS
1904–2004
"The Beauty of the North"

ROWENA (LAVETTE) FALLS
1909–2009
"Fifty-five Years with a Broken Heart"

NATHANIEL FALLS
1901–1975
"He Took the Helm—Grandly"

EDGAR FALLS
1896–1916
"Noble in Life, Noble in Death"

MARIA (CRUISE) FALLS
1958–2007
"Her Smile Consoled Us"

NORDBRIDGE FALLS
1936
"A Worthy Successor, a Friend to All"

GRACELLA (FALLS) WINTERS
1936–2016
"An Enigma"

WINIFRED (FALLS) SOMERS
1983–2009
"Gone Too Soon"

FERLAND SOMERS
1981–2009
"Gone Too Soon"

SELENA (WINTERS) HIEMS
1977–2017
"She Went Astray"

ALEISTER WINTERS
1977–1977
"We Pray for Him"

MICKELSON FALLS
1933–1954
"He Remains a Light to Us"

ELIZABETH SOMERS
2005
"Book Lover and Puzzle Solver"

LAMBERT FALLS
1862–1926
"The Relentless One"

MORENA (DALTON) FALLS
1865–1965
"The Kitchen Was Hers"

SERENA (VALE) FALLS
1895–1995
"She Loved Flourishes"

DONALD FALLS
1893–1967
"He Traveled the World"

DOMINIC FALLS
1891–1896
"The Ice Took Him—Too Early"

MILTON FALLS
1890–1966
"Visionary, Scholar, Builder"

CLARICE (LIDELL) FALLS
1896–1996
"She Saw the Best in All"

MARSHALL FALLS
1916–1994
"Our Unrivaled Chronicler"

CASSANDRA FALLS
1920–??
"A Devout Soul"

NOT SPECIFIED

KIONA FALLS
1918
"An Artist of Unusual Grace"

ERNEST FALLS
1915–1933
"The Mountain Took Him, Too"

EUGENE FALLS
1914–1933
"The Mountain Took Him"

LENA FALLS
1934
"With Singular Vision"

"Freddy?" Elizabeth said.

He opened his eyes and smiled. "Nova Scotia," he said. "Avocations."

"Whoa," Elizabeth said with awe. "Seriously?"

"That, sir," Norbridge said, slowly and crisply, "may be one of the most incredible anagrams you have ever created."

"You just did that on the spot?" Hyrum said. "Right now?"

Norbridge held up both hands. "This has been a most diverting and wide-ranging discussion. Elizabeth, thank you for your observations on the renowned Granger poem." He winked at her. "However, right now I need to check on dinner. Please, all, note that the famous Tuvan throat singer Sainkho Mongush will be performing in Grace Hall at seven thirty, and you won't want to miss her." He gave a general salute and departed with Leona.

Elizabeth was about to say something by way of fare-well, but the silence in the corridor seemed suddenly over-powering. She looked to Freddy—but he, just like Hyrum, was staring up at Riley Granger's poem, studying the eight lines.

"Interesting poem," Hyrum said, to no one in particu-lar. "There's a lot to it."

Elizabeth nudged Freddy. "We better get going," she said.

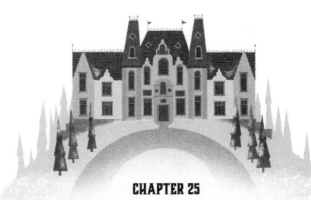

CHAPTER 25

DISCOURAGED, CRESTFALLEN, AND UNSETTLED

Tuesday evening and Wednesday morning were a frustration for Elizabeth and Freddy—they could make no headway on solving Riley Granger's puzzle even though they spent two hours painstakingly examining his four paintings in the portrait gallery; they'd also fallen way behind on their project. They'd targeted Thursday afternoon to complete the brochure so that Norbridge could have it available by Easter, but it seemed they would need more time. All of the locations in Winterhouse had been decided on days before, but it was proving more difficult than they'd imagined to write about each one in ways that would be appealing and concise. An hour before lunch on

Wednesday, the two of them sat in the workshop, writing away.

"How about this?" Elizabeth said, reading from her notebook: "The autographed copy of *Six Years' Wanderings in the Sáhreev'ah Tea Plantations* by Paxton Rumidello, can be found in a display case along the southeast wing of the corridor on the ninth floor. You'll find this book of interest because, ten years after it came out in 1952, Paxton Rumidello broke the world record for longest amount of time enclosed in a box of ice (forty-seven hours and thirty-two minutes). He did this in Casper, Wyoming, and after the ice blocks around him were sawed away, he spent three weeks in a hospital and never ate ice cream the rest of his life. He visited Winterhouse in 1974 and stayed inside the whole time."

"I like it," Freddy said. "I think it has just the right tone."

"Short and sweet," Elizabeth said. She sighed. "We sure have a way to go, though."

"We'll get it done. What we really have a way to go on is just about everything else around here." Freddy peered at his screen. "I've been keeping a list, believe it or not. *Who stole the book? What picture is Riley Granger talking about? Why is Lena wandering around, and what does she want to do for Elana?*"

"And *who set the fire at Gracella's cabin?*" Elizabeth said.

"I'll add that one."

"Also, *how did Miles hear Gracella's name?*"

"I have that one already," Freddy said, "plus *what is causing the earthquakes?*"

"Wow," Elizabeth said. "That's a lot. And we don't even have *who is Lena's father?*"

"Or *how many of Sir Reginald's stories are true?*"

Elizabeth began to laugh, and Freddy jiggled his laptop for emphasis.

"At least nothing strange has happened today," Elizabeth said.

"Not yet," Freddy said.

"If we can just find the third item, or make sure no one else finds it—"

"Hey!" Freddy said, sitting up straight. "I have an idea. You know how the Dredforth Method would need to be done on Saturday night when the moon is full? Why don't we ask Norbridge to host a special little dinner party that night? He could invite everyone on our list, and that way he could keep an eye on all of them. Like, he'd make it a really fancy dinner in his apartment, and there would be special entertainment. Everyone would stay until midnight, and then no one could do the ceremony to bring back Gracella because they'd be with Norbridge."

"That's a good idea," Elizabeth said, picturing the scene. "That's a *really* good idea."

"Can you say that one more time?" Freddy said. "A little louder? Write it down, maybe?"

Elizabeth was already thinking through the ramifications of Freddy's plan and how it would mean several of the things that were troubling them would be resolved: If no one could perform the Dredforth Method, then it didn't matter who had stolen the Anna Lux book or what Riley Granger's picture was: Gracella would be unable to return and could never threaten Winterhouse again. If Freddy's idea worked, it would neatly solve all their worries.

"I promise to give you most of the credit when I run things by Norbridge," Elizabeth said.

"Credit," Freddy said. "Direct."

Elizabeth rubbed her forehead in mock annoyance. "Just work on the brochure, okay?"

That night, after a thrilling display of paper folding by the renowned origami artist Aristotle Schliemann in Grace Hall, Elizabeth said good night to Freddy. The afternoon had been so full with working on the puzzle and the brochure and then an hour of skating at the rink beside Lake Luna, that Elizabeth was worn out. She had, though, run Freddy's idea by Norbridge, and he told her he would start planning out Saturday evening immediately.

"Brilliant plan," Norbridge had said. "We'll do it. I can even get Phuong Nguyen to give a private concert on her lithophone that evening. She's giving a recital on Easter day in Grace Hall, but if I bring her in the night before, that will make the gathering even more special."

"A lithophone?" Elizabeth said.

"It's like a vibraphone, but with rocks. She's one of the best in the world on the thing, and we're lucky to have her at Winterhouse this weekend, because she has an engagement in Novosibirsk three days afterward. Anyway, I love the plan. We'll do it!"

Elizabeth couldn't get to sleep that night, and so she sat on her sofa reading *Nevermoor: The Trials of Morrigan Crow*, until late. When the midnight chimes sounded from the Tower, she stood and looked out her window at frozen Lake Luna and thought of her mother's statue on the far side. From the first time Norbridge had used his telescope to show her the white marble monument—set on a pedestal on the distant opposite shore of the lake—Elizabeth had been eager to see it up close. In summer, she'd been told, this was an easy enough thing to do by rowing across the lake or hiking through the woods, but in winter, with snow covering the trails more deeply the farther away they were from Winterhouse, a trip was out of the question. If there was no more snow for a few days, though, Elizabeth thought perhaps Mr. Obrastoff could clear the trail all the way to the opposite end of the lake and she'd be able to ski there. She thought of her mother's statue, beautiful and pure white, standing beside the icy shore of the lake, waiting.

Elizabeth turned and stared at the book she'd left on her sofa. *The feeling* arose in her, and the book began to tremble as she focused on it. She was about to cause the volume to leap off the sofa when a peculiar agitation came over her and she cut off what she'd begun. She turned to the window and looked out once again—and there, on the stone bridge, the strange crimson haze she'd seen once before was hovering. Elizabeth watched and waited—the fog disappeared, and just like the last time, she wondered if she'd really seen anything at all. The chimes ended; a slight rumbling arose from the earth far beneath, a faint tremor.

Midnight, she thought. *The hour I brought Gracella's spirit back two Christmases ago.*

She listened as the shaking subsided. It seemed she could hear—in the distance—the same humming she'd heard at the wall in Freddy's workshop, the buzzing she'd followed months before when she'd let herself into the passageways beneath Winterhouse and discovered the secret of Riley Granger's second item. She stood completely still, waiting.

Something's happened, she thought as she moved to open her door. The sight that met her in the corridor was so disorienting, Elizabeth wondered if her confusion and fear had made her lightheaded: A thin crimson haze wafted through the hallway, a smoky mist that had, somehow, taken on a reddish tint. Elizabeth shook her head—and the haze was gone. Something dreary and forlorn, though, remained, some evil residue, and Elizabeth felt a knot of despair inside her that she didn't understand. Her eyes began to water as if irritated by the fouled air.

She pulled her door closed and raced down the hallway; as she reached the stairwell and passed it, she realized she was heading for Room 333. She slowed and peered

down the corridor. As she rounded the last corner, there, in front of Gracella's door and facing her, was Lena, standing as if waiting for her to arrive.

"Lena?" Elizabeth said, though she knew Lena couldn't hear her. "Is everything okay?"

The old woman lifted her arm. In her hand was a small book with a black cover.

"What is that?" Elizabeth stepped forward. Lena continued to hold her arm out, and Elizabeth moved even closer. With a small motion of urgency, Lena extended the book.

"You want me to have this?" Elizabeth said.

Lena remained fixed in place and gave the book a tiny shake. Elizabeth took it from her, Lena dropped her hand, and then a sound came from the rear of the corridor.

"Everything all right?" Gustavo said as Elizabeth turned around.

"I found Lena here," she said, clutching the book. "I don't know what she's doing."

"This has been happening a lot," Gustavo said quietly. He looked to Lena. "Miss Falls? I can get you back to your room, okay?"

Lena looked to the floor; she seemed entirely defeated, and when Gustavo came to her, she simply allowed him to take her arm and steer her forward.

"We'll help you out, Miss Falls," Gustavo said. Over his shoulder, he said, softly to Elizabeth, "I'll take her. Maybe you should get back to your room."

When they disappeared, Elizabeth examined the thin black book, which was very old and frayed, with no markings on the cover. She opened to the front page and read the words "Kiona Falls—Journal."

Why did Lena give this to me? she thought, and she realized she would need to return it at the first opportunity. Elizabeth guessed Lena had, out of some disorder in her mind, taken the book from Kiona's shelf and then, in an extension of her confusion, handed it off on a whim.

A red bookmark extended just above the pages at the midpoint of the book, and Elizabeth opened to it and read the following:

December 26, 1938—The old Granger gentleman continues to ramble around everywhere, without purpose, it seems. Patricia trails after him and tries to get him to settle somewhere, but her efforts are unsuccessful, and, besides, he is harmless. Today, however, he came up to me in the lobby and spoke words with so much insistence, I can't help thinking there is something important behind them. He held up a finger and said, "Faith eliminates." Then he held up a second finger and said, "A triple-egg buzz." I nodded and wished him a good day. He checked me by grabbing my wrist and repeated the entire thing: One finger, "Faith eliminates." Second finger, "A triple-egg buzz." Then he repeated it once more. Very curious. I've learned he duplicated this exercise with Milton, Rowena, Ravenna, and Marshall, and so I'm certain there must be some meaning in it.

From a story Leona had once told her, Elizabeth knew of Riley Granger's final visit to Winterhouse. It had occurred in 1938 for Christmas, when he'd been accompanied by Elana's grand-aunt, Patricia Powter, though he'd been so old and senile, it seemed he wasn't certain where he was. Now, from Kiona's old journal, a strange fact—something Elizabeth hadn't known—was being revealed.

Is this what Lena wanted me to see? she thought. *Something about Riley Granger's last visit here? And what does "faith eliminates, a triple-egg buzz" mean?*

"Elizabeth!"

With a start, she looked up to see Norbridge approaching.

"What are you doing here?" he said.

Elizabeth's thoughts were so jumbled, and she'd been so surprised at Norbridge's appearance, she nearly couldn't find her voice. "Something strange happened," she stammered. "I felt the ground shake again, and then . . . there was a red fog in the hallway. At least, I think there was. And I came here, and Lena gave me this book! It's Kiona's old journal." She held it out to Norbridge, who glanced at Gracella's door and then took the book from Elizabeth's hand and examined it anxiously.

"Let's get you to your room, please," he said, his voice barely louder than a whisper.

"But—" she began.

"Please," Norbridge said. "I'm not upset, I just need you to get to your room."

"What's going on?" Elizabeth said. She thought of the crimson haze in the hallway.

"There was another rumbling." He glanced behind him. "And there's a strange mood in the hotel tonight. I can't put my finger on it."

"I felt it, too. And look at that page with the bookmark in it. It's about Riley Granger."

Norbridge examined the page quickly. "'Triple-egg buzz'?" he said, looking to Elizabeth.

"It has to mean something."

"I agree." Norbridge lowered his brow. "I better get this book back to Kiona and check on Lena myself. And Elana."

"Is she okay?"

"For now, all seems steady."

"Is there something I can do to help?" Elizabeth said.

Norbridge patted the top of his chest, right where Elizabeth's pendant typically lay. "Keep the faith," he said, which were the words echoing in Elizabeth's thoughts as she entered her room a few minutes later. As she closed her door, though, the anxious feeling she'd had earlier returned. She went directly to her window and looked at the bridge across the creek. The thin crimson mist was there again, but it was something else—something new— that sent a chill through her. Elizabeth peered into the darkness: Someone appeared to be standing on the bridge.

The buzzing sound arose once more, insistent and steady. Elizabeth stared out her window—and then she closed her eyes and shook her head. The sound stopped. When she looked again, the bridge was as it had always been, with no red haze and no figure.

Elizabeth listened for a moment, waited to hear if any sound or echo arose or any strange sight appeared—and then she sat on her bed thinking.

Faith eliminates. A triple-egg buzz.

There was some interlacing of things, Elizabeth felt, and they seemed to be tightening: Elana and Lena and Riley Granger's picture and the cabin and the Anna Lux book. All of it. And Gracella.

Easter evening is in three days, she thought. *I have to figure out what's going on. I have to keep Winterhouse safe.*

PART FOUR

ONE FINAL ASTONISHMENT

CHAPTER 26

STEPS FOR ESTABLISHING A THEORY

Midway through breakfast the next morning, Norbridge came and sat with Elizabeth, Freddy, and Mr. and Mrs. Knox. After some small talk that, to Elizabeth, seemed Norbridge's way of indicating all was close to normal now that a new day had begun, he extended an invitation.

"I'd like our two scholars to take a break from their work and join some of our guests on a cross-country outing," he said. "The group departs at ten o'clock from the ski shed."

"That sounds like great fun," Mr. Knox said. "Why, Mrs. Knox and I went out hiking on the eastern trail just yesterday. Wonderful to get that fresh, brisk air in your lungs."

"But we have to finish the brochure," Elizabeth said.

"The outing includes a trip to the far side of the lake," Norbridge said. "The trail has finally been cleared, and, if all goes well, the group should be able to make it all the way around." He raised his eyebrows at Elizabeth. "And even make a stop at a famous statue. The one of a certain Winifred Falls—or, rather, Winifred Somers."

"Your mother?" Mr. Knox said. "There's a statue of her?"

Despite all that was weighing on her mind, the prospect of a visit to her mother's statue thrilled Elizabeth. It seemed, after a week without snow, Mr. Obrastoff had been able to clear the trail all the way around the lake.

"There is," Norbridge said. "I erected it some years ago. It depicts my daughter, Winnie, when she was just about the age Elizabeth is now."

"I'd love to ski over there," Elizabeth said. "You really think today's a good time for it?"

"I do," Norbridge said. "And I think if Freddy joins, it will be the perfect time for it."

"Frederick," Mr. Knox said, "is this something you'd like to do?"

Freddy rolled his eyes. "Yes, Dad," he said dryly.

"Such intrepidity!" Norbridge said, teasing Freddy. "Such boldness! It's settled, then. Bring your backpacks, too, because I understand individual thermoses—thermosi?—

of hot chocolate and lunch sacks with sandwiches and brownies will be provided. Au revoir."

❄

One hour later, Elizabeth and Freddy were gliding along the well-groomed trail that skirted the western shore of Lake Luna with a group of seventeen other skiers, including Hyrum. Their guide, a college student named Uchenna Bello who'd worked at the Winterhouse ski shed for two seasons, was at the front of the line of skiers. She'd made sure everyone had enough warm clothes to wear, a backpack with lunch in it, and a clear understanding that the trip would cover at least a dozen miles and last till midafternoon.

"Everyone can go at their own pace," Uchenna had said at the outset, "and from time to time we'll stop and regroup."

"If you need any help," Hyrum said to her, "I'm here to assist."

"Maybe we can take our first break at the cabin where the fire was," Elizabeth said.

"Good idea," Uchenna answered. "We'll all stop there."

Elizabeth and Freddy skied through the fir and hemlock trees—many of which had shed patches of the snow that had lain on them for months—and fell to the rear of the pack as Elizabeth shared with Freddy everything that had happened the night before.

"*Faith eliminates. A triple-egg buzz?*" Freddy said. "What was he talking about?"

"No idea." Elizabeth, through her labored breathing, kept an eye out for Gracella's cabin.

"Question," Freddy said. "You know how Elana told us Gracella's trying to control people? I started thinking: Do you think she would limit it to only one person?"

"I guess she could try to get as many people as possible to help her."

Freddy slowed and halted, and Elizabeth glided to a stop behind him. "I just thought of something weird," he said. "What if Norbridge is helping her?"

"Norbridge?" Elizabeth said. "That's impossible. Why would he do that?"

"I don't mean on purpose. I mean in a way he doesn't realize. By doing something or finding something . . . Well, I don't know. I'm not saying Norbridge would do it on purpose. It just sort of would happen. It would seem like nothing out of the ordinary. Like Elana said."

"But then that could mean other people are doing things to help Gracella without realizing it." Elizabeth stopped, an alarming realization coming to her.

"Like us, even," Freddy said.

A whistle sounded in the distance.

"That's Uchenna." Elizabeth was rattled by Freddy's words. "They must have stopped."

When Elizabeth and Freddy skied up to the clearing beside the frozen creek down from the charred ruins of Gracella's cabin, the members of the group were standing around talking and munching on snacks from their bags. Everyone seemed in a good mood.

"Hey, you guys," Uchenna said. Hyrum was beside her, and he raised a hand in greeting.

"You made it," Hyrum said. He offered his bag of peanuts to Uchenna, who took a handful and began chewing away.

Elizabeth gazed up the slight grade to the field where Gracella's cabin stood, one side of it completely charred and a portion of the roof caved in. This place had been the scene for two troubling encounters she'd had with Gracella's spirit, and Elizabeth had thought she'd be glad to see it damaged. But now, standing before the cabin, she felt oddly saddened to consider this place—the only spot Gracella had been able to find peace when she'd been a bit older than Elizabeth herself was now—had been ruined.

"Wow," Freddy said. "That cabin's in bad shape."

Elizabeth turned to glance at Hyrum, but he seemed completely oblivious of the cabin and was chatting happily with Uchenna.

"It's practically destroyed," Elizabeth said to Freddy.

One of the skiers, a man about forty years old and wearing a red ski jacket, began trudging up the grade toward the cabin.

"Gonna take a quick peek," he called back to the group.

Elizabeth watched as he moved away, and as he drew closer to the cabin, something unexpected came over her: She didn't want the man to encroach on Gracella's cabin. It was as though she, Elizabeth, held some secret and didn't want anyone else to learn of it. A flutter arose in her stomach, and a buzzing came into her head. With a slight extension of her arm, she pointed to the limb of an alder that rested atop a charred beam of the cabin. The tree branch lurched and then slid off the beam and plopped into the snow with a loud noise.

"Whoa!" the man called out, stopping in place.

"You should come on back," Uchenna called, and the man turned around and returned with a sheepish look on his face.

Freddy looked to Elizabeth, and she gave him a side-long glance in return.

"What?" she said quietly, turning fully to him and forcing a smile on her face.

"Was that another little joke?" he said.

Elizabeth shrugged. "I just think we should leave her place alone."

Freddy looked to the cabin. "And I think . . ." He shook his head, everything about his expression indicating he disapproved of what Elizabeth had done.

Hyrum laughed loudly at something Uchenna said, and the sound distracted Elizabeth.

"Hey, everyone," Uchenna called. "Let's hit the trail."

"There wasn't anything dangerous about it," Elizabeth said to Freddy. "I just didn't want him going up there." She hoped he would smile or do something to indicate he wasn't bothered, but he simply pointed ahead and said, "Let's go see your mother's statue."

As the skiers drew closer to the far end of the lake, and as Elizabeth tried to put the incident at the cabin behind her, she found herself captivated by the view of Winterhouse. Across the vast white plain of snow-covered Lake Luna sat the golden bulk of the grand hotel like a dollhouse nestled among the surrounding forest. Elizabeth could hardly believe she and the others had come so far—and that Winterhouse looked so stately across the iced-over expanse of lake.

She was glad to have this distraction, because she wasn't certain what she might feel once she stood before her mother's statue, and she was hoping to arrive quickly and find out what the moment would hold. And then the group rounded one last bend, someone shouted, "There it is!" and a few minutes later, all nineteen of them stood gathered before Winifred's statue.

"In case everyone doesn't know," Uchenna said softly, "that's Elizabeth's mother there."

The group made a space to allow Elizabeth to draw near; everyone was quiet. She looked at the white marble figure, which was set on a low pedestal, and studied her mother's features. A puff of a breeze arose, and for a moment, Elizabeth thought she heard—in the light wind—something like the humming sound she heard when she listened at the walled-off doorway in Freddy's workshop. But the sensation passed, and the mood was

too happy and too full for Elizabeth to allow anything distressing to intrude. She placed a hand at the top of her chest and felt the impression of her necklace—her mother's necklace—there.

"I miss you," she mouthed soundlessly. "I wish you were here."

"She looks like you!" Freddy said, his timing just right so that—somehow—his words eased the emotions of the moment. Everyone began to laugh, Elizabeth included.

"I hope so," she said.

"Winifred Somers," Freddy said. "Wisdom Refiners."

Elizabeth turned to him and shook a finger, though she was laughing enough that it was impossible to look angry. "You've been waiting to use that one for a long time, haven't you?"

"You got me!" Freddy said, and everyone began taking off their packs and removing their lunches. As Elizabeth drank her hot chocolate and admired her mother's statue, it seemed all the troubles at Winterhouse—stolen books and anxious nights and crimson-haunted dreams—were farther away than the miles separating her from the hotel across the silent and frozen lake.

The skiers continued past the statue and made a loop around the lake, and it was about halfway along this eastern trail that Elizabeth realized they would intersect, at some point, the trail to the East Range near where she'd come across the sealed Ripplington Mine. Everyone had been skiing close together for a while, but when the group took a break just after one thirty, Hyrum said he didn't want his legs to cramp up and he wanted to get some strenuous exercise in.

"I'm gonna air it out a bit and press on," he announced. "I'll see everyone back at Winterhouse." With a few strong glides, Hyrum disappeared into the trees ahead.

"Five minutes, and we'll get going," Uchenna called.

Elizabeth tired rapidly over the remaining stretch along the lake, even after the trail veered eastward and then wound through the trees. She and Freddy fell behind the others, and she began struggling so much to keep up, she nearly didn't notice when the lake trail connected to the East Range trail and angled back to the west. She was moving slowly, thinking of the moment she would arrive at Winterhouse and head straight for one of the comfortable overstuffed chairs before the fireplace in Winter Hall, when Freddy shouted, "Look!"

He'd stopped on the trail and was pointing to a red kerchief tied to the branch of an alder.

Elizabeth halted. "This is right where I was before. And that looks just like the other red cloth I told you about."

"That's what I was afraid of." Freddy turned from her to scan the trail ahead. "Why don't we catch up to the others? We can get back to Winterhouse and tell Norbridge what we saw."

The fatigue that had consumed Elizabeth a moment

before had disappeared, replaced by a sharp unease. She tugged at the cloth; it was bound tightly.

"Someone was here again," she said, glancing down to see tracks in the snow leading toward the Ripplington Mine. "Look at those boot prints."

As she spoke, she began removing her skis; all she wanted to do was follow the tracks and see what she could find at the sealed entrance of the mine.

"You've got to be kidding me," Freddy said. "No way you should go up there, Elizabeth. Let's get moving and find the others."

"Wait here," Elizabeth said. "I'll be right back."

"You shouldn't go up there. That's crazy."

"It's crazy to try to make sure nothing bad happens to Winterhouse?" Elizabeth presented Freddy with the deepest look of disbelief she could summon. "I'm worried about what's going on. I thought you were, too."

"There's a difference between being worried and just rushing into things. Doing something dangerous isn't smart. We should go find Norbridge."

Freddy glared at Elizabeth, and neither said a word. The silent white valley seemed more hushed and more deserted than it had a moment before. A feeling of regret ran through Elizabeth for what she'd said to her friend, but she was in no mood to abandon her plan, and the tracks in the snow were too enticing for her not to follow.

"I didn't mean to say you weren't worried," Elizabeth said. "I know you are. But I'm not just going to leave here when there's a chance I can figure something out." She leaned her skis against the tree closest to her. "I'm going to go take a quick look at what's up there."

She turned and began walking briskly toward the mine.

"Elizabeth," Freddy called. She looked back. "I'll wait here."

Elizabeth smiled at him.

"But please hurry," Freddy said.

CHAPTER 27

ANIMOSITIES WEAR THIN

By the time Elizabeth scrambled down to the DANGER sign she'd come across the week before, she knew something was wrong at the mine. Patches of snow had melted across the broad bowl of the sealed entrance, as though the earth had warmed from beneath; the expanse seemed to have already been touched by spring and was halfway toward a complete thaw.

Something moved just beyond the far rim of the snowy berm that surrounded the mine. Elizabeth peered and saw a person walking, but the distance was too great and there were too many trees in the way for her to tell who it was. She stood motionless—and had a momentary impression that whoever the person was, he was as tall as Sir Reginald and walked with a similar gait. The figure moved out of sight beyond the rise. Elizabeth watched for a moment, and then, alarmed by the melted snow, she raced up the embankment and down the other side. As she reached the bottom, she noticed something move on the periphery of her vision.

"Elizabeth?" Hyrum stood in the trees twenty yards off.

"You scared me!" she said, putting a hand to her chest. "What are you doing here?"

"I was going to ask you the same thing." He looked behind her to the rim at the edge of the mine. "You were up there?"

She nodded, uncertain how much she wanted to share.

"Did you see all the melted snow?" he said. "It's like something's warming the ground."

The way Hyrum said this—with such apparent perplexity—calmed her slightly. He certainly didn't sound as if he was up to anything suspicious.

"I saw it," Elizabeth said. "But what made you come out here?"

Hyrum approached, eyeing the rise above them warily. "I was cruising along when I thought I heard someone yelling, and then I saw a red cloth on a tree next to the trail. When I stopped to look at it, I saw someone up over this way running through the trees, but whoever it was didn't answer when I called. I took off my skies and started tromping around." He shrugged. "I didn't find any-one, but, gosh, that sealed-up mine sure is weird. It makes you wonder what's under the ground." He looked toward the trail. "Is the rest of the group waiting over there?"

"I think they're way ahead. Freddy and I stopped when we saw that cloth."

"Why'd you leave the trail, though?" Hyrum said.

"I saw prints in the snow coming up here, so I just thought I'd take a quick look." She shrugged. "Maybe we should head back to Winterhouse."

"Definitely," Hyrum said. "I need to get a few more hours of studying in anyway."

He was beside her now, and they began walking toward the trail. Elizabeth felt so strange about things, she didn't know what to say.

"Very important days ahead," Hyrum said.

A jolt went through Elizabeth. "What do you mean?"

"I've got to finish my paper," Hyrum said nonchalantly.

"Hey, you guys," Freddy called as Elizabeth spotted him through the trees. Uchenna, and—to Elizabeth's surprise—Freddy's parents were with him.

"Hi!" Elizabeth called as Hyrum did the same.

"We came back to find you," Uchenna said as she waved. "And look who joined us."

Elizabeth felt a rush of relief as she and Hyrum joined the others. The Knoxes explained they'd ridden with Mr. Obrastoff on his grooming vehicle and been dropped off nearby so they could enjoy a little hike back to Winterhouse; Uchenna had become concerned when Elizabeth and Freddy didn't catch up, and so she'd backtracked and found Freddy by the trail.

"Frederick said you went to investigate something?" Mr. Knox said to Elizabeth.

"We saw this red cloth," Elizabeth said, gesturing to the kerchief, "and I saw something here just like it over a week ago." She turned and pointed behind her. "There's an old mine up there. I guess I was wondering if maybe someone was marking this spot for some reason."

"And I actually did see someone up there," Hyrum said. "About fifteen minutes ago."

"Very brave of you to go off on your own," Mrs. Knox said to Elizabeth.

A peculiar silence came over the group, and everyone glanced at one another as if waiting to see who would speak next.

"Who's that?" Freddy said, pointing eastward along the trail. Everyone turned to see Sir Reginald Eton-Pailey striding toward them on snowshoes and looking as self-assured as if he were walking down the corridor to Winter Hall for an evening's dinner. As he came closer, the expression on his face didn't change a bit—he appeared completely unsurprised to come across this group of six standing on the trail before him.

The *crunch-crunch*ing of his snowshoes grew louder. Elizabeth had no idea what to expect, given that Sir Reginald and Freddy's parents hadn't spoken all week.

"Good afternoon," Reginald said flatly as he stopped. "Lovely out here," he added, his voice steady and somber.

Elizabeth, Freddy, and Uchenna greeted him politely, while Mr. Knox merely grunted something nearly inaudible.

When the silence resumed, Mr. Knox, with a note of accusation in his voice, said, "And what brings you out this way?"

Without hesitation, Sir Reginald lifted his right foot to display the snowshoe affixed to his boot. "This elaborate footwear, my good man," he said. "One on each foot, you'll notice. That's what brought me out this way." He lowered his leg, adjusted his jacket, and began to move past the group. "Good day, one and all. I must make my return to the hotel."

"You just *happened* to be snowshoeing out here?" Mr. Knox said.

"Sir," Reginald said, turning sharply to him, "I once snowshoed from Ilulissat to Qeqertaq in the middle of the third coldest December on record, and so this little traipsing about today amounts to little more than falling out of bed for a man like myself." He pulled himself up tall and straight. "Good day!"

"Let's stop with all the games, Mr. Eton-Pailey!" Mr. Knox said. His tone was so deliberate, and the look on his face was so penetrating, Elizabeth felt intimidated even though it was Sir Reginald to whom he was speaking. "We have a strong suspicion you broke into Gracella's room and, if there was a Crowley book there, removed it. Do you deny this?"

Sir Reginald's expression turned doubly grim; it looked as though he might whip a broadsword out from some scabbard at his back and begin menacing Mr. Knox until he apologized. Instead, he took two steps in his direction, unfastened the top button of his wool coat, and snatched at the sash across his torso to display a row of medals.

"Sir!" he yelled. "The award on the extreme upper corner of this band nearest my shoulder belonged to my great-great-grandfather and was bestowed in honor of his bravery and service to country in the Battle of Tysami!" Sir Reginald was in a fury now, his face red and his voice loud. He clutched the indicated medal tightly and said, closing his eyes, "On my sacred honor and in the name of all that the line of Eton-Paileys hold most dear, I swear I neither entered that room belonging to Gracella Winters nor removed any book whatsoever in any way, shape, or form!" He popped his eyes open and glared at Mr. Knox. "And now," he yelled, "do you find yourself satisfied?"

Freddy's father stared blankly at Sir Reginald. Beside him, Mrs. Knox reached a hand to her neck and fished out the necklace strung there. She pinched a small pendant between her thumb and forefinger and, displaying it, said, "This medallion of Saint Francis de Sales belonged to my mother, and she gave it to me the day I turned nineteen. I swear on it that I did not break into Room 333, and I also have not stolen anything from anyone at Winterhouse ever."

She gave her husband a firm stare, and he scooted beside her and set a finger on the medallion she held. "That goes for me, too," he said. "I swear it by Francis de Scales."

"Sales," his wife said.

"Yes," Mr. Knox said.

"Same for me!" Hyrum said, and everyone turned to see him holding up what appeared to be an ancient and rusty sardine tin.

"Is that a can of sardines?" Freddy said.

"Pilchards, actually," Hyrum said. "They're a little bigger than sardines. But I carry this tin in my outdoor bag always, in honor of my father, Caesar, who, my mother used to tell me, always brought a can with him on his travels through India and China—for good luck. This tin belonged to him, and I swear on it the exact same thing the rest of you have sworn. I didn't steal any books at Winterhouse or break into any rooms. And neither did Professor Fowles."

Silence once again fell upon the group, though a new mood had been established; some diminishment of tension had occurred, some evaporation of enmity and suspicion. Sir Reginald removed his hand from his sash and straightened his coat. Mrs. Knox and Hyrum put away the items they'd brought out. Elizabeth and Freddy stood waiting to see who might speak; Elizabeth was recalling that both Mr. Wellington and Mr. Rajput had, two days before, sworn to her at the puzzle table that neither they nor their wives had broken into Room 333.

"I don't know what happened that caused all of you to quarrel," Uchenna said, "but I don't think anyone here did anything wrong. It sounds like just a bunch of confusion to me."

"The young woman is entirely correct," Sir Reginald said quietly. "It seems we are all blameless." He glanced about, his expression soft. "I'm inclined to believe each one of you. And I would like to offer an apology for harboring any suspicions."

Mr. Knox moved to him and extended a hand. "Same goes for me," he said. And then his wife and Hyrum moved forward and repeated the gesture. As Elizabeth watched, everyone's mood lightened, and it seemed Sir Reginald was suddenly friends once again with one and all.

"This is a most welcome development," he said as he prepared to walk back with Mr. and Mrs. Knox, and the others moved forward to begin skiing. "Because Mr. Falls has invited all of us to a special gathering in his rooms two evenings from tonight, and I am very much looking forward to the occasion."

Everyone began talking about the upcoming evening with Norbridge and how glad they were to have a few more days at Winterhouse; within minutes, Uchenna and Hyrum were skiing back to the hotel, Elizabeth and Freddy behind them. After a brief silence, Freddy turned to Elizabeth and said, "If no one at the table that night took the book, then who did?"

It was the exact question that had been running through her mind.

CHAPTER 28

THE DEEPEST A RUMBLING CAN SOUND

The rest of the day was, for Elizabeth and Freddy, a mix of work, fatigue, and consternation. Before continuing on the brochure, they shared everything with Norbridge and Leona during a brief conference in the library. Following dinner, Elizabeth assisted at the puzzle table—around which was now a perpetual crowd of nearly two dozen, as Mr. Wellington and Mr. Rajput approached the final stretch. Afterward, she and Freddy attended the very interesting lecture by an archaeology professor named Hediyeh Salafani, who spoke about the Antikythera mechanism, a mysterious, two-thousand-year-old computing device found in the wreckage of a ship near Greece in 1900. Elizabeth was fascinated by the talk, though her thoughts kept returning to the events of the ski trip and her hopes for completing both the brochure and the puzzle. There was Elana, too—Norbridge was not allowing any visits, although he insisted she was doing well.

At eleven o'clock the next morning, Elizabeth and Freddy completed their brochure and headed to the library to meet Norbridge and Leona.

"Summer's here!" Miles cawed as the two kids appeared in the doorway to Leona's office. "Summer's here!"

"It's Somers with an 'o,' little guy," Elizabeth said.

Leona was scowling at the bird, who was bobbing on the stand in his cage. "For the hundredth time, Miles," she said, "you should say 'winter's here!'"

"But it's spring now, Leona," Freddy said. "It should be 'spring's here!'"

"Leona always gets cranky when the days get longer," Norbridge said.

"That I do!" Leona said. "More people curl up inside and read books when the weather's nice and gray, rather than tromp around outside hiking or swimming or whatever young people do nowadays when the weather warms up." She pointed to Freddy's laptop. "And then there's those things!" She looked ceilingward and gave out a low sound of exasperation.

"Tea too strong this morning, Miss Springer?" Norbridge said.

Elizabeth laughed. She loved to see Norbridge and

Leona tease each other, not only because it was enjoyable in itself but because it spoke to a friendship the two had developed over decades. The thought of having a true friend, someone with whom she could feel this easy—and having it persist for years and years—made her feel happy.

Elizabeth gestured toward Freddy. "Well, even if you don't like computers, Leona, we finally finished the brochure, and Freddy has everything ready to go on his laptop."

Leona peered at Freddy's computer as if somehow the brochure might materialize atop it. "Everything's inside there?"

Freddy nodded. "We just have to print it out."

"I'll get Sampson on it right away," Norbridge said. "But can you give us a preview?"

Freddy set his laptop on Leona's table, and the four of them gathered around. Over the next twenty minutes, Elizabeth and Freddy walked the two others through each entry—the diorama room, the ice castle, the bakery, the murals outside Winter Hall, the display cases in each hallway, the basement swimming pool, the ski lift beside the lake, and all the rest.

"Well," Norbridge said, "this exceeds anything I'd hoped for. Our guests will love it."

"I'll second that," Leona said. "The two of you have done an absolutely fantastic job." She jabbed a finger in Norbridge's direction. "Your boss here ought to award you a bonus in appreciation for your outstanding work."

"How about extra pie and ice cream after dinner tonight?" Norbridge said.

"Hold on!" Freddy said, closing his eyes as though he couldn't contain his excitement.

"He's done this one before," Elizabeth said, grinning.

"Pie and ice cream," Freddy said, popping his eyes open and overenunciating each word. "Paramedic niece."

Leona smiled. "That is a real talent."

"Talent," Norbridge said. "Latent."

"Hey," Elizabeth said. "Not bad!"

"I love the write-up about the stained-glass windows here in the library," Leona said. "Shakespeare, Milton, Dante. It's amazing to think that—"

"Gracella!" Miles cawed. Everyone turned to the bird in his cage. "Gracella! Gracella!"

Leona looked to Norbridge. "You see? I told you he was saying that name."

"What do you think is going on with Miles?" Freddy said.

"I don't know," Norbridge said. "Though it obviously means something that he's saying that name." He glanced toward the doorway. "Something's . . . *off*. My hope is that we make it past this full moon. If the third item isn't found, and if everyone who might have Crowley's book is in my apartment tomorrow night for our little celebration, maybe we'll stave off any final assaults from Gracella. That's if she's really stirring."

"But it really seemed like everyone was genuine about being innocent yesterday," Freddy said.

A thought came to Elizabeth. "What if the person isn't even aware of doing it? Like how Elana said? What if Gracella is controlling someone—or *someones*—so there's no memory the person has of doing anything wrong?"

Leona looked to Norbridge and then turned to Elizabeth. "Your point is a good one. Which is why our little party tomorrow night will be a wonderful safeguard against mischief."

Elizabeth couldn't help feeling there was some hole in the plan. "I just wish we could figure out what the last item is," she said, though even as she spoke the words, a thought came to her, one she'd been trying to suppress all week. She thought of how she'd once held The Book—Riley Granger's first item—and then how she'd clutched the second item, her own pendant, in the underground passageway a few months before, right after it had become imbued with a powerful force. And although, on both occasions, she'd made the choice to render the items inert, it had been exhilarating to possess each one—to feel its power—if only momentarily. As she considered the possibility of discovering the third and final item, a notion formed in her mind: If the picture—whatever it ended up being—was truly the final item hidden in Winterhouse, the discovery of it would represent her last opportunity to claim a power that would be staggering.

Three wishes, she thought. *All to myself.*

"Are you all right?" Norbridge said.

"I'm fine," Elizabeth said, surfacing out of her thoughts. "Just thinking."

"Well, let's get this brochure to Sampson," Norbridge said. "I'll make an announcement this evening at dinner, too, and we can begin passing the things out to everyone."

"We'll have guests crawling around the hotel till midnight," Leona said.

"What's wrong with that?" Norbridge said.

"Who said anything was wrong with it?" Leona said. "I'm looking forward to the fun!"

Elizabeth and Freddy spent part of the afternoon at the sledding hill before Elizabeth joined Mr. Wellington and Mr. Rajput at the puzzle table for two hours. A crowd of nearly thirty people had gathered, and the two puzzle men did a thorough job of enforcing quiet and making certain the onlookers didn't interfere with their efforts.

"Please," Mr. Wellington was in the habit of saying if a member of the audience blurted out a hint or tiny cheer, "we must once again request *absolute* silence from the gallery as we tread onward. Observe but do not comment, please."

The remaining puzzle pieces had dropped below one thousand, and the work was accelerating steadily. Elizabeth herself located twenty-three pieces during her two hours, generating so much excitement among the audience, it was palpable. When the chimes sounded for dinner, Mr. Rajput looked up as though he'd hardly noticed the minutes had ticked forward past noon.

"We shall break for the evening meal," he announced, "and then resume our work." Everyone waited for the usual pessimistic addendum to Mr. Rajput's comments, but instead he merely examined the puzzle itself and said, "I am encouraged by our progress and daresay we might bring the project to conclusion tomorrow."

Mr. Wellington's eyes widened. "A most rare and welcome expression of confidence from Mr. Rajput!" he said, and the audience laughed. "By seven thirty, expect us back here at our stations, buzzing along."

Buzzing, Elizabeth thought. And then: *A triple-egg buzz.*

"Will you be joining us later?" Mr. Wellington asked Elizabeth as the crowd dispersed.

"Count me in," Elizabeth said.

Elizabeth was glad when Norbridge stood to deliver his post-meal speech. Conversation at the dinner table—filled, once again, with the Knoxes, the Wellingtons, the Rajputs, Sir Reginald, Hyrum, Professor Fowles, Leona, and Freddy—had been subdued, even after the reconciliation on the trail the day before and the air of festive expectancy that had taken over Winterhouse now that the Easter weekend had begun. Mrs. Rajput mentioned a strange noise in the hallway that had awakened her early that morning; Freddy's mother said she'd wanted to visit the Tower after lunch but had felt unaccountably hesitant;

Mrs. Wellington announced she'd been struggling with a bad headache and was surprised she'd felt up to coming to dinner.

"Did you hear that someone in the sauna saw a reddish tint to the steam?" Mr. Knox said.

"Prolonged exposure to heat," Egil Fowles said, "can prompt visual aberrations."

"That is absolutely correct," Sir Reginald said. "Heat can bewitch the human mind. Why, once when I was in the Taklamakan Desert with only a canteen half filled with water, I became convinced, after eight days of temperatures exceeding one hundred and twenty degrees, that I saw fifteen spiders the size of elephants approaching me—"

"Good evening, one and all!" Norbridge said from behind his lectern at the front of the hall. "And I hope you enjoyed that wonderful dinner."

"Here we go again," Freddy said. His father scowled at him. "But he says the same jokes all the time," Freddy added, before settling in with the others to listen to Norbridge's speech.

Elizabeth was surprised when, two minutes into her grandfather's address, he wasn't speaking with his typical levity but, instead, had moved through a very plain round of welcoming comments. He seemed much more serious than usual—just as he had at the dinner table itself.

"I always look forward to the Easter holiday," Norbridge said. "I have a certain preference for the winter months, but I also appreciate that time of year when the days become brighter and a feeling of renewed life permeates everything—the earth, the sky, the trees, the mountains. A feeling sinks into me that makes me think of times long ago, and it fills me with gratitude not only for the season but for this wonderful life we are so fortunate to experience."

Norbridge looked to Leona, who was, Elizabeth noticed, deeply focused on the words spoken, without an ounce of the wry, teasing expression she would typically have on her face—it was as though Norbridge was speaking directly to Leona herself, in a way Elizabeth had never heard, or maybe never understood, before.

"I'm grateful for the wonderful people in my life who have helped me and loved me." Norbridge paused and surveyed the audience. "And I'm fortunate to be able to share this hotel with all of you. Winterhouse is a magical place, not merely because of the beauty of the setting or the loveliness of the building itself, but because the spirit at its heart is beautiful, because there is a fundamental goodness here. This hotel offers this gift of goodness to you." He looked to Elizabeth. "And it's my hope that it will always do so, that people will come to this place to renew their spirit and their faith, and leave feeling a little more hopeful than when they arrived."

He hesitated once more. "But I was, actually, working up to . . ." The lights in the hall dimmed. "This," Norbridge said softly.

The audience was rapt with expectation as Norbridge stood, his hands clasped. The lights dimmed even more, so that, aside from the fire blazing in the hearth behind him, Norbridge was in shadow. He raised both hands and then lowered them slowly; the flames in the fireplace sank so that the logs quieted to embers. It was like watching the sun drop below the horizon and seeing the sky transform from golden-bright to a softening orange, and the crowd gasped in awe.

"How in the world did he—" began Mr. Knox.

"Shh," said his wife. Everyone at the table—at all the tables—kept watching.

"Well over a century ago," Norbridge said, "a small group of devout men spent two years circling the earth." He raised a hand and, in the air before him and above his head, gave a tap at the empty space. A small disk of light—an orb of flame no bigger than a quarter—materialized where he'd touched, and it remained hovering, fixed in midair. "They went to places around the globe." He moved his hand out from one hip and tapped the air; another flame sprouted, and he did the same thing on his opposite side. "Locations they'd selected after great consideration." Three thin lines appeared, connecting the three dots, so that Norbridge—from the waist up—was framed by a golden triangle floating before him.

"Their purpose was to make certain there were places throughout the world where a special *spirit* could persist." Norbridge tapped the air to the side of his shoulder, and then down near his knees, and then to the opposite side above his belt. Three more points of light blazed in the air, and then another triangle swelled into view connecting the three disks. Two interlocking triangles glowed before him.

"And by some mysterious magic, they accomplished what they'd set out to do." He repeated his previous three taps, though this time in the air at points opposite, and when the third triangle blazed alive connecting these last three flames, Norbridge stood within a nine-pointed star. "They provided nine places around the world with an undying yearning to serve as centers of goodness. Places that would stand as ongoing sources of something essential."

The star blazed brighter, illuminating Norbridge. He stood with both palms facing out, and then the star began to rise. Norbridge moved his hands as if pressing at the shape through the air, steering it so that it continued to lift toward the ceiling. He gave a tilt of his hands, his palms turned upward, and the star, too, shifted from the vertical to the horizontal and drifted toward the ceiling. It remained hovering several feet above Norbridge's head, and then he began to spread his hands apart—and the points of the star began to move apart as well. Within seconds, as Norbridge extended his hands fully, the star stretched above and across the entire hall, blazing over the guests like beams of fire held in the air on invisible lines.

"If you take nothing else with you when you leave Winterhouse," he said, "take this moment. Remember that you were here and how you felt just now." He clapped his hands once. "Because these moments sustain us." He

clapped once again. "They inspire us." He clapped one last time. "And it is so easy to forget."

The star blinked out. The room was absolutely dark and absolutely silent.

"I am having brochures delivered to each table," Norbridge said as the chandeliers flashed on, and everyone glanced about as if stunned to find themselves still in one piece and still in Winter Hall, now brightly lit. He was speaking in the most ordinary and conversational tone, as if the magic of the past few minutes hadn't happened at all.

Elizabeth sat in disbelief. It wasn't so much that the spectacle of it was amazing—she'd seen her grandfather perform feats like this often enough to know he had more magic and more surprises in him than he let on. It was, rather, that his words and the mystery of the star had been more profound and moving than anything she'd ever seen from him.

"These brochures," Norbridge continued, "were created by my granddaughter, Elizabeth, and her good friend Mr. Freddy Knox at my request and for your pleasure."

The kitchen servers were fanning out among the tables and depositing stacks of the brochures—nicely printed and folded on silver paper—at each one, and the diners, slowly recovering after the thrill of Norbridge's display, began examining them appreciatively as Norbridge explained what they were.

"And so I hope you will enjoy discovering new locations and artifacts and bits of history as you use these wonderful little guides to familiarize yourselves with the hotel . . ."

The feeling came over Elizabeth. She saw Norbridge's expression change slightly, and she heard the tiny catch in his voice—and she understood he had sensed something, too.

"That is," he continued, "as you . . ."

The ground began to rumble, a low churn that sounded like distant thunder and then rolled and roiled and grew, as though a vast ocean wave was about to crash down upon the hotel. The tables shook and the chandeliers clanked and the pictures on the walls trembled and then a few people here and there let out yelps and some glasses crashed onto plates and the entire hall became a jarring, shaking scene of uncertainty.

"Stay seated, please!" Norbridge called. "It's the permafrost settling!"

But by then, the entire hall was gripped with fear, and it didn't seem that any amount of consoling would calm things. As everyone at Elizabeth's table gaped or stood or gripped the arms of their chair, Elizabeth found herself looking to Freddy.

"It's Gracella," he said to her. "It has to be. Somehow she's coming back."

CHAPTER 29

CRYPTIC RIMS ON A CRYPTIC NIGHT

After Norbridge had scurried off to check his seismo-graph, and after the anxious questioning had subsided at Elizabeth and Freddy's dinner table and all of the guests had departed, the two kids found themselves alone.

"Somehow Gracella's breaking out of the mine," Freddy said. "There's the rumbling and the melted snow and all the weird things going on. She's trying to come back."

"But if no one performs the Dredforth Method," Elizabeth said, "it won't matter."

Unless someone finds the third object, she thought, *and decides to give Gracella one last chance.*

"Greetings!" Sir Reginald called as he entered through the side door of Winter Hall and surveyed the nearly empty room. He waved to Elizabeth and Freddy as he strode toward them.

"Oh, no," Freddy said under his breath. "Get ready for a story about a journey across the Mojave with only a bag of potato chips and a can of ginger ale."

"Be nice," Elizabeth said.

"Still here?" Sir Reginald said. "I would have thought the two of you would be guiding visitors about the hotel or elaborating on the amusing entries from your remarkable guide."

"I'm about to go help with the puzzle," Elizabeth said, sliding her eyes to Freddy. "And Freddy's been talking backward for the last ten minutes."

"Own I vah tahn," Freddy said. "I mean, no, I have not."

"Very good!" Reginald said, pulling a chair out from the table and plopping down onto it.

"So where are you heading after you leave Winterhouse?" Freddy said. "Somewhere interesting, I'm sure."

Sir Reginald drummed his hands on the table with excitement. "The Estonian secret service has requested a refresher next week in the safecracking course I give. After that, I'm joining friends on a raft journey down the Amazon before leading a tour of the so-called fairy chimneys in Cappadocia. So, a rather light month ahead." He lifted his chin nonchalantly, stretched his back, and glanced around the hall. "I most certainly will miss this lovely hotel." He looked to Freddy. "But you say your skills at backward speaking are improving?"

The three of them launched into a conversation about palindromes and anagrams that almost took Elizabeth's mind off all the strange things that had occurred over dinner. As Freddy and Sir Reginald worked through some anagrams with the words "least" (slate, stale, steal, tales) and "scrape" (capers, pacers, parsec, recaps, spacer), an idea came to Elizabeth.

"Sir Reginald," she said, "can you make any sense of these sentences?" She opened her notebook before him to display the two lines: *Faith eliminates/A triple-egg buzz.*

The elderly man bent his head over the page and examined it for a moment.

"Nothing resolves at first glance. But I'll give it some thought. What is this from?"

"Something Kiona wrote in her journal a long time ago," Elizabeth said.

"Elizabeth!" someone called, and she and Freddy turned to see Sampson approaching. "Glad I found you."

"Hey, Sampson," Elizabeth said.

"Elana wants to see you," he said, his face lined with worry. "Norbridge is with her, but she's asking for you. Can you guys come with me to her room?"

Elizabeth stood immediately. "Of course," she said, looking to Freddy. "Come on."

"I hope everything's all right," Sir Reginald said, standing as well. "At any rate, I have your two sentences locked in my brain and will mull things over."

Elana, whom Elizabeth hadn't seen for three days, didn't appear to have diminished since Elizabeth had last visited. She was sitting upright in her bed, and Norbridge was on a chair beside her. The two of them were in quiet conversation when Elizabeth and Freddy arrived.

"Good to see you both," Norbridge said.

Elana shifted her head to look at Elizabeth and Freddy; she was so stiff, she had to move her entire torso rigidly to adjust her gaze.

"Hey, you guys," Elana said. Her voice was weaker, Elizabeth thought, and raspier, too.

"Great to see you, Elana," Freddy said.

"Yeah, we've been wanting to visit," Elizabeth said.

"We were having a little discussion here," Norbridge said. "Elana tells me Lena came to the room this evening while the rest of us were at dinner." He looked to Elana, whose eyes dimmed slightly as she tightened her lips.

"She sat here," Elana said, indicating Norbridge's seat with a tiny tilt of her head, "and began signing letters to me. 'Tomorrow night' is what she spelled."

Elizabeth turned to Norbridge; he bit his lip and looked to Elana.

"Nothing more?" Norbridge said. "Just 'tomorrow night'?"

"That's all," Elana said. "But she had a strange look on her face. She didn't look mean or anything, but it scared me."

"Anyone would be scared by that," Elizabeth said, moving to Elana and taking her hand.

"Yeah, Elana," Freddy said, pushing at his glasses. "Did anything else happen?"

Elana lifted her chin slightly toward the hallway. "She just stood and left. Do you think she knows something about . . . my condition? What if tomorrow night . . ." She began to sob quietly. Elizabeth squeezed her hand, although she felt that she, too, might begin crying.

"Can someone stay with me tomorrow?" Elana said.

"I will!" Elizabeth said. "I can stay right here, okay?"

Norbridge looked flustered. "Of course, someone will be with you, Elana. Mrs. Trumble and some of the other staff, absolutely. And Elizabeth can certainly join you for a portion of the time, as well." Elizabeth shot him a pleading look. "I can assure you that nothing is going to happen tomorrow night. I'm going to make certain of that."

A distressing unease remained with Elizabeth the rest of the evening—after Freddy left for his room at his parents' request, after Elizabeth helped Mr. Wellington and Mr. Rajput find twenty-nine more pieces in just over an hour, and after she stopped by the portrait gallery to admire her mother's painting. By the time she reached her room at eleven o'clock and then sat on her sofa to consider all that the evening had brought, she felt anxious.

The buzzing noise arose in her head.

"No!" Elizabeth said aloud, lifting both hands. The noise stopped.

She moved to the cherrywood desk and slid her drawer

open. The puzzle piece lay where she'd left it. Elizabeth plucked it up and tossed it toward the ceiling. When it landed on the carpet, she took two steps back, pointed a finger at it, and allowed her vision to focus and her mind to clear. As if some invisible force were stretching from her extended finger directly to the piece itself, it lifted off the carpet and into the air under Elizabeth's pinpoint control.

With a steady motion, Elizabeth guided the piece through the air and above the open drawer; then she snapped closed her concentration, balled her fingers into a fist, and allowed the piece to drop into the drawer, which she slammed shut.

That was perfect, she thought, and a novel feeling of delight moved through her at the idea that she had done something so delicate and precise: Her power was strengthening. She turned to the window. A crimson tint colored the light snowflakes drifting by the window.

Could Gracella really help me? she thought. It didn't feel wrong at all to use her power, despite those moments of disapproval she'd experienced with Norbridge and Freddy. *They don't understand. Maybe if Gracella came back . . . Maybe Norbridge is right—she's not beyond all hope.*

The buzzing noise erupted in her head once more; Elizabeth squeezed her eyes closed and lifted both hands before her to hold an intense focus in her mind. When she looked again, only white snow, ordinary snow, was falling beyond the window. The sound was gone.

"Tomorrow night," she said aloud, and after the two words left her mouth, she realized she wasn't sure if she'd uttered a warning or a promise or merely echoed what she'd heard from Elana. She looked to the window and then pressed at the desk drawer to make certain it was closed.

It was only after she crawled into bed and was falling asleep that the thought she'd been considering all day— the exhilarating thought, the terrifying thought—came to her once more: *The third item will be my last chance.*

CHAPTER 30

THE NAIL IN THE COFFIN IS HARDLY SECURE

The next morning, Saturday, Elizabeth felt exhausted, though she knew she needed to work up energy to face the day. She forced herself out of bed, showered and dressed, and headed to the lobby to begin on the puzzle.

When she arrived, she was amazed to find over thirty people clustered about the table; Mr. Wellington and Mr. Rajput were both lost in deep concentration as they surveyed the remaining pieces. The puzzle, a long rectangle of sky blue and mountain white, on whose lower half was a slate-gray stone temple adorned with a few pale flags, was nearly complete.

"Good morning," Elizabeth said softly as she made her way through the crowd.

"A very good morning to you, Miss Somers," Mr. Wellington said. "And a morning I consider a prelude to what seems poised to be an extraordinary afternoon." He looked to the puzzle and beamed. "I'm confident today is the day we find our efforts rewarded with the ultimate resolution—completion of the puzzle."

"Though obstacles might yet arise," Mr. Rajput said. His gaze was locked on a small open space at the upper right of the puzzle. "One of us stumbles, say, and breaks an arm, or a water pipe bursts and floods the lobby, or—"

"Sir, please!" Mr. Wellington said huffily. "That is more than enough."

"Keep working, you guys!" someone from the audience called.

Mr. Rajput jerked his head up and scowled. "Cajoling will prove an unsuccessful strategy," he said. "Please refrain from placing undue pressure on us." He gestured to Elizabeth. "Our associate has arrived now, and even I believe we might—just might—see our puzzle finalized before the dinner chimes ring."

Elizabeth smiled; her morning fatigue was passing. "Well, let's get to it!" she said.

The remaining pile of pieces diminished quickly as the morning hours proceeded. Elizabeth ducked out for a quick breakfast, and then, later, a quick lunch, too. She told Freddy she would do her best to join him on the sledding hill no later than three o'clock if she could pull away.

"It's almost done," she told him. "This is probably going to be the very last day I'll be working on it."

"And tomorrow's my very last full day here at Winterhouse until I don't know when."

Elizabeth wanted to spend the afternoon with Freddy—already she'd passed hours in the lobby rather than with her best friend—but she couldn't bring herself to leave the puzzle table.

"I promise tomorrow will be different," she said. "Plus, we have the big party with Norbridge tonight. I'll meet you at the sledding hill just as soon as I can, okay?"

"Okay," Freddy said, giving Elizabeth a curious look. "I'll check back after a little while."

She smiled. "I'm going to get back to work."

Three o'clock passed and then four—Elizabeth lost track of time as she and the two men toiled away. A crowd of forty people remained gathered around the table, and even many of the hotel staff stopped to watch as the puzzle moved ever closer to completion.

"About fifty pieces left," Elizabeth said at one point. "I really think we're going to do it."

"Overconfidence may be our undoing," Mr. Rajput said.

Norbridge visited a few times, as did Leona and Professor Fowles. Freddy stopped by twice, and on each occasion, Elizabeth signaled him to indicate it would be a little bit longer. Mrs. Wellington and Mrs. Rajput had put up an all-day vigil and been admiring the effort from chairs off to one side throughout. Whenever one of the three puzzlers fit a piece into a slot, the crowd erupted in applause— and even Mr. Rajput had ceased trying to quiet them.

"Elizabeth," Norbridge said, drawing up beside the table and gesturing to her. The afternoon was growing late. "Elana's requesting a visit from you."

She looked up. "Elana," she said. It suddenly struck her as unbelievable that she'd allowed nearly the whole day to pass without visiting Elana—or, in truth, even thinking much about her. "Is she okay?"

Norbridge nodded. "But I know she's been hoping to see you."

Elizabeth moved a hand idly to her necklace. "I'll go really soon. We're just about done here."

From the periphery of her vision, she noticed Hyrum approaching from the direction of Winter Hall. Even as Norbridge stood before her, Elizabeth felt her attention diverted, and she watched Hyrum scan the crowd at the puzzle table and then slow to a stop. His face had an expression of worry on it.

"Elizabeth?" Norbridge said.

She turned back to him. "Sorry. Yes, for sure. I'll go see Elana. I don't know what I was thinking." She turned to look at Hyrum again; he put a hand to his forehead and closed his eyes. His body began to sway, and he reached out to steady himself.

"Is Hyrum okay?" Elizabeth said, pointing to him. Hyrum's knees buckled and, with a sluggish motion, he

dropped onto the carpet. Several people nearby let out a
cry, and Elizabeth rushed over to him.

"He fainted!" someone called. A cluster of several
people gathered around Hyrum, who appeared to be lost
in a deep sleep.

"Let's get him to the infirmary," said Norbridge, making motions to someone at the clerk's desk. He looked to
Elizabeth and said quietly, "Come with us."

Several minutes later, Hyrum lay on a bed in the small
Winterhouse infirmary. Someone had located Professor
Fowles, and he and Norbridge and Jackson stood beside
Hyrum's bed as Elizabeth sat off to the side.

"He collapsed?" Professor Fowles said. "Just like that?"

"Apparently," Norbridge said.

"We'd seen him wandering around the hotel through-out the afternoon," Jackson said. "He seemed very distracted. Leona told us he stopped by the library several times but never stayed more than a few minutes."

"The poor boy's been under so much stress with his studies," Professor Fowles said.

Hyrum stirred on the bed, his eyes fluttering open slightly, though he didn't appear to know where he was. With a lurching motion, he swung a hand toward Norbridge as if to find something steady to grasp.

"My mother," Hyrum muttered. "She's here?"

Elizabeth felt her skin go cold. A sudden terror ran through her, something that made some bizarre sense but also seemed so improbable she could hardly hold the idea in her mind.

"She's on the way, Hyrum," Norbridge said. "I'm hopeful she'll arrive tonight."

"What?" Elizabeth said. "What do you mean?"

Hyrum opened his eyes and tried to lift up on his elbows.

"Stay resting, dear boy," Professor Fowles said. "You took quite a fall, and you don't want to discombobulate yourself once more. Just lie there and regain your equilibrium."

Norbridge turned to Elizabeth. "Over the past few days," he said, "in conversation with Hyrum, I realized we may actually know his mother, Zarina Crowley, and I invited her to join us for Easter. She's due to arrive today. I hope she'll make it for dinner."

Hyrum lay with his eyes closed, recovering himself. "So she's on her way?"

"By all accounts, yes," Jackson said.

"I don't know what happened to me there in the lobby," Hyrum said, putting a hand to his forehead. With a quick shift of his body, he looked to Elizabeth. "Are you okay?"

The question was so unexpected, Elizabeth was startled. "Yes, for sure. Why's that?"

"I saw Lena in the hallway this afternoon," Hyrum said. "And she looked really worried. She started spelling your name, and then Gustavo showed up and took her to her room."

A knock sounded at the door; when Jackson opened it, Sampson stood before them.

"Sorry to bother everyone," he said as he glanced at Hyrum on the bed. "I just wanted to let everyone know they're done."

"They're done?" Elizabeth said, a wave of excitement and perplexity rushing through her. "The puzzle?"

Sampson began nodding. "Yeah, the puzzle. They finished."

"That's absolutely magnificent!" said Professor Fowles. "After all this time. We knew the end was approaching, and look here—they've done it."

Elizabeth stood. Sampson's face wasn't nearly as enthusiastic as she would have thought.

"They're finished with their work, yes," Sampson said. "But the puzzle isn't done."

"What?" Norbridge said.

"They used up all the pieces they had on the table," Sampson said. "But the puzzle isn't done." He looked at each of the five faces before him.

"What do you mean?" Egil Fowles said.

"There are some pieces missing," Sampson said. "Two of them."

Elizabeth rushed to the lobby with the others to confirm that, indeed, two pieces—a patch of blue in the sky, and a piece of the temple itself—were missing.

"You can hardly expect that a puzzle of thirty-five thousand pieces would remain intact over all these years," Professor Fowles said to Mr. Wellington and Mr. Rajput, both of whom sat slumped in chairs off to one side of the puzzle and looked as though they'd just been informed their homes had been obliterated by a typhoon.

Elizabeth felt awful as she considered the sky blue piece in her room. But the main thought she had was: *Where is the other piece?*

CHAPTER 31

A SUPPER FOR MANY GUESTS

Freddy had been friendly to Elizabeth when he and his parents arrived for the gathering in Norbridge's apartment, but she sensed he was being standoffish. It didn't surprise her—she knew he had every right to feel put out.

"I'm sorry I didn't spend time with you today," Elizabeth said as the two of them, before sitting at the dining table, admired Norbridge's collection of ceramic figurines on a shelf in his living room. He had a set of nine players from the 1927 New York Yankees, the five children from *Charlie and the Chocolate Factory*, twelve Greek gods, and the comic-strip characters Calvin and Hobbes, all done in elaborate detail and paint.

"I understand," Freddy said nonchalantly as he

examined a small figure of Augustus Gloop. "I just organized some stuff in the workshop and went sledding. It was fun."

Elizabeth felt hurt to hear this, though she could hardly blame Freddy. She caught him up on Elana and Lena and what she'd heard about Hyrum's mother.

"Anything about the missing book?" Freddy said.

"Nothing. I just hope tonight goes quickly." She gave Freddy a faint smile. "Then we can hang out tomorrow."

"Sounds good," he said, though he didn't sound very enthusiastic. When the two of them sat at the dinner table, Elizabeth hoped the evening would proceed without incident.

"It's hard to believe our time here is winding down," Mr. Knox said as the guests enjoyed their dinner. "The week has absolutely flown by."

Mr. Wellington looked up. His eyes were red-rimmed, and he appeared to be completely oblivious of the conversation. "Where could they be?" he said, his voice pleading and sad. "Two pieces. After all this time. *Two* pieces!" He lowered his gaze to his plate and resumed poking at his ham with his fork. He'd barely taken a bite of his dinner.

"Dear," Mrs. Wellington said, "I'm sure they'll turn up."

"I doubt that," Mr. Rajput said. He, too, had spent most of the meal moping and picking at his food as his wife alternately rubbed his shoulder or gave his arm a consoling pat. "Some efforts are doomed to fail, and it's clear we should have foreseen this eventuality. All that time wasted. All the hours now come to nothing. All our hopes dashed as—"

"Mr. Rajput, please," Norbridge said kindly. "No journey is without a setback or two. We can't expect perfection in all things, but you should rejoice in the magnificent work you've done."

"Absolutely," said Professor Fowles. "We applaud what you and Mr. Wellington have accomplished. It is a marvelous example of fortitude that the rest of us can admire— and from which we can take inspiration." He raised his hands to clap as he looked around the table, encouraging the others to join him—which they did, in a prolonged and hearty applause that brought the two puzzle men to tears, though it wasn't clear to Elizabeth if they were crying out of joy or a deepened disappointment over their failure to bring the puzzle to an absolute finale.

"You're looking better, Hyrum," Leona said as the clapping subsided. "Much better."

"Thank you. I feel fine. I don't know what happened back there, and I'm kind of embarrassed for all the fuss." He looked to Norbridge. "You really expect my mother to show up?" There was an empty chair beside Hyrum, and he tilted his head in its direction.

"I hope so," Norbridge said. "She's due sometime tonight."

"She's been living where, again?" Mr. Knox said.

"Marbella," Hyrum said. "Way down south. She used to teach at the big art institute there."

"I became intrigued by the connection you have to Damien Crowley," Norbridge said to Hyrum, "and, well, I'm a bit of a genealogy buff, and so I started poking around."

"You might know more than I do," Hyrum said. "Mom was always tight-lipped about things. I'm sorry to say she was a bit estranged from her family."

"We can learn more, perhaps, about your family tree once your mother arrives," Norbridge said.

A knock sounded at the door.

"Maybe that's her now," Norbridge said.

The visitor turned out to be Phuong Nguyen, who arrived accompanied by Jackson and also Gustavo and Sampson carrying Phuong's lithophone. She greeted the group and set up in the living room as everyone ate Key lime pie and drank Nilgiri tea and listened to her explain the interesting history of lithophones. Once she was sure the rock slabs of her lithophone were secure, she began to play, song after song of the loveliest music Elizabeth had ever heard. It sounded something like bells, but so resonant and airy at the same time, it was unlike any music she could recall. When Phuong Nguyen concluded her concert and everyone stood to applaud for several minutes and then asked questions about how she'd learned to play and what the songs meant and where she would be giving recitals in the future, Elizabeth felt as if nothing dangerous or difficult could possibly trouble the evening.

"It's certainly getting late," Mr. Knox said, yawning. "We might head back to our room."

Professor Fowles glanced at his watch. "But it's only ten twenty-six, my good man. Surely you're not thinking of leaving at this early hour." Egil turned to Norbridge, who was in the kitchen, and yelled, "How about some more tea and sparkling cider, Mr. Falls?"

"I suppose we can stay a bit longer," Mr. Knox said.

"I'll put on one of my old Stan Getz albums," Norbridge called. "We can all enjoy ourselves for a bit. Besides, I have a surprise to share."

Before long, everyone was sitting around laughing and talking and drinking tea and having seconds or thirds of pie. Even Mr. Wellington and Mr. Rajput were in the spirit—the former more than the latter—as though the pleasant meal and good company and lovely music had washed away their disappointment over the puzzle, at least temporarily.

Once all the guests were occupied, and as Norbridge's music played loudly, Elizabeth gestured to Freddy to join her, and they came and sat beside Sir Reginald at the dinner table where he was peering down at his sash and polishing one of his many medals with a napkin.

"Ah, Miss Somers and Mr. Knox," he said, idly drumming a hand on his knee to the music. "These bossa nova tunes bring back so many fond memories. I spent seven months in Rio de Janeiro years ago overseeing operations

at a prominent glass foundry. Sand casting, kiln, graphite—
we did it all there. Beautiful works of art. Mostly of my
creation."

Freddy glanced at Elizabeth as if to say, *Maybe we
should leave him by himself.*

"Oh, I nearly forgot," Reginald said, reaching into
a pocket of his shirt and drawing out a piece of paper.
He unfolded it and spread it on the table. "That unusual
inscription of yours." He leaned over the paper and examined it as if to make certain it was the correct one.

"That's a lot of writing on there," Freddy said, peering at the columns of sprawling words Sir Reginald had,
apparently, jotted on the page.

"Because there are a multitude of possibilities,"
Reginald said. "That's under the theory that we are deal-
ing with an anagram, as I believe we are. If we start with
'Faith eliminates,' and restrict ourselves to two-word anagrams, we come up with several options, including 'filthi-
est anemia' and 'fishtail matinee.' Three-word anagrams
offer 'the finite salami' and 'leafiest mini hat.'" He shook
his head. "All dead ends, I believe."

Freddy shot a quick glance at Elizabeth as if to say,
This isn't going to help at all.

"The second line, though," Reginald said, examining the page, "seems a more fruitful line of enquiry. The
double 'z' there is a rarity. Two 'z's in a single sentence
would be quite unusual." He peered at the page once more.
"Perhaps the word in this anagram—if, indeed, anagram
it is—would include a double 'z,' which simplifies our

efforts immensely. As you may be aware, there are only three hundred fifty words in the English language with a double 'z.'"

"Time for presents, everyone," Norbridge called, clapping his hands.

Sir Reginald snatched up his piece of paper and stood quickly. "Perhaps we can delve into this more in a bit." He smiled. "Time for presents!"

"*Double* 'z,'" Freddy mouthed to Elizabeth, whose thoughts were racing furiously.

CHAPTER 32

THE DAUGHTER WHO CHOSE TO DISAPPEAR, RIVEN BY HATE

Norbridge dragged out the next thirty minutes by giving humorous gifts to each person—thousand-piece puzzles each to Mr. Wellington and Mr. Rajput, along with spa certificates for their wives; Winterhouse snow globes to the Knoxes; an old paperback entitled *The Librarian Who Was a Grump* for Leona ("It's a real book!" Norbridge said, laughing, as Leona glared at the volume as if it were a toad); a digital clock for Egil P. Fowles; a TEACHER OF THE YEAR T-shirt for Hyrum; five boxes of Flurschen for Phuong Nguyen (who departed shortly thereafter to get a good sleep before her Easter performance); and one Winterhouse brochure apiece for Elizabeth and Freddy— each autographed by the entire hotel staff. And then it was eleven o'clock, and still nothing unusual had occurred. Elizabeth felt that all danger might be averted, even as she continued to consider the anagram Sir Reginald had begun to explain.

"We really should be going," Mr. Wellington said, taking his wife's hand and rising.

"But I have a letter I wish to share," Norbridge said.

"A letter?" Mrs. Wellington said. "From whom?"

"My sister, Gracella," Norbridge said quietly, and the astonishment that enveloped the gathering was so entire, it felt as though time had stopped for an instant.

"But she's . . ." Hyrum began.

"I'm not saying it just arrived," Norbridge said. "But I did just find it."

Everyone settled back into their seats and waited for Norbridge to explain.

"A few days ago, these two," he said, gesturing to Elizabeth and Freddy, "discovered a hidden compartment under the lid of an old crate that belonged to my grandfather Nestor. Inside we found some letters he'd received over the years—as well as some letters sent to my father, Nathaniel."

"They didn't tell you about it?" Mrs. Rajput said.

"I believe my father intended to," Norbridge said, "but by the time he got around to it, his mind was very confused. It wasn't until the kids here discovered the compartment that I put two and two together." He reached into his breast pocket and removed a letter. "And found this."

Norbridge displayed a small envelope for Nathaniel with no return address on it. "From my sister. To my father."

Norbridge slid a single page from the envelope, unfolded it, and began to read:

January 1, 1966
Father,
I write to you from the small home I occasionally visit outside of Alcobar to let you know I still despise your hotel, the entire Falls family, Mother, and you.

Norbridge sighed and looked up. "Can you imagine reading such awful words? Or writing them? When I opened this letter, I felt terrible all over again for my father. And my sister—for whatever dark emotion had twisted her so terribly." He returned his eyes to the letter.

I don't know why you wrote to me or how you discovered where I'm living, but I will burn—unread—any future letters you send to me, and this is the only time I will write to you.

None of you at Winterhouse ever understood me or made the effort to try. My interests differed from those of the others in the family, and for that I was made to feel like an outsider, like someone who was letting the family down. I couldn't see a life for myself in that miserable palace of yours, spending my days acting polite to paying idiots. It all seemed false and pointless to me, and I couldn't leave soon enough. Worse, you lorded over me—you, Mother, Mickelson, Norbridge, and all the rest. I hate you for it. And I will not rest until I've captured the power of Winterhouse for myself and destroyed every member of the Falls family who stands in my way. I will continue to secure power, and I will ruin anything that opposes me. I've committed my eternal soul—by sacred oath—to this end. Which is why I can never turn back.

At Winterhouse, I was informed my destiny was already defined for me. I hoped to follow my own interests and develop my own talents, but I was met with scorn. In short, I wanted to find my own path— and, in short, I was advised to abandon it.

Is it any wonder I have nothing but hatred for all of you and the place you love?

I defy and despise you—I am your resolute adversary. You will never understand me.

—Gracella Winters

Norbridge sat staring at the letter. No one moved; no one spoke.

Elizabeth felt stricken. *You will never understand me.* These words, more than the rest, echoed in her head— absent the hatred behind them, she felt as though she might have uttered them herself, and for a moment they overwhelmed the bitterness of the previous lines. She let this distressing thought pass. The letter was venomous and elaborately hurtful, but there was, too, a shred of logic to it, something behind or beyond the hatred: Gracella's pain was understandable, if just barely.

"I'm sorry you had to see that letter, my dear man," Egil Fowles said finally. "Awful sentiments there. Just awful."

A few of the guests cast furtive glances at one another, uncertain what to say or do.

"It just kills me to think of my poor father reading those words," Norbridge said. "But it also makes me feel sorry for my sister. To think that she harbored these feelings and they warped her so completely."

"Frankly, Mr. Falls," said Mrs. Wellington, "even when we visited decades ago, she displayed all the signs of someone easily enraged."

Norbridge looked up wearily. "Absolutely, Mrs. Wellington. But she's my flesh and blood. I wish there was some way to—"

A knock sounded on the door.

"That must be Zarina," Norbridge said, tucking the envelope into his pocket. "Let's welcome a new friend to our circle."

When Norbridge opened the door, a short, black-haired woman with glasses and an expression of meek uncertainty on her face stood before him. Jackson was just behind her.

"Mr. Falls?" she said, extending a hand. "I'm Zarina Crowley."

"And I'm Norbridge Falls," he said. "It is my pleasure to meet you." He turned to look at Hyrum approaching. "I think you know this gentleman well enough."

"Mom!" Hyrum said, and as his mother stepped into the room, they hugged tightly.

"My little man!" Zarina said, pinching Hyrum's cheek. "Looking all grown up!"

Norbridge ushered her forward and introduced her to everyone as she stood with her arm around Hyrum and responded

with small nods and smiles. Elizabeth thought she was one of the most immediately charming women she'd ever met, all the more so because she wore a lovely purple dress and kept tapping at her glasses in a way that reminded her of herself.

"This is a beautiful hotel, Mr. Falls," Zarina said, once everyone had welcomed her, "and I'm most appreciative of your generosity in bringing me here." She pinched Hyrum's cheek once more. "I also needed to check up on this guy."

Hyrum smiled bashfully, and after a moment he and his mother were sitting on one of the sofas and the entire crowd had settled back into a circle, eager to hear about Zarina's lengthy journey to Winterhouse and more. There was an abundance of laughter and questions as Zarina held forth. Hyrum looked so happy to have his mother beside him, it seemed his fainting spell and odd behavior from earlier in the day were long forgotten.

"Norbridge," Mr. Wellington said, "you mentioned something earlier about genealogy and our new friend, Zarina Crowley, and whatnot. Perhaps you can explain what you meant."

"Well," Norbridge said, "after a conversation several of us had the other day regarding my cousin Cassandra, along with a comment or two Hyrum made, I became curious about things. Freddy, actually, shared a web spot with me."

"Website," Elizabeth said.

"Yes," Norbridge said. "What was it called again, Freddy?"

"The name is sojustwhereyoufrom.com," Freddy said.

"Yes, that's it," Norbridge said. "So, I began to fiddle around and see what I could find. Hyrum had mentioned his mother, Zarina, to me, and so it was a fairly quick process to make a few connections, and, well, Mrs. Crowley, perhaps you would like to explain."

"Certainly," she said, adjusting her glasses. "But first, I must say I knew very little about my husband's side of the family. Even just hearing from Mr. Falls a few days ago has filled in several gaps for me." She pressed her hands together and tipped them forward in Norbridge's direction, a small gesture of gratitude.

"My husband, Caesar," she said, "rest his soul, passed

away in '97, just before little Hyrum was born. I always knew about Caesar's famous father, the great writer Damien Crowley, and we saw him on several occasions—even after Caesar died. He lived in a nursing home in West Schtrunken, which is upstate from me. We used to visit him a few times a year, as Hyrum remembers. Well, Damien had three sons—Alexander, then Benito, and, last, Caesar, though the first two died when they were very young. My poor Caesar died at the tender age of forty-one." She dabbed at her eyes with a napkin. "I miss him still." Hyrum pulled her closer to him with an arm around her shoulders, and she shrugged as she tried to regain composure.

"I'll be all right," she said. "Well, Caesar's mother—Damien's wife—was named Cassandra. We knew her as Grandma Sandra, but she died in 1962, and Damien hardly ever spoke of her. I didn't even realize until Mr. Falls himself informed me, that—based on his research on the internet thingy . . . You'll have to forgive me, I'm terrible when it comes to gadgets. Anyway, Mr. Falls discovered that my Caesar's mother was Cassandra Falls, originally from right here. Winterhouse."

Elizabeth felt a shock go through her. "Wait a minute," she said. "If Damien Crowley married Cassandra Falls, then that makes Hyrum . . ." She turned to look at him.

"Your cousin!" Leona said, looking just as amazed as Elizabeth felt. "A bona fide member of the Falls family."

Hyrum was staring at his mother in disbelief. "Are you sure, Mom?" Zarina sat nodding her head furiously.

"So, I'm related to you?" Hyrum said to Elizabeth.

"I guess so," Elizabeth said, looking to Norbridge. One part of her felt she should be ecstatic over this news—it meant there was another young member of the Falls family after many, many years when it had seemed the line was all but ending. But another part of her felt conflicted—Gracella's surest route to working her mischief seemed to reside with relatives. "We're cousins, aren't we?"

"That you are," Norbridge said. "And he's my . . ." He glanced at the ceiling momentarily. "Second cousin twice removed. Welcome to the family, Hyrum."

"Amazing!" Mr. Knox said. "Why, to think that no one put this together before."

"So what happened to Cassandra?" Elizabeth said.

"Like I said," Zarina said. "She died. Back in 1962."

"And I feel very grateful to have learned this," Norbridge said. "I never knew her fate. No one did. Zarina has filled in the blanks for me."

"Do you know how she died?" Mrs. Rajput said. "She wouldn't have been that old."

"Well, that is a mystery," Zarina said. "Caesar never talked about it, and I never got a word out of Damien on it. In fact, I never got much of anything out of Damien. Frankly, he had a number of odd pursuits. Some even a little disturbing."

"Odd?" Sir Reginald said. "Meaning what?"

"The older he got," Zarina said, "the more serious he became about magic. Not coins and card tricks, but real magic. Truth be told, I found him strange. And anytime

I asked him about Cassandra, he just shook his head and went silent. There was one time, though, when he was very old and his mind was going, that I asked him about Cassandra, and he looked at me and said, 'That little girl from the hotel took care of her.' I have no idea what he meant."

Elizabeth put a hand to her forehead and looked to Norbridge, who had an expression of concern on his face that, just as she caught his eye, became composed.

"Well," Norbridge said, "we have a happy reunion here tonight. Glad we're all together."

"I did have an ulterior motive in accepting Mr. Falls's invitation," Zarina said. "Aside from finally getting to visit Winterhouse, I wanted to check on my little Hyrum."

"Oh, Mom, please," Hyrum said. "You always get so worried about everything."

"Mothers never stop being mothers," Mrs. Wellington said, and everyone laughed and began making conversation. Five minutes later, the midnight chimes sounded. Whatever anyone was doing—midsip on a cup of tea, poised with a fork over a plate of pie, explaining something about Easters past or vacations to come, laughing at a joke—came to an immediate halt, as one and all listened to the low chimes strike twelve times. It was as though a spell had fallen over the room, something pleasant and lulling.

"Happy Easter!" Norbridge said as the echo of the chimes faded. "To each one of you!"

The guests began to cheer and hug and call out good wishes.

"We made it to midnight," Leona yelled. "And no one tripped on the carpet or got sick from sparkling cider!"

Elizabeth felt tentatively optimistic—it seemed the danger really had passed. Midnight had come and gone.

"I guess everything is going to be okay," Freddy said to Elizabeth. He had a wry smile on his face, as though astounded that nothing bad had happened.

"I think so," Elizabeth said.

With an exaggerated motion, Freddy lifted his arm and then swung it forward to offer Elizabeth a hearty handshake. But she ignored his hand and leaned into him with an enormous hug.

"We really made it," she said.

"Hey!" Freddy called, laughing. "Watch the glasses!"

Elizabeth pulled away as Freddy dramatically repositioned his glasses on his nose. With a little press of his fisted hand, he offered her his knuckles to bump.

"This is much safer," he said, and she whammed his hand with her own.

"Ouch!" Freddy said.

"Eepah Retsee!" Elizabeth said. "It's finally here!"

"Oh," Freddy said. "And about that anagram? The second line is 'great big puzzle.'"

Elizabeth tapped the side of her head. "That's what I came up with, too."

"But the first line . . ." Freddy began, yet just then another knock—harsh and urgent—sounded, and the merriment in the room ceased.

Norbridge strode to the door and opened it to find Gustavo standing before him looking stricken.

"What is it?" Norbridge said.

"It's Lena, sir!" Gustavo said, so loudly the words echoed across the room. "Come quickly! Please!"

Norbridge wheeled about and surveyed his guests with a grim face. "I'm drawn away, all. Please excuse me." His eyes sought Elizabeth's. "And, with no exceptions, do not follow me."

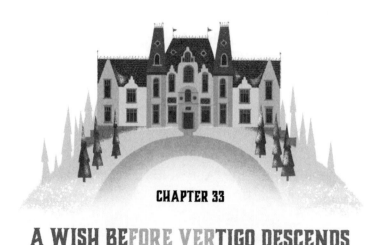

CHAPTER 33

A WISH BEFORE VERTIGO DESCENDS

The Knoxes, the Wellingtons, and the Rajputs departed immediately. Hyrum left with his mother; Sir Reginald accompanied them. Only Leona and Egil Fowles remained in Norbridge's apartment, and as the door was about to close behind Hyrum, Jackson appeared.

"Please, Miss Somers," he announced somberly. "I will take you to your room."

Once Elizabeth had closed the door to Room 301, she sat at her desk and—after glancing inside her drawer at the puzzle piece—took out a piece of paper. At the bottom of the page, she wrote "triple-egg buzz"; next to it she wrote "great big puzzle." At the top of the page, she wrote "faith eliminates." She understood so thoroughly where she was headed that—after a few scrawls and crossings-out—beside it she wrote "The final item is a." And then she scratched everything out and wrote, simply, "The final item is a great big puzzle."

The puzzle is Riley Granger's "picture," she thought. *We've been working on the final item all this time.*

A familiar and draining feeling of guilt came over her—mingled, once more, with the realization that if she herself completed the puzzle, its power would be hers.

"Three wishes," she said, and then thought, *But where is the last piece?*

She stood, drank a glass of water, and then paced her room, checking out her window and seeing nothing other than the snowy field that rolled toward the lake. No buzzing sound came, no eerie crimson lights or mist or anything of the sort appeared. The night felt quiet—oddly quiet. A thought of Lena came to her, and then Elana; she wondered how it was she'd put both of them out of her mind so completely from the moment she'd left Norbridge's apartment.

Elizabeth opened her drawer once more and stared at the puzzle piece—and then she picked it up, put it in her pocket, and left her room. She walked to the stairwell, went quickly downstairs, and took several steps down the corridor in the direction of the room Kiona and Lena shared. No one was in the hallway there, and, although she stood listening for a moment, she heard no voices coming from that direction. She reversed her steps and headed to the lobby.

When she arrived, the vast space was, as she'd hoped, deserted and still. The same ghostly light as always fell gently through the high windows, and the shadows and quiet seemed palpable; everything was under a hushed spell. She moved to the puzzle table, lit only by a dim lamp at this hour, and examined it. Sure enough, two spaces remained unfilled—one in the sky and one on the temple itself. Elizabeth put a hand to her pocket and felt the piece within.

Without the other piece, she thought, *mine is useless. The puzzle has to be complete.*

She admired the nearly whole picture before her. The scene was dramatic and lovely: a windswept stone temple at the base of a towering and snowy range of mountains, with an endless blue sky above. This was the very temple Nestor Falls and Riley Granger had inhabited for several years, the very place from which all the magic of Winterhouse had originated. Now, seeing the picture before her in this way—immense and uncluttered, spreading across the broad table—she felt she was looking at it for the first time.

"The last item," she said, and the thought of possessing it herself, of discovering the other piece and placing them both within, felt so stirring, she became dazzled by the sight of the temple. She leaned closer. A crimson sheen came over the puzzle, a glow that made it look spectral.

A sound came from the corridor, and Elizabeth looked up, her breath catching. Someone was approaching. Out of the darkness Hyrum appeared, moving with an odd sluggishness.

"Hyrum?" she said. "Are you all right?"

He stepped into the lobby and stopped. His face was drawn and slack; his hair was disheveled. Although he lifted his head at the sound of her voice, he seemed not to be focusing on the words or even on the fact of Elizabeth's presence. He appeared lost in a dream.

"Are you okay?" she said, but he simply stood looking at her blankly. She wondered if he was sleepwalking, if he'd risen from his bed and come to the lobby without being fully awake.

Hyrum opened his mouth with a twitching motion, but no words came. The sight was so uncanny, Elizabeth felt afraid. She was about to shout or turn and run—anything to alleviate her panic—when Hyrum's eyes widened and he darted his hand into his shirt pocket. As he did, his body began to sway, and his eyes became unfocused once more. But from somewhere deep inside his strange fog, he forced himself to draw an object from his pocket and hold it up.

"The puzzle piece!" Elizabeth said.

Hyrum's eyes closed as he attempted to speak. His body swayed more roughly this time.

"I don't know . . . why I took it," he said, through labored breaths. "I—"

Hyrum's knees buckled, he crumpled to the floor, and then he lay sprawled on the carpet convulsing, as though trying to catch his breath after an exhausting run. The puzzle piece he'd held lay on the floor beside his hand. Elizabeth began to rush to him—but then she saw something that made her stop in place. In the corridor that led to Winter Hall, a crimson light was blazing, filling the hallway with an intense reddish light.

"Who is that?" Elizabeth said.

"You know who I am," came a voice so low and hushed, it was barely more than a whisper, even though it echoed eerily from within the hallway.

"Gracella?" Elizabeth said, her panic rising so rapidly, she could barely maintain focus.

"I knew one of you would help me," came the voice.

"What do you mean?" Elizabeth said. "No one's helping you."

"Yes, you are," came the voice—level and low. "And yourself, too. You know very well what's happening. You have the power, just as I do. And you know I can help you."

"Stop saying that!" Elizabeth yelled, her confusion flaring.

The crimson light blinked out, and the lobby became dark and still once more. Hyrum remained motionless; Elizabeth waited. She felt certain something awful was about to happen, and she braced herself. As she stood, her body trembling, a thought came to her: *What if I'm imagining this?* She'd heard Gracella's voice and sensed her proximity, but there was an undeniable difference from the two other times she'd seen Gracella. Now something felt insubstantial, partial—maybe even unreal.

After a full minute of silence, Elizabeth moved warily in Hyrum's direction, trying not to make a sound. Hyrum didn't shift, though he was breathing steadily.

With absolute resolve, Elizabeth focused her attention on the puzzle piece beside Hyrum, concentrating fixedly as she pointed to it. The piece shot up and into her hand. Elizabeth held her palm open and stared at the two pieces that now lay there. She glanced at the corridor—dark still—and at Hyrum, and then she moved directly to the puzzle table.

"Finish it," came the voice, a whisper. "Complete the puzzle. Those wishes belong to you."

Elizabeth pinched her eyes closed, willed herself not to hear anything. She took a deep breath, opened her eyes, and locked the piece of the stone temple into place. The remaining piece—the one of pure blue that had been in her drawer for two weeks—lay in her palm. She took it up, pressed it into the vast sky of the puzzle, and then kept her thumb against it as she stared at the now-complete picture. And she waited.

Elizabeth had expected exactly what she'd felt in the underground passageway when she'd discovered the magic of her pendant—an intense rush of feeling, a moment of clarity and exhilaration that nearly carried her away with its force—and yet this time, as she stood touching the puzzle, she felt nothing like that previous emotion. Instead, she felt only a strange tremor in her chest, a tight flickering of motion that, as she stood, grew faster—it felt as though her heart had begun to beat too fast, and then faster still, and then a throbbing came into her ears that she recognized as the insistence of her own pulse. The noise grew quickly and steadily, a piercing sound that, combined with the racing of her heart, made her feel afraid. She pulled her hand away from the puzzle and clamped it and her other hand to her ears—all to no effect, because the noise kept on.

And then it stopped. All was quiet again. Elizabeth heard her heart beating now, but slowly, deliberately. She heard it in a way she'd never heard before—a steady pulse of sound inside her head, inside the center of her.

"Bring me back," came the voice once more. "I'm the only one who can help you. And I'm the only one who understands."

"Understands what?" Elizabeth called, lowering her hands. "What do you mean?"

"Understands you."

Elizabeth peered toward the corridor. Before it stood Gracella, staring at her. Only this wasn't the woman Elizabeth had seen before but merely a wisp, some airy shape that both looked like Gracella—dressed in her same black and flowing clothes, and with her same spume of white hair, and with her same piercing eyes—and did not look like her, a dull crimson glow surrounding her insubstantial form. Elizabeth stared—she could see right through.

"It's you I understand," Gracella said, without emotion. "Because we are alike. As you know very well."

Elizabeth turned to her and then, unaccountably, took several steps in her direction.

"The power is mine now," Elizabeth said. "Three wishes."

Gracella's expression remained fixed. "Grant me life once more. Haven't I suffered enough? Simply because I sought my own path?" She glanced down at herself. "I'm only a shade of what I was. Bring me back. I'll share every-thing with you."

Elizabeth stepped closer. "Why do I need you? I don't need to know any of your secrets."

"I allowed you to bring the picture to life," Gracella said, her eyes softening slightly. "To complete it, to earn its wishes. I could have let him do it, but I chose you."

"How do I know that? Besides, I'm the heir to Winter-house." A stab of doubt ran through her. "I don't need you."

"You don't believe what you're saying," Gracella said. "You're like me—and you've always known it." She reached out a hand. "I'm asking you to save me." She stretched her hand out farther. "Please. I'm a Falls, just like you."

Hyrum stirred but then fell still once again. Elizabeth pointed to him. "He's a member of the family, too, but you used him to steal a piece of the puzzle."

"To bring about my restoration." Gracella stared at her. "I can still exert my will, even with my physical form use-less. You see the sort of power I can teach you?"

"You had someone call your name, didn't you? Just like I did once."

"Reginald. In the library, and at the entrance to the

mine. Your friend's parents tied the red cloth there to mark it, after Damien's grandson left another one there weeks before and burned down my cabin so I would come here rather than there. Those two at the puzzle have been doing my work all along. All of them have. With no knowledge of it. No recollection at all. Yes, I controlled all of it and all of them—and you, to the extent I could." She reached out her hand once again, a pose that mirrored Morena's in the painting by Riley Granger.

A deep uncertainty filled Elizabeth. "We may be alike," she said, "but why should I bring you back? I can learn about my powers on my own."

"You know you don't believe that." Gracella stared. "And I'm asking for your mercy."

Elizabeth felt herself about to make a declaration, to utter a wish. Just how she would do it or what she would say or consent to inside herself was an absolute blur. The line from the Anna Lux book about a girl who decided to become a witch came to Elizabeth's mind, and she felt she could simply assent to this desire and it would be so—she could will herself to become whatever she desired, to take any path, to claim what she wanted.

An image of Elana came into her mind.

Moved by intuition, Elizabeth set her hand on the pendant at her neck and glanced at the puzzle. She closed her eyes and spoke: "My first wish is to make Elana young again—just like she was before she was transformed."

An immense wave moved through her, and she kept her eyes closed.

"My second wish is to keep Winterhouse safe for all time," she said as she thought, *I have one more left.*

"Elizabeth." Gracella's voice was low and calm. "It makes no sense to return hatred with hatred."

"What did you say?" Elizabeth felt she was falling. That Gracella had uttered these words was as disorienting as anything that had happened yet.

"Don't hate me," Gracella said. "Let me live once more."

Elizabeth removed her hand from her pendant. "One more wish," she said.

Hyrum groaned—and Elizabeth thought of the pain Gracella had caused to so many people over so many years. A dark yearning came over her: to make Gracella pay for all she'd done, for threatening Winterhouse again and again, for harming Elana so awfully, for undermining all of Norbridge's attempts to keep Winterhouse safe—and for killing her parents. Elizabeth felt welling inside herself the need to punish Gracella.

"You don't really want to see me suffer," Gracella said, her voice steady, her eyes fixed on Elizabeth's. "I've given my soul for power. If you don't bring me back, I will suffer forever."

"All you've done is hurt people," Elizabeth said. "And killed some of them, too, like my mother and father. And now you're asking me to save you?" She tried to work up as much anger as she could, but Gracella's words— Norbridge's words—throbbed in her head: *It makes no sense for a person to return hatred with hatred.*

"I'm asking for another chance," Gracella said. "Let me help you."

Elizabeth heard the words, but even as she did, she was searching for something else Norbridge had told her, something about Gracella that had made little sense when she'd heard it—that Norbridge wanted to see his sister freed from the evil she'd created for herself. That he hoped, somehow, Gracella could be saved.

She took two more steps forward and now stood directly before Gracella. "You think I only have two choices: either punish you or bring you back," Elizabeth said softly, with complete composure. "But there's something else."

Gracella kept her eyes on Elizabeth as she put a hand to her pendant. "My final wish: Let Gracella pass out of life with goodness in her heart." A buzzing arose; Elizabeth closed her eyes and continued to speak. "Even though she did awful things, she still had the love of her brother, and he hoped for the best for her. He wanted to give her what everyone wants—love and forgiveness." The sound grew louder; Elizabeth felt a hot wind on her skin. "Give Gracella peace. Let her be surrounded by the goodness she didn't ask for or even want. Let it be with her as she leaves this life. And let her soul have peace." The sound was deafening.

"Forever," Elizabeth said—and the noise stopped.

Elizabeth opened her eyes and drew her hand from her necklace. Gracella was gone. The corridor was dark, the puzzle lay dimly on its table, and the lobby was silent. She looked up to see the shafts of lamplight streaming in through the high windows.

"Elizabeth!" She turned to see Norbridge rushing to her from the far corridor.

"The last item," she said. "It was the puzzle."

Norbridge stood before her. "The puzzle? What do you mean?"

"Gracella was here." A rush of emotion came over Elizabeth, all of the fear and panic and confusion she'd been holding back. "She tried to . . . I don't know what, Norbridge! I put the last pieces in the puzzle and made a wish, and then she disappeared. I made her go away."

Norbridge reached for Elizabeth to pull her to him. After a moment, she drew back and clamped both hands to her eyes to stanch her tears.

"What happened to Lena?" she said, surprising herself with the question.

Norbridge looked stricken. And then Hyrum made a sound and began to sit up slowly.

"Elizabeth," he said, his voice coming haltingly.

"Hyrum?" Norbridge said as he moved toward him. "What are you doing here?"

Hyrum put a hand to his forehead and slumped again. "I don't know."

"Gracella made him come here somehow," Elizabeth said. "And then he blacked out."

"You're all right?" Norbridge said to Hyrum, who shook his head as if to clear his confusion. He took Norbridge's arm and stood unsteadily.

"I think so," he said.

"Let's get you both some water," Norbridge said, keeping a hand on Hyrum's shoulder. "You should sit, both of you."

"What happened to Lena?" Elizabeth said again.

"I'll clear everything up," Norbridge said softly. "Please, for now, let's get you off your feet."

A fog entered Elizabeth's brain; she wanted to explain to Norbridge every minute of what had just happened, but she felt as though she couldn't quiet the confusion racing through her.

"What about Elana?" Elizabeth said.

Norbridge's face took on the most peculiar expression Elizabeth had ever seen. This was the final blow, something she couldn't take in.

"Is she . . ." But those were the last words Elizabeth uttered—everything went dark, and silence claimed her.

CHAPTER 34

FRIENDSHIP'S GRASP RINGS IN THE DAY

Easter day blossomed like the true start of spring—the morning was cold and clear and crisp, but a new freshness was in the air, even though the hotel and the lake and the nearby forest and the mountains beyond were as snow-covered as they'd been all winter. A corner had been turned; warmer days and brighter nights were ahead. Elizabeth sensed all this even as she lay in her bed, because the light fell through her window so cleanly, and her view of Lake Luna and the mountains was bathed in a crystal clarity she hadn't seen during her previous weeks in Room 301.

She read—for the fifth time—the note that had been waiting for her on her table when she'd awakened:

The events of the evening overwhelmed you—you fainted, my dear. When you're fully rested, please come to my room. We'll be waiting.—N

At ten o'clock, Elizabeth was sitting at the dining table in Norbridge's room with him and Leona, both of whom had hugged her and reassured her and told her all would be clear soon.

"Eat, dear, just a bit," Leona said once Elizabeth was situated. "You'll feel better."

"Please, I want to know what happened last night," Elizabeth said. "To Lena and Elana."

"I need your coconspirator here with us," Norbridge said as he sat at the table, "and then we can talk everything through. It's only fair that we include Freddy."

Leona was drinking from a mug of tea, while Norbridge nibbled on walnuts and raisins he picked out from a small bowl. Elizabeth glanced at the door. "Is he on the way?"

"Not yet," Norbridge said. "But look at this." He held up a cell phone that appeared to be about ten years old and had buttons four times bigger than anything Elizabeth had ever seen. "Sampson loaned this to me. It's a self phone."

"Cell phone, Mr. Senior Citizen," Leona said. "Even I know that."

Norbridge glowered at her and then turned to Elizabeth with a kindly look. "Can you send a texter to Freddy and ask him to come right away?"

"A text?" Elizabeth said. "Yes, of course."

Leona shook her head as Elizabeth tapped out her

message. "We used to pass notes in my day," Leona said. "Or just come right up to someone and yell at him. Everything's different now."

"What's going on?" Freddy said when he arrived five minutes later. It was clear, as he sat at the table with the others, he had no idea what had happened after the party had ended the night before. "We've been in our room all morning. Is everything all right?"

Norbridge looked to Leona, who gestured to him with a flourish of her hand as if to say, *This is your story to tell.*

"First," Norbridge said, "everything is, let's say, *contained*. I'll elaborate in a bit, but I need to hear Elizabeth's account of last night before I fill you two in." He looked to her. "From the time Jackson took you to your room. Please, start there."

Elizabeth drew in a long breath and exhaled. "I actually need to start a little earlier. Like, two weeks ago." She glanced at her bowl of oatmeal. "When I took one of the puzzle pieces."

"You stole a piece of the puzzle?" Freddy said.

"Well, sort of, I guess." She sighed. "Let me just explain, and maybe it will make sense."

Over the next twenty minutes, Elizabeth walked the others through every twist and turn in the story, working her way up to the encounter with Gracella in the lobby. No one spoke; no one ate their food or sipped their hot chocolate. They simply listened to Elizabeth detail how Gracella had manipulated the various hotel guests—without their awareness—to advance her scheme and then she explained what had happened after midnight beside the puzzle table.

"Three wishes," Freddy said quietly when Elizabeth was done. "Like out of a fairy tale."

Leona's eyes were glassy as she sat looking to Elizabeth. "You figured out the last item, and gave a gift to the soul of that wicked woman. It's stunning, dear." She looked to Norbridge. "Absolute kudos to the young lady, Mr. Falls. This is maybe the most remarkable thing I've ever heard of among the vast number of remarkable things at this hotel."

"I thought I had an interesting tale," Norbridge said, "but yours tops everything, Elizabeth."

"Did the wishes actually work?" Freddy said. "I mean, the third one did. And I guess we won't know about the second one for a while. But what about the first one, the one for Elana?"

Leona lifted her glasses toward Norbridge in invitation. "You really better explain."

"Explain?" Elizabeth said. "What do you mean?"

"I'll start from the beginning myself." Norbridge rubbed his forehead, sat back, and began. "After Gustavo broke up our gathering last night, he and I went to Elana's room."

"But I thought something happened to Lena," Elizabeth said.

Norbridge raised a hand. "Gustavo informed me that Lena had been wandering the halls again, and that she'd gone to Elana's room for a visit just before midnight. When she was done, Mrs. Trumble walked her out into the hallway, and at first Lena started to leave. But then she turned around, closed the door on Mrs. Trumble, and locked herself inside Elana's room."

"Why would she do that?" Freddy said.

Norbridge remained silent, though he gave a meaningful look in Leona's direction.

"To help Elana," Leona said.

Elizabeth shook her head. "I don't get it."

Norbridge stood and went to the nearest bookshelf; he picked up a book that lay there. After studying its cover as though making certain it was the right one, he held it up.

"*The Secret Instruction of Anna Lux*," Elizabeth said, astonished. "Where'd you find it?"

"Under Lena's pillow," Leona said.

Freddy turned to Elizabeth. "Lena had the book all this time?"

A flicker of realization began to stir in Elizabeth. "I think I know what happened." Norbridge lowered his chin in her direction, inviting her to continue.

"Lena somehow got into Gracella's room and stole the book," Elizabeth said. "I don't know how she knew it was there, but however she did, she took it because she knew there was something about the Dredforth Method in it. Maybe she thought she could help Elana?"

"You've got the outline," Leona said. "Though it's a bit more complicated."

"Why don't you try to untangle things, Miss Springer?"

Norbridge tucked the Damien Crowley book inside the inner pocket of his suit jacket.

Leona bowed her head and began to speak. "Late last night we learned something very interesting from Kiona. She finally told us, after all this time, who Lena's father was—the man she met here at Winterhouse before she ran off and disappeared for two years." She paused and looked in turn to each of the three before her. "Aleister Winters."

Elizabeth gasped; Freddy's mouth dropped open.

"That was our reaction, too," Norbridge said.

"Gracella's husband?" Elizabeth said. "That's not possible."

"It certainly is," Leona said. "Gracella met Aleister twenty years after Kiona knew him. There's nothing to stop a man from marrying two women in the same family."

Elizabeth put a hand to her head. "That's just too bizarre. So, Lena is the daughter of the same man who married Gracella and taught her the worst of her black magic."

"That's more than bizarre." Freddy stared at the table with glassy eyes. "Bizarre squared, or something. I don't know the right word, but whatever it is, that's what this is."

"Take it for what you will," Leona said. "Lena probably always knew more about Aleister and Gracella's magic than we did. Regardless, she removed the book from Room 333."

"And she decided to work the Dredforth Method to help Elana," Norbridge said.

"Help her how?" Elizabeth said. "I'm still not following."

"To make her young again," Leona said.

Silence came over the room. "Can a person just work the Dredforth Method?" Elizabeth asked. "I've been thinking that it seems like in order to perform it, someone else has to . . ."

"Die?" Norbridge said.

Elizabeth didn't say the word "yes" because it seemed she didn't need to.

"Or give years of their own life," Leona said.

An even deeper silence settled over the room, something somber and forlorn.

"What happened?" Freddy's voice was barely louder than a whisper. "Something happened to someone."

"Lena locked herself in that room," Norbridge said, "and by the time we got the door open, she was gone."

"Gone, like . . ." Freddy began.

"Passed away," Leona said. "Lena died last night."

A flood of sorrow came over Elizabeth. It had been impossible to know Lena, lost as she was in her own world, but it was still deeply saddening to know she'd passed away.

"We haven't yet shared the news with Kiona," Norbridge said softly. "It may be too much for her just now. But, yes, Lena has passed away."

"She still had sixteen years to go," Freddy said.

"She gave her life." Elizabeth looked to Norbridge with a confused expectation. "She must have thought that would make Elana young again."

"And it did," came a voice from the far side of the living room.

Elizabeth and Freddy turned, and there, in her white pants and blouse, and with a white ribbon once again tied into her long black hair, stood Elana, looking as radiant and beautiful—and as young—as she ever had, and smiling more brightly than Elizabeth could recall.

"Elana!" the two kids shouted as they scrambled out of their chairs. In a flash they were hugging Elana and calling her name again and again as she stood crying happily between them.

"You guys are gonna suffocate me!" she said finally, and the two others began laughing before redoubling their grip on Elana as she laughed even through her tears.

"I can't believe it!" Elizabeth said. "You're okay!"

"Come over here, all of you," Norbridge said, beaming, "and sit down."

It took twenty minutes and several detours into questions and explanations and a few more hugs and tears, but eventually all was explained. Lena had, indeed, locked herself in Elana's room and then—as Elana watched helplessly—scrawled circles and symbols on the carpet with a piece of coal before soundlessly uttering words and making strange motions with her hands. That was all Elana could remember—because at that point, she lost consciousness and only woke up just before dawn in Norbridge's guest room, which was when she realized she was the girl she'd been three months before. Norbridge had even had the Havenworth doctor visit Elana that

morning just to make sure she was well—and all checked out perfectly.

"I couldn't believe it," Elana said. "I still can't. I never thought in a million years this would happen."

"Elizabeth wished for it, too," Freddy said. "Once she solved the puzzle. She had three wishes, and one of them was to make you how you were."

"Maybe the two things together added up," Leona said with a quizzical look. "Elizabeth's wish and Lena's magic."

Norbridge gave her a sidelong glance and then smiled at Elana. "Whatever the causes were behind this, here you are, back to the lovely young lady we knew. Elana Powter."

"Elana Vesper!" Elana said. "That's what I want to be called from now on. That other name is . . ." She turned to Elizabeth and reached for her hand. "That's the person I used to be."

"Elana Vesper it is!" Leona said, and Elizabeth lifted their clasped hands above the table as if to finalize the decision.

"But what about Lena?" Freddy said.

"We found her on the floor of Elana's room," Norbridge said. "It's sad, absolutely. But it's a noble thing she's done. Somehow, with what little spark of connection she had in her, she wanted to save someone else. Maybe, in some way, because of her links to the Winters side of the family, she wanted to atone for all they've done. It's a remarkable gift she's given."

Elana squeezed Elizabeth's hand. "It is," she said. "All of this is. I feel so lucky to be here with all of you. To be back the way I was."

"Was that a bookmark I noticed in that book?" Freddy said, pointing to where Norbridge had tucked the book inside his jacket.

"Observant as always," Norbridge said. "It was a bookmark." He bobbed his head twice. "It marked a part of the story that was, well, unpleasant."

"Oh, just tell them," Leona said. "Do you really think they can't hear it after all they've gone through?"

"It's not often I admit that Miss Springer is correct,"

Norbridge said, "but I'm going to admit that she is, indeed, correct this time." He squinted at Leona. "But don't get used to it."

Leona lifted her chin regally, and the three kids laughed.

Norbridge set both hands on the table. "This little book of Damien Crowley's is a mess, frankly, the product of a severely confused mind. He must have been in the grip of all his magical nonsense at this point. Anyway, it's clear he's woven in some events from real life in his book, and that bookmark—left by Lena—is on a page that describes a particularly awful act performed by the magician in the tale. He lures a young woman out on a snowy night, and then steals her powers of speech and hearing, all to enhance his own abilities."

"That must have been what Aleister did to Lena all those years ago," Elizabeth said. She turned to Freddy and added with a gasp, "His own daughter."

"It certainly seems that's the case," Norbridge said. "And it seems Lena must have thought so, too."

"I'm lost," Elana said. "Can someone tell me what this is all about?"

"In time, my dear," Leona said. "In time. My goodness, you just dropped eighty years in one night, so no need to rush things."

Everyone laughed once again, and the morning turned into a series of questions and explanations and clarifications—until the chimes sounded for lunch, and

Norbridge announced that the great Easter meal in Winter Hall was about to be served and they would need to join in.

"After eating breakfast here all morning?" Freddy said.

"We just need to put in an appearance," Norbridge said. "All except for you, Elana. I want you to stay here and get some rest. Besides, it will save all of us a lot of explanation."

"I'll be here." Elana looked to Elizabeth and Freddy. "You'll come back after lunch?"

"Of course!" Elizabeth said. "We'll be here before you know it."

"Well," Freddy said, "technically, that's not possible—but you know what she means."

Everyone laughed some more—Elana loudest—and then quick farewells were offered as the others left Elana to rest and headed to Winter Hall.

⊷⁂⊷

Lunch passed pleasantly as the Knoxes, the Wellingtons, the Rajputs, Reginald, Egil, and Hyrum were joined by Zarina and the four from Norbridge's room at a single congenial table. Lena's passing cast a sad light on the proceedings, at least at the outset. But the circle of friends took their lead from Norbridge, who urged all to think of the event as the inevitable progression of a woman well past the age of eighty, and a person whose incapacities had already distanced her from the life of the hotel years before.

"I prefer to think of her death as a relief from the burdens of her existence," Norbridge said. "And I take solace in the fact that she passed on a day we associate with new beginnings. There will be a memorial service on Tuesday evening."

"To Lena Falls!" Professor Fowles lifted his glass of milk, and everyone at the table followed suit.

Conversation was varied and full as the hour passed. The Wellingtons and Rajputs, relieved to learn Elizabeth had finished the puzzle before dawn as an Easter gift to all after locating the two missing pieces in one of Nestor's crates (so Norbridge said), were leaving that afternoon for a stay in Upper Swabia, Germany ("Home of the Ravensburger puzzle company!" Mr. Rajput informed everyone, with uncharacteristic enthusiasm). The three Knoxes were heading home the next day but were already making plans to spend a month at Winterhouse in the summer. Egil Fowles and Hyrum were returning to Havenworth after lunch to make sure they were ready for the resumption of classes in the morning ("First period at seven fifty sharp," Egil said to Elizabeth, glancing at his watch); while Zarina was looking forward to staying at Winterhouse as Norbridge's guest for the next week. And, finally, Sir Reginald Eton-Pailey informed everyone that, before heading to Estonia to lead the safecracking seminar he claimed he'd provided to government agencies in "seventeen countries on four continents" over the years, he would be visiting the great library in the palace at Mafra, Portugal.

"Do you know," Reginald said, "that in that remarkable library, they encourage the habitation of tiny bats in order to combat the bookworms and bugs that would otherwise devastate the remarkable collection of volumes within?"

"Bats live in the library?" Elizabeth said.

"They *protect* the library!" Sir Reginald said. "At night they swarm the place."

"We'll have to visit, Elizabeth," Leona said. "But during the middle of the day."

"To the perpetual safety of all books everywhere!" Egil Fowles said, lifting his glass of milk once more, and the entire table joined in the toast again.

"Especially at Winterhouse!" Elizabeth called, and everyone added, "Hear! Hear!"

By two o'clock, Elizabeth, Freddy, and Elana were in the Tower at the very top of Winterhouse, admiring the views on all sides—the sparkling mountains, the valley far below, Lake Luna gleaming white with snow and ice. The sky was an endless blue, and the day felt as full of Winterhouse magic as any she'd ever experienced.

"You're sure you're not getting tired?" Elizabeth said to Elana, who was gazing through a window at the far peaks.

"I feel great," she said. "I was lying on that bed for so long, now I feel like I have all the energy in the world."

"It's amazing that you're back to how you were," Elizabeth said. "It's almost like you were never 'away,' you know?"

"I'm just glad it's over," Freddy said. "But I feel bad about your family and everything. How they, you know . . ."

"Abandoned me?" Elana sighed. "I've been thinking about that so much lately, wondering why they did that."

"You're not to blame, you know, Elana," Elizabeth said.

"Maybe someday I'll be able to figure it out," Elana said. "For now . . ." She shrugged. "I don't know. I really don't. I hope someday to talk to them and understand everything."

A silence came over the room, something heavy and sad. As Elizabeth considered the difficult thoughts Elana was sorting out, something arose in her mind that had been working its way through her since morning: If Lena had given her life for Elana prior to Elizabeth uttering her wish to bring about the same thing, had the wish—the third and final one—really been used?

"Do you guys know how unbelievable it would sound," Freddy said cheerfully, very obviously trying to undo the somber mood, "if I tried to explain any of this to people back home? 'Hey, so my friend Elana was, like, ninety for a few months, and now she's back to being twelve. And that's after my other friend Elizabeth defeated a wicked sorceress.'"

The two girls laughed, and Elizabeth shook her head in wonder.

"Sometimes it's hard to believe *any* of it," she said. "It really is like something out of a story. Like something you'd read in a book."

"You should write it someday," Elana said. "You love to write."

"And read," Freddy said. He caught Elizabeth's eye. "But you still have a lot of time to figure out what you want to do."

She smiled at him. "I've been thinking about that. About what I want to do."

"You mean, like, for a job?" Elana said.

"Kind of," Elizabeth said. She turned to Elana. "Hey, has Norbridge mentioned to you anything about what's going to happen now? Like, for you?"

Elana shrugged. "We haven't talked about that yet. He said I could stay here for as long as I want, though. I guess that's what will happen." She shrugged again, and her face brightened. "I mean, it sounds incredible to just keep living here at Winterhouse."

Elizabeth looked at Freddy. "I don't even need to ask you if that sounds like something you'd like to do, too."

Freddy gave Elizabeth a look that was half wary and half glad, as though a realization was growing in his mind, but he wanted to make sure he wasn't jumping too far ahead. "What are you thinking? You have that look you get when the wheels are spinning in your brain."

"Well, someday someone will have to run the hotel," Elizabeth said.

Freddy turned to Elana and, with an exaggerated display of his hand, raised it as if to block Elizabeth's view. With his other hand, he pointed dramatically toward

Elizabeth and whispered loudly to Elana, "She's gonna do that!"

Elizabeth laughed in spite of herself and pointed right back at Freddy. "And someone will need to help run everything here," she said, "as well as invent all sorts of cool new things to make sure Winterhouse is always interesting and up-to-date."

Elana turned to Elizabeth and did a good imitation of Freddy's playacting by indicating him just as he'd indicated Elizabeth. "He's gonna do that!" Elana said.

"I see where we're going," Freddy said. "Because someone will need to run the library, and what if that person is you, Elana?"

"Seriously, if all of that happened," Elana said, "that would be like a wish come true."

It was exactly what Elizabeth had been thinking. She reached her hands to the other two, and the three of them formed a small circle.

Elizabeth closed her eyes; a flutter moved through her, some tremor of *the feeling*, and the pendant around her neck gave off the slightest throb of heat.

"I want the three of us to grow old here together at Winterhouse," she said softly. "That's my final wish."

A tiny ripple—a breeze or shift in temperature or something beyond words—moved through the room and through Elizabeth, Freddy, and Elana; they stood holding hands, connected by something momentous and definite and sweet. It felt as though everything had turned very serious, very important, and no one wanted to unclasp hands or make a motion or stop feeling what they were sharing just then.

Freddy's phone buzzed.

"Oh, come on!" he said with a groan, and they all let go of one another's hands as Freddy removed his phone from his pocket. "They are always doing this! Why can't they just—"

He stared at his phone and looked startled.

"What is it?" Elizabeth said.

"It's not my parents." Freddy held the phone up for the two girls to see. "It says, 'Freddy, this is Norbridge sending this texter. Please tell Elizabeth to come see me in my office.'"

"Texter?" Elana said.

"Norbridge doesn't always know the right words for things," Elizabeth said.

Freddy was staring at his phone. "Wow, I'm just impressed he didn't misspell any words." He turned the screen toward Elizabeth again. "I guess you better go see him."

Elizabeth put a hand to her pendant. "What are you guys going to do?"

Elana gave Freddy an eager look. "You want to go skating?"

"Can I really argue with you on a day like this one?" he said. "Let's do it."

"I'll come find you guys when I'm done, okay?" Elizabeth said. And after quick hugs with both her friends, she departed the Tower—only to find herself stopping

halfway down the corridor when she heard Freddy's voice behind her: "Elizabeth!"

She turned around to see him following. "Didn't we just say good-bye, like, five seconds ago?" she laughed.

Freddy pushed at his glasses and smiled awkwardly. "I know." He glanced back toward the door to the Tower. "It's just, I wanted to tell you . . ." Freddy stopped speaking; he seemed unable to figure out how to finish his sentence.

"What?"

"You were right, you know," Freddy said. "Out there when we saw that red cloth. About making sure we looked into things, and keeping Winterhouse protected, and all of that."

Elizabeth shrugged. "You and I both love this place. We're a team, right? We want to make sure Winterhouse is okay."

"But you really put yourself out there to make it happen. You're the one, Elizabeth. You saved Winterhouse. Just like you did twice before. I guess I just wanted to say, I don't know, thank you or let you know I think it's cool, everything you've done."

Quickly, as if to conceal something he felt but couldn't say, Freddy lifted an arm and held his fist out for Elizabeth to tap. Instead, she leaned forward and, with all the delicate and tender precision she might use to turn a page in a precious book, put a kiss on Freddy's cheek.

His eyes widened as Elizabeth backed away, smiling.

"Wow," Freddy said, putting a hand to his face.

"Nice palindrome," Elizabeth said. She resumed

walking down the corridor. "I'll see you at the skating rink!" she added, before bursting into a run.

Elizabeth sat with Norbridge on the sofa in the main room of his office just behind the telescope. She'd noticed when she came in that there were pieces of blue and white tile scattered on the floor and the smell of glue or turpentine in the air. The door to Norbridge's office was closed.

"What's been going on in here?" she said, once they were seated and after he'd asked her how Elana was doing.

Norbridge surveyed the small mess on the carpet before them. "Of all the days for this to happen," he said, "Fortinbras Antunes, my good friend and the master tile maker I work with from Portugal, arrived early this morning to complete a project I'd asked him to finalize."

"On Easter?" Elizabeth said.

"The gentleman is so absentminded, I'm not even sure he knows what month it is sometimes. But that's what makes him such a supreme artist. The focus! He is obsessed with his craft. Anyway, he came this morning at dawn and was working until an hour ago." Norbridge gestured around him at the living room. "In here only. No one goes in the office, of course. He brought all his tools, the mini kiln, the paint, all of it."

"But for what?" Elizabeth said.

Norbridge put a hand to his beard. "First, my dear, how are you feeling after the events of the last day? It's a lot to soak up."

"Honestly, I feel all right. I mean, so much has happened, but I'm feeling okay."

"'So much' is right. Gracella, Elana, the puzzle . . ."

"Damien's book and all the guests and . . . everything! All of it. I don't even know where to start." She paused. "Is Kiona okay?"

"She took it hard, as you can imagine. But she's doing as well as can be expected. I'm concerned about a shock like this when, well, her time is growing short. I think one part of her is glad to know her daughter gave her life to preserve Elana's. Maybe the two of you can visit her once things calm down a bit."

"I'd love that."

"Oh," Norbridge said, reaching into his pocket. "How about one more surprise while we're at it?" He removed an envelope and extended it to Elizabeth. "For you. It came yesterday, but Sampson just got it to me this morning."

Elizabeth took the letter and examined it—the postmark indicated the town of Drere, and suddenly the return address made sense to her.

"My aunt and uncle?" she said, looking to Norbridge with astonishment. He nodded and then moved his finger toward her to encourage her to open the envelope. Once she did, she found only a single piece of paper with three sentences on it:

Dear Elizabeth, we miss having you here with us, and we want to apologize for the way we treated you for so many years. Our son, Carothers, died when he was ten, and I guess that just made us feel so awful, we didn't know how to be nice to anyone afterward. Now that you're gone, we really realize how mean we were to you, and we regret it and hope you can forgive us.

—Aunt Purdy and Uncle Burlap

Elizabeth felt her eyes flooding with tears as she tried to read the note a second time but couldn't make it through. She set it in her lap and put a hand to her forehead, recalling a photograph of a boy she'd once found in a book that belonged to her aunt. It all made sense now.

"Are you all right?" Norbridge said softly.

"They're apologizing," Elizabeth said. "For being mean to me."

Norbridge remained quiet for a moment, and Elizabeth finally looked at him.

"I'm very glad to hear that," he said. "We never know the influence we might have on other people simply by showing them some kindness, by trying to remain in good spirits as best we can. By not returning hatred with hatred."

"It's just so hard, Norbridge. Some people are just . . . bad." She glanced at the envelope. "I'm really surprised by this letter, to tell you the truth."

"Sometimes maybe people are just waiting to be touched by a little bit of goodness from someone else. I really don't think most people want to be unhappy." He glanced around at the room as if to take in the entire hotel. "Which is why I hope this place of ours can help just a bit."

"So do I," Elizabeth said.

Norbridge tapped the top of his chest to indicate the pendant around Elizabeth's neck. "Just keep the faith, Miss Somers. I'm counting on you." He smiled as he stood. "Come on. Let me show you the office."

Elizabeth followed Norbridge down the short hallway to the door there, and when they entered, all appeared as it had on the few other occasions she'd been inside. She scrunched up her nose and sniffed.

"Paint?" she said, glancing around.

"A type of glue," Norbridge said. "To affix tiles to the wall."

He pointed to a section off to one side, and Elizabeth saw a mural where there had been only blank space before.

"New tiles," Norbridge said. "For a new addition to the Winterhouse story."

Elizabeth stepped toward the wall and gazed at it, her mouth opening in astonishment. Before her, in lustrous blue and white, was a depiction of a girl—herself—standing beside a table and extending a hand to press a piece into a massive puzzle on it. Beneath the mural was a caption: "The Greatest Easter Ever at Winterhouse—Elizabeth Somers Solves the Puzzle."

As her eyes filled with tears once more, Elizabeth turned to Norbridge and threw her arms around him. She tried to say something, but the words couldn't form.

"It's okay, Elizabeth," Norbridge said, hugging her tightly. "It's okay."

"Everything that's happened," Elizabeth said against him. "I feel like the luckiest person. I just love all of this—you, Winterhouse, all of the people here, everything." She pulled away from Norbridge slightly, and he reached to wipe the tears from her face.

"I love you just as much, Elizabeth," he said, and then he gestured toward the wall. "And I'm so glad I was able to have that picture there for you today. It's another wonderful Winterhouse story that's come to an end."

Elizabeth stared at the tiles, and then back to Norbridge. She stood tall and straight, and she placed a hand against her pendant and looked at her grandfather with fearless eyes.

"Not the end," she said. "Not at all. It feels like everything is just beginning."

ACKNOWLEDGMENTS

Thank you to Christy Ottaviano for her expertise, generous guidance, and friendship; Chloe Bristol, for her deep artistry and vision; the great folks at Macmillan—in particular, Jessica Anderson and Brittany Pearlman, for their untiring support; and Rena Rossner for her constancy and fine counsel. As ever, thank you to Jacob, Olivia, and Natalie; and, above all—always—gratefulness in the extreme to Rosalind.

THE WINTERH